Take Me Down

Lauren H. Kelley

LOVESPIN PUBLISHING | ATLANTA

LOVESPIN PUBLISHING | ATLANTA

This is an original publication of LoveSpin Publishing, LLC.

Copyright 2014 Lauren H. Kelley.

Published by LoveSpin Publishing
ISBN 978-0-9898714-5-7

Cover design by LoveSpin Publishing.

Contents

Acknowledgments

To my fabulous editor Yolanda Barber who challenged me every step of the way. To my husband, friends and extended family members who encouraged me to pursue my dream. Thank you all.

TAKE ME DOWN

Third in A Series | A Suits in Pursuit Novel

Lauren H. Kelley

LoveSpin

LOVESPIN PUBLISHING | ATLANTA

Chapter One

"It's not what you think, Ash. Hear me out, babe. She doesn't mean anything to me. I screwed up." Paul groveled on his rusty knees, kneeling near the bedside as Ashley shoved past him. "I was vulnerable. Weak. Babe, please don't do this. I promise I won't mess up again."

Ashley whipped her head around and shot fiery daggers at Paul with her eyes. "The sad thing is that you don't even care, and that's a problem for me. I'm tired of your bull. I won't do this with you anymore. We're done. Get out!"

Paul crawled across the floor, his bare pasty ass crack covered with a crumpled sheet as he wrapped his lower half. The rail-thin skank, whom he'd been screwing senselessly when Ashley walked into the room, crouched naked in a corner, scrambling to dress. Arms and legs flailed wildly as the skinny redhead shoved her freckled face through the neck hole of a pink shirt and yanked a pale gray skirt up around absent hips. She grabbed her checkered Mary Jane pumps and tacky leopard-print bra and panties.

"You'd better move faster like you don't want my foot up your ass," Ashley snapped. "Can't even look at me, can you?" Tucked away in his crate, Copper yipped and circled in time to the commotion.

Her head kept down. "I... I'm sorry. I... I'm leaving now," the woman stammered. Her large round eyes darted wildly as though looking for the fastest escape route. A hand shielded her beet-red face from Ashley, and her pace quickened.

Ashley's scathing glare trailed that sleazy hoochie's hasty steps as she made a scandalous escape through the front door of the loft apartment.

Finally on his feet, Paul yanked up his underwear and stalked over to Ashley. Sweat-drenched biceps snaked around her waist and pulled her to him. Taking a deep breath, she squelched the nausea building in her belly.

"Ashley, you know this is your fault. If you didn't hold out on me last week, I wouldn't have..."

She jerked out of his grimy grip and spun around. With the full force of breath in her lungs, Ashley's scream bounced off the twenty-foot ceiling. "Get your goddamn hands off me! How dare you blame me, you piece of shit! Get out! Now!" Trembling hands clenched into fists. "Get your shit and get the hell out."

Paul stilled. He backed away. Kept quiet. A smirk smeared across his face. He meandered across the room in his boxers and leaned against the speckled granite kitchen countertop. "Ash, come on. I swear. I'll never cheat on you again."

A coy smile relaxed the tension in her lips. "Last time, huh?" Her stare idled on perfect bleach-white teeth that he dared to bare.

"I swear. This is the last time. You're my beautiful mocha princess."

Moving at a snail's pace, she recovered his black slacks and dress shirt tossed carelessly to the floor near shiny new loafers. Shiny new loafers that his broke ass couldn't have purchased. *Deadbeat!* He hadn't held a steady job or paid a single bill in six months. She slinked past him and wiggled her voluptuous ass. With a slight turn and a flippant tilt of her head, she glanced over her shoulder. "You're damn right, asshole." She tossed his belongings through the large industrial window nine stories to the ground below. "I said get out, and that's what I meant. Now!"

Suddenly Ashley lunged forward, her clawed hands aimed at Paul's jugular. He stumbled, crashed into a leather stool, and landed on the cold concrete floor.

Paul clambered to his feet. Backing away from Ashley, he slammed into the gritty exposed brick wall. "You crazy bitch!"

"Crazy?" she said, her laugh deranged, mocking his words. "Oh, you haven't seen me at crazy, but I'm about to show you crazy." She stepped out of her right shoe. Then her left shoe. Bent over, Ashley retrieved a four-inch stiletto and then rose to her full five-foot-seven-inch height, heel aimed at Paul.

He slithered along the wall's surface, trying to flee. "Agh!" he cried out when the brick grated his flesh.

Ashley charged again. Paul scurried to the front door. The sound of him fiddling with the doorknob assaulted her eardrums until finally the chambers in the lock clicked and he made a hasty escape.

Paul stood half-naked in the hall. The door slammed shut. Ashley laughed, thinking about him running through the interior of the building in his boxers. He hadn't been wise to tempt her sanity.

Paul evicted from her apartment and her life, Ashley sank to the floor. Her knees pulled to a heaving chest, her head lowered into them. Her anger burned hot. She had forgotten to breathe. Stewing in her reality, Ashley sobbed hard and tears flowed in streams down her face like a waterfall.

Ashley and Paul had met at a bar. That first night of heated passion had been a deceptive lure. The explosive sex that started with midnight booty calls quickly fizzled into a year of pure hell. Paul came equipped with a heartbeat and a hard cock, barely a step up from dildo sex. They had nothing in common, he was rude, and frankly the man was dumber than the loafers that hit the pavement when she tossed them out the window. He just happened to have the right male apparatus to soothe the empty ache between her thighs on lonely nights. Ashley turned to men whenever the loneliness in her life was too overwhelming, echoed too loudly, and reminded her that fairy-tale endings didn't always happen— though her best friend Kerrigan proved to be the exception. *Bitch.*

After her pity party, Ashley reveled in a sense of relief. The thought of that bargain-basement hooker in her apartment having sex on her bed made Ashley's stomach twist. She pulled herself up from the floor. With puffy eyes, she entered the bathroom to clean up, dabbed tears away from her swollen brown eyes.

After returning to the loft's main living area, Ashley slid on a pair of flip-flops. She grabbed the keys and Copper's leash from the wooden console table. Releasing Copper from the crate, she scooped him up and exited the apartment.

She always used her knuckles to punch elevator buttons. Hundreds of thousands of filthy fingertips came into contact with those archaic buttons, including those of Paul and his little skank. Ashley pressed a hand to her belly. The thought made her stomach revolt. "Dirty knuckles," she muttered and rubbed the back of her hand on her pants.

The elevator ride to the building's lobby didn't take long. At least the oversized tin can didn't lodge between floors today. She could skip her typical breathless sprint down nine flights with Copper tucked under one arm.

A quick flick of the wrist, she waved to Carl, the door attendant who always wore headphones, head bopping to the beat. The twitch in his jaw hinted at a smile. He didn't lift his head or wave back. Ashley nudged the old rickety doors of the Carlisle, forced them open, and stepped outside. She dialed the number and then pushed a button on her hands-free earpiece.

"Hello," the winded husky male voice answered.

"Hey, Axel. This is Ash. Is Kerri home?"

"Hi." He paused. "Uh, yeah. Hold on a minute." His exaggerated sigh didn't faze her.

Ashley's Yorkie circled brightly lit lampposts and yipped at strangers strolling down the dark sidewalk in front of her apartment building. She tugged Copper's leash. Understandably, he was more hyper than was usual.

A small breathless voice whispered in her ear. "Hey, Ash. You never call this late. What's going on? Are you okay?"

Kerrigan didn't sound like herself. "Kerri, did I catch you at a bad time?" Ashley's eyes stretched wide, and her jaw dropped. "Oh. No. You and Axel are fu..." Ashley halted her words as she caught the crumpled frown of a craggy old woman who resembled Maxine, sprung to life from the cover of a Hallmark greeting card. "Oh. God. You are screwing." Ashley stared brazenly and rolled her eyes at the old hag who stood at the building's entrance, puffing on a cigarette. She imagined the woman, like the Carlisle building, must have been beautiful once. "I'm sorry I called after ten. I forgot married people with an infant only have sex at night. I'll call you tomorrow."

Kerrigan let out a guilty giggle. "Ash! You know I'm always here for you. Let's talk now. What's wrong?" Ashley heard Axel grumbling in the background.

"Kerri, go take care of your man. Axel is still my boss. You don't have to deal with him at work now that you're off running your boutique. I don't need your grumpy husband after me on Monday."

Kerrigan laughed again. "Don't worry about Axel. I've already taken care of him. We can talk now. Do you want me to come over?"

Ashley let out a sigh, and tears pooled in her eyes. "Oh, Kerri. My life is a mess, and… and… I… shit!" The leash slipped from her clammy fingers.

In a frenzied rush, Ashley bolted down the sidewalk, her legs carrying her as fast as she could move them. "Copper, come back! No, no! Oh my God. No! Copper!" Her smartphone crashed to the sidewalk, the face cracked, and the device landed on the concrete.

Ashley held her breath. She watched Copper dash into the road, cross to the other side, and scamper down a dark alley. His bark faded into silence. She loved Copper, but she knew better than to chase him into an alley at that hour of the night. The last time he escaped, she found him the next morning scurrying in front of the building, waiting for her to appear.

She retrieved the battered phone. "Hello. Kerri, can you hear me?"

Nothing. Three minutes and counting displayed on the screen indicated a connected call, but there was utter silence. Out of breath, tears trailed across Ashley's cheeks, and tangled hair whipped across her face. She clutched her sides and bawled like a two-year-old whose favorite toy had been snatched away. If anyone deserved to have a mental breakdown at ten thirty on a Wednesday night on Peachtree Street, she did.

With rapid steps, Ashley paced up and down the block. "I can't believe this is my life," she muttered under her breath, helpless like a sailor adrift a tattered raft and without the mental strength to plan next steps. Attempting to skirt a man who jogged past her, their shoulders grazed and she nearly fell. The jogger didn't stop or offer an apology.

"Excuse you, asshole."

She trailed behind the man, quickened her gait to a stride. The jogger raised a hand and presented his one-fingered salute over his shoulder. His legs carried him full sprint. The red, five-fingered hand halted her pursuit at the end of the block as the crosswalk signal changed. Two lanes of idling cars were the great divide between Ashley and her assailant.

From the opposite side of the road with his chest puffed out, he yelled, "Lunatic," and then continued on his way.

Ashley's heart pounded in her chest. She glared at the man's back getting smaller and smaller until he vanished into the night. Breathless, she limped back to the front of the Carlisle building and leaned over, open palms pressed against her knees.

Two minutes later, Ashley's shallow breathing returned to normal and she stood up. She moved her hand to her tear-stained face and wiped the moisture away. Suddenly a warm sensation blanketed her right shoulder.

Ashley jumped. "Ah!" She whirled around, arm arched back and ready to throw a punch. "You can't rob someone on one of the shittiest days of their life! I don't have any damn money."

The stranger snatched his masculine hand away and stepped back. Slowly her eyes settled on his Nike sneakers, crawled up his navy jogging pants to a muscular chest and then landed on a face so perfect that she had to lift her jaw up from the sidewalk.

"Miss, I'm not going to hurt you. Are you okay?" The handsome stranger's voice soothed her fear.

She stared into his gray eyes. *Gorgeous.* "Yes, I'm okay. I've just had a bad day. Thanks."

"Me too." His eyes were dark and sunken. "Do you live in this building?" He pointed at the towering Carlisle building behind them.

She gave a cautious half nod.

"I was watching you. Saw you hunched over. I thought you might need some help."

"Well, that's a little creepy," she blurted out.

He frowned, wrinkled his brow. "You're welcome," he said with a smirk.

His snappy quip triggered Ashley. "Maybe you should mind your own business. I'm not a damsel in distress who needs rescuing. If I want to cry or scream in the middle of the night, that's none of your business."

The stranger's eyes widened, and he took a step back. "It is my business when there's a crazy woman chasing people down the block and throwing a tantrum in front of my building."

Ashley's hand mounted her hip. "You don't own the building. I live here too. I can stand here. I'll cry whenever I want. Asshole!"

"I do…" He paused midsentence. Waved a dismissive hand. "Forget it. Good-night, miss. Obviously you're the source of your own problems." The pesky stranger turned and stalked away, giving her a final glance, and he tossed the

Dogfish Head beer bottle into the trash bin and then
disappeared into the building.

Before he could punch the elevator button,
Sebastian's cell phone rang. He couldn't help but roll his eyes
and release a sigh that accompanied the gesture. "Hello,
Garrett. I know why you're calling."

"Good. How soon will the proposal be ready?"

Sebastian huffed. "Couldn't this wait until morning?"

"Probably, but I'm worried. I don't trust Stephen, and
neither should you. You missed the meeting today, and the
board is becoming impatient."

His voice rose. "You do remember who I am?"
Sebastian circled the small, dingy lobby, shaking his head at
mucky carpet stains that trailed from the entrance to the
elevator. "Stop worrying. I have a plan," he said, his voice
returning to a natural cadence. Glancing through the large
lobby window, Sebastian eyed the Chinese restaurant across
the street. "Some of the people who live here…" He paused,
his encounter with the ranting woman still fresh on his mind.
Her small frame curved in all the right places. Too bad she'd
opened her mouth. "I have my work cut out for me, but yes,
I do have a plan."

Harsh light filtered into the living room and pried
Ashley's tired swollen eyes open. She lay in the streaming
daylight, empty sorrow ripping her heart in two. A loud

banging at her front door jolted her into an upright position. Both pieces of her torn heart hammered. She froze. Paul would be the last person she wanted to see. She lifted herself up from the sofa where she had fallen asleep last night. One step, two steps, three steps, and slowly she made her way to the peephole.

"Who's there?" Her strong voice didn't give away her frayed nerves.

The knot in Ashley's stomach loosened when she peered into the world on the other side of her door.

"Hey, Ash. It's Kerri. Open the door."

Ashley twisted the knob, and the door opened. Kerrigan shoved her way past, whirled in, and glanced around at Ashley's disheveled apartment. Kerrigan hopscotched across the room toward the kitchen, avoiding a shattered wineglass and the remnants of Ashley's cell phone scattered on the floor.

Nearly stumbling on top of an overturned stool, Kerrigan paused her steps and grabbed the edge of the breakfast bar for support. "What happened last night?" She spun around, leaned down, and grabbed Ashley's shoe dangling the stiletto in the air by its snapped heel. "Ash, are you okay?" Her nose crinkled as her eyes landed on Ashley.

Ashley clutched her stomach. "Nothing." She shook her head. "I kicked Paul's sorry ass out. I caught him in my bed with some random chick. I can't sleep on that bed. I want to burn the whole freaking mattress."

"You were yelling and screaming last night, and then our call disconnected. I tried to call you back, but you didn't answer. I was worried about you."

Ashley lowered her gaze. "Sorry." Her shaky voice pitched. "I took Copper out last night, and he broke lose. When I went after him, I dropped my new phone. Broke it. No insurance. My life is awesome." Ashley sneered and then rolled her eyes.

Heat rushed to her cheeks. "Only I could lose a man and my dog in an hour. Honestly, I'm more upset about Copper's running away. You know how much I love that little fur ball." Her anger being so intense raised her temperature ten degrees. Ashley dabbed her forehead, drying light perspiration.

Kerrigan reached out and wrapped Ashley in her arms. "Oh, Ash. I am so sorry."

Ashley sobbed on Kerrigan's shoulder.

"You're better off without Paul in your life. You and him, the whole relationship, was toxic. You're a knockout—absolutely gorgeous. Smart. Sassy. Any man worth anything and with half a brain would be lucky to have you. You deliberately put yourself into relationships with jerks to avoid getting too close. Is this about Chris?"

Ashley squirmed out from Kerrigan's embrace. "Damn you, Kerri. That's not fair. You can say whatever you want, but you know talking about Chris is off-limits." Dragging heavy feet, Ashley dawdled into the kitchen. She sank into a chair at the round glass table.

Kerrigan followed and sat next to her at the kitchen table. "Ash, I'm your best friend and nothing I say is ever meant to hurt you. You need to let him go. It's been six years." Her voice softened, and tender eyes met Ashley's.

Ashley squeezed her eyes shut, fighting back conflicted emotions. She inhaled a deep breath. "I know you're right. I'm trying." Sharing her vulnerability, even with Kerrigan, had been rare and difficult.

"Take a long weekend, go on an exotic trip. I'd go with you if I could leave my family, but Alexa is so young she needs me." Kerrigan consoled Ashley, patting her hand with graceful fingers.

Ashley's gaze landed on Kerrigan's wedding ring. The massive diamond probably had its own atmosphere. Envy stung her eyes again. "You have a different life now—husband, baby, your own boutique. I get that. Kerri, you know I'm happy for you." She stared at the photo deliberately placed at eye level where she could see him whenever she sat at the table. "Chris and I always talked about going…"

Kerrigan shifted in her seat and took Ashley's stiff hands into hers. "Ash, Chris is gone. You had a wonderful life with him. If he were still alive, I know he'd want you to be happy. You need liberation from the past, from him—a new happiness."

Ashley blinked wide, watery eyes.

Kerrigan reached across the table and yanked a tissue from the box. "You always talk about going to Europe." She handed the tissue to Ashley.

Ashley dabbed her wet eyes dry. "You can't be serious. I can't go to Europe by myself." She shook her head.

"Okay, what about taking a weekend trip somewhere closer to home?"

Ashley shrugged her shoulders. "Kerri, I… I know you mean well, but I can't."

"Yes, you can. You should talk to Dr. Martin. Find out what he thinks."

"I know what he thinks, and I happen to disagree with him too. I can't go."

"No. You mean you won't go because you're afraid of living your life. That's the reason you keep sabotaging any chance at a meaningful relationship by picking losers like Paul."

Ashley's lips twisted into a crooked, quivering, nervous line. "I know you're right, Kerri, but I can't."

Kerrigan frowned, her index finger pointed at Ashley. "Yes, you will. I'll pick the destination and buy your ticket. All you have to do is show."

Ashley plastered herself against the chair's backrest, arms folded across her chest, sulking.

"Well?" Kerrigan asked, pushing Ashley for an immediate answer.

"Your damn husband is rubbing off on you. I don't think I can take time off from work. You know how busy work is with the McBride account. If I'm going to land that promotion, now isn't the best time for me to take vacation." Ashley replied.

"Enough with the excuses, Ashley Ann Turner. Taking one or two weeks off won't put A.C. Advertising out of business or jeopardize your promotion."

The fog that had dampened Ashley's mood began to lift. "Fine. I'll think about taking a trip, but I'm not making any promises. I'm doing the best I can."

"I know you are, Ash. I just want to see you happy again. Besides, it's my turn to return the favor. Without you, I would have never moved to Atlanta or met Axel. Without you, I'd still be running from my man."

Ashley narrowed her eyes at Kerrigan, silent for minutes. "Okay. Okay." She let out an exasperated sigh. "Do your thing. But just so you know, this trip is not about me finding romance. I like my arrangement. Sex without expectations works for me." She twirled a stray hair around her finger as her chest tightened. Filled with anxiety, Ashley gasped for air, her constricted breaths made her lightheaded.

Kerrigan rolled her eyes. She rose from the chair and then strolled across the stained-concrete floor to a built-in bookcase. "When are we going to take these down?" She held up a photo of Chris that sat on the shelf. "I like Dr. Martin's idea about a memory box. Might help you move on."

"I'm not ready for that either." Ashley's frantic head nod forced Kerrigan to place the photo back on the shelf.

"Okay. Baby steps. Whenever you're ready, just call, and I'll come over. We can take them down and create a memory box together."

"If I fall in love again, that's when the photos come down."

Kerrigan's heels clicking against the concrete floor, she walked toward Ashley and stretched her arms out wide.

Ashley returned the hug. "Thank you, Kerri, for everything," Her words poured out from twisted lips.

"I'm going to make this easy for you. I'll schedule a date, time, and location."

Ashley hoped her smile masked the fear. Kerrigan was right. The time to move on had come, but she had no idea how to let go of the man she had thought she would spend a lifetime loving. Her chin placed on Kerrigan's shoulder, Ashley scanned the room. She met Chris's ghostly gaze, peering at her from a large frame seated on the shelf. His memory delighted and tormented her. Then suddenly, she heard his voice.

"Time to let go."

A chill ran up Ashley's spine. She clutched Kerrigan tighter, determination to move on dissolving her fear.

Chapter Two

Ashley paced the kitchen floor and then strutted to the large window. Her thumb twitched against her outer thigh as she scanned the street with a careful eye, watching for familiar car lights. She glanced at her cell phone. The time was five o'clock in the morning. Kerrigan and Axel would arrive at any moment. She was reeling inside. After all she had been through the past six years, Ashley wanted to move on, but guilt, like a hard knot, settled in her belly. Guilt bore down, hard and heavy, keeping any forward momentum stalled. How had Kerrigan talked her into going to Florida? When Kerrigan mentioned the trip two months ago, Ashley thought she had been bluffing, but Kerrigan followed through on her promise.

Five minutes later, a knock at the door jolted her up from the sofa.

"Come on in. I need to grab my suitcase," Ashley said, nervous fingers clinging to the door's edge refused to unloosen.

Kerrigan reached out, swept Ashley into an embrace. "Hey, Ash. Axel is keeping the car warm for us. Do you have everything you need?"

Ashley backed away and held up a small garment bag. "You know I do, including my lingerie and condoms." She winked at Kerrigan.

Kerrigan snatched the bag away and peeked inside. Her mouth dropped open. "Really, Ash? Black lace corset with matching thong, garters, and stockings. There's no way you're going to have casual sex with some random stranger in the Keys." Her self-righteous tone made Ashley laugh.

"Probably not, but in case an opportunity presents himself, then I'll be ready." She shoved the smaller bag into a slightly larger carry-on masquerading as luggage.

Kerrigan shook her head. "Are you sure you have actual clothes in that tiny duffel bag?"

She mounted her side with a hand. "Maybe," she said with a tease tickling her vocal chords. "But since you've decided to come with me, you can keep an eye on me."

"Someone has to keep an eye on you," Kerrigan muttered as she tugged Ashley's so-called luggage into the hall and closed the door.

Ashley and Kerrigan moved through the crowd of people and eventually made their way to the terminal. Although the flight to Key West would be short, only two hours from Atlanta, Ashley hated to fly. They had little more than an hour to kill at the airport before the flight would begin boarding.

"Hey, Kerri, I'm feeling a little restless, and my bladder is about to explode. I'm going to the restroom. Wanna come?"

"No, go without me. I'll stay here with Axel." Kerrigan nodded and leaned into Axel's side. He wrapped his arm around her, pulling her close.

Ashley rolled her eyes and shoved her finger halfway down her throat. "Uck! Didn't you two have a three-month honeymoon?" She scoffed and gave a disapproving head shake. "I'll be back soon. Try not to make a scene or get a room," she said. Her words trailed off, and distance separated her from the lovebirds.

Ashley made her way from the restroom to the first gift shop she spotted. She stopped in front of the magazines and books, perusing the titles and headlines. For minutes, she contemplated one tabloid after another, each smeared with the latest headlines on Hollywood's drama, mayhem, and trysts. A magazine featuring the year's sexiest men in film caught her attention. *Yum!* Her eyes glided across the cover that graced a nearly shirtless and ripped Henry Cavill. She stooped and picked up the magazine, searching the table of contents.

Turned to the spread featuring delicious photos of her favorite actors, gorgeous men leaped off the pages into Ashley's imagination. *Idris Elba, OMG!* She knew she had been ogling the movie gods for far too long. *Damn, I need a man.* Self-conscious about her lusty ruminations, she glanced around, biting her bottom lip and avoiding eye contact with would-be prosecutors. She looked to the right, and no one was there. Thank goodness. Then she looked to the left. There stood the most beautiful man she ever laid eyes upon. Ashley's cheeks warmed.

Eyes a deep bluish gray. Dark golden hair framed a perfectly sculpted face. There was something familiar about that strong jawline and those firm, shapely lips. Slowly her eyes slid down the rest of him. Veins pulsed in his sinewy arms as large hands slid into denim pockets. Whoa! He came to life from the pages of the very magazine she held.

Ashley stared at the stranger far longer than was polite. As lonely and horny as she had been, she might attack the man where he stood. Turning, she decided to head back to the terminal, or else she might orgasm right there in the store. Before she could reach the exit, firm fingers clamped around her forearm. Jostled by the strong grip on her arm, she whipped around. She hadn't paid for the magazine still in her hand.

"Oh, I'm sorry. I was lost in thought. I didn't mean to…" she said, lifting her eyes to meet her captor. Rattled, a small tingle started in her feet, crawled up her legs, and spread through her trunk, bursting like fireworks from every pore. She was met by the intense gaze of the provocative stranger who stood mere inches away, his fingers wrapped around her arm.

A wide grin spread across his face like stars spanned across the evening sky. "I know, me too," he said in a deep voice as smooth and as sexy as his swagger, and then he released her arm.

"I'm sorry. What?" Her words came out dull, dazed.

"I meant, I was lost in thought too." His eyes roved her frame. A pink short-sleeved sweater hugged round, perky breasts and dipped low. "You look familiar. Have we met?" He had seen those fiery brown eyes before.

"I don't think so. I would remember you," she said, her voice springing to life as she tilted her head, exposing a long slender neck.

He grinned and arched a brow. *Hmm.*

The tips of their fingers grazed each other as she handed the magazine to him. "I didn't mean to take the magazine." The sensation of her touch hit him in the gut. "Do you work here?" she asked.

He kept his eyes glued to her. Her curvy, fit frame was familiar too. "Nope. I don't work here." Pondering her acquaintance, his eyes scanned her face. He imagined rummaging his fingers through her straight dark hair and then fondling naked, tawny-colored flesh. A rogue tongue skittered across his lips as he entertained the thought of capturing full, pouty, glossed lips with his. "I never forget a face. Are you sure we haven't met before?"

She squinted and then paused before speaking. "I'm pretty certain we haven't," she replied.

"That's a shame. You're beautiful." Like a bolt of lightning, the memory struck him. He remembered where they had met.

Her broad smile faded when a flight attendant's voice filled the air. "Thank you. Sorry, but I have to go. My flight's boarding." Frantically, she turned away and fled. He watched her slip into the crowd, and then she was gone.

Ashley didn't head back to the terminal immediately. She had been too shaken. She ducked into the restroom, locked herself in the first empty stall, back pressed against the cold tile wall. A hand to her chest, she waited for her breathing to calm. She had never been so awe-stricken by a man, a stranger at that. *He called me beautiful.* She gulped oxygen into her lungs and opened the stall door.

By the time she reached the gate, first-class and business-class passengers had been boarded.

"Now boarding passengers seated in zone four." The perky blond behind the counter placed the handset into the cradle.

Ashley weaved through the hoard of people assembled at the gate.

"I was worried you wouldn't reach the gate in time. We're boarding next." Kerrigan stood. "Hello, are you here with me?" Kerrigan waved her hand in Ashley's face.

"Hmm?"

"Ash, you okay?"

"Yeah, I'm fine. It's nothing."

"Now boarding passengers seated in zone five," the flight attendant said.

"That's us." Kerrigan tugged Ashley's arm. "I know you. Something's up."

Ashley didn't plan to tell Kerrigan about the sex god in the gift shop. There was no point. "I'm just a little nervous about flying. I'll be fine."

Thirty minutes into the flight, passengers began moving about the cabin, some headed to the restroom while others visited with neighbors. A pale-faced, red-haired boy stood in the aisle with his mother and played with a red and white toy airplane. Kerrigan had fallen asleep.

Ashley swiped the screen of her iPad and stared blankly at the words of a client's proposal she had planned to read. She could fool Kerrigan, but she couldn't fool herself. Her mind returned to the man whom she had met in the gift shop. *He was beautiful.* Folding the protective cover over the device, she tucked the tablet into her bag. She closed her eyes, remembering how his deep gray eyes returned admiration and the tingle that ran up her spine. Suddenly she felt a presence hover near.

A slight caress on her forearm jarred her from her musing. The toy plane the red-haired boy played with had rubbed against her arm. Ashley smiled and closed her eyes again, returning to her bawdy thoughts of the mysterious man. Suddenly a thick, deep voice startled her and demanded her attention.

"You again," the voice said. Ashley's eyes landed on a broad grin stretched from ear to ear. "The stars must be aligned."

Ashley's heart raced. Mr. Sexy-as-hell from the gift shop stood directly over her.

Her eyes raced up his tall, muscular frame. "Hi. Are you going to Key West too?"

"It would appear so. This is a direct flight, and mid-flight drop-offs are heavily discouraged."

Her stomach clenched. She recognized that sarcastic tone.

Thin lips spread into a devious grin. "I'm Sebastian." He extended his hand to her.

She reached up to accept his handshake, but this time not so eager to return a smile.

"I'm Ashley." Their hands locked. Ashley warmed, an exchange of mutual attraction obvious by his dilated pupils. He kept clamped fingers around her hand.

"It's nice to meet you again, Ashley. Are you going to Key West for business or pleasure or both?" The seductive growl in the hum of his deep voice made her insides quiver.

Clumsily she rammed her elbow into the seat's sidearm when he released her hand from his clutch. Pain shot up her arm. *Ouch!* She winced. "Pleasure... to meet you. I'm taking a vacation from life. You?"

"Hmm." He smiled down at her. "That's interesting. I'd say the same, but I'm going for business mostly, although"—he raised a brow—"I'm hoping to find a little pleasure too."

Her eyes widened. Before she could think of a smart response, the line in front of him began to move.

"I'll see you around, Ashley." She liked the way her name rolled off Sebastian's tongue. The heavy Southern drawl gave her goose bumps. There was a dangerous swagger in his stride as he stepped off. He glanced over his shoulder, caught her stare, and flashed a wicked grin her way.

Ashley breathed erratically, and her heart pounded hard. *Sebastian.*

"Who was that?" Kerrigan piped up, her voice muffled by a yawn.

"Just some guy. I didn't realize you were awake."

"I wasn't until you started carrying on with Mr. Sexy-and-Southern. Do you know him?"

"Uh, well… yeah, sort of." Ashley frowned.

Kerrigan frowned back. "Sort of? Either you know him or you don't. Which is it?"

"I sort of met him in the gift shop at the airport… and before." Ashley's words trailed off, muffled. She thought about those black jeans he wore. The way the denim hugged his thick thighs. *Amazing.*

Kerrigan shot up in her seat. "Gift shop? And before?" Her tone escalated. "Ash, what aren't you telling me?"

Ashley sank into her seat and twisted guilty lips into a smirk. "I think we met the night of my meltdown in front of my apartment building." She had told Kerrigan about her ballistic outburst on a man who had tried to help. "His name is Sebastian. I just realized where we first met. I haven't seen him since that night."

"Did you see his shoulders and those arms? Wow! I think this trip is just what you need." Kerrigan's excitement tamed Ashley's grimace and made her blush.

"He is something, isn't he?" Ashley conceded with a smile that faded dim.

"Are you going to do anything about it?"

"I... I don't know. I'm not going to chase him, if that's what you mean." Ashley shifted in her seat and glanced in Sebastian's direction, making certain he was out of earshot. "Besides, that one is dangerous."

"Dangerous? How?" Kerrigan asked.

"He's not fling material. I know fling material." Ashley pursed her lips and wagged a finger. "One word... Paul."

Kerrigan rolled her eyes. "Yeah, well Paul was a jerk, and you knew that going in. If Sebastian isn't fling material, what is he?"

Ashley twisted around, looking back again. "He's danger. Did you see the Rolex on his wrist? And those jeans he's wearing cost more than my entire wardrobe times three," she said.

"Rolex? Expensive jeans? Sorry, but I fail to see how that makes him dangerous. You're prejudiced."

"Kerri, don't be naïve. Those are clues, not fashion statements. A man like Sebastian probably has an ego and a sense of entitlement bigger than the price of that watch and those jeans combined."

Kerrigan shrugged her shoulders. "So he's got an ego. Some people call that confidence."

Ashley rolled her neck. "Sebastian's the kind of man addictions are made of. The worst kind of drug. He'll wine you and dine you, and you can't get enough. He'll possess you as one of his expense trinkets. And then, bam! He'll drop the ax, and he's done with you." Ashley shook her head, feeling sympathy for all the women who had fallen victim to

Sebastian in the past. "I'm nobody's trinket, and I can't be bought."

Kerrigan narrowed her eyes. "He's a game player. I thought you specialized in handling his type."

Ashley smiled a crooked grin, remembering how Sebastian's pants hung from his waist and the feeling that knotted her belly when she shook his hand. "He's the kind of man who will take a sista down." She nodded her head. "I can handle the little league players. Sebastian is major league. Dangerous."

Kerrigan leaned in and whispered in Ashley's ear. "Danger can be fun. You taught me that, remember?"

Ashley rolled her eyes. "Yeah, but Danger fell in love and married you."

"You never know what could happen. Give him your number at least."

"Or maybe I'll ask for his number." Ashley arched an eyebrow.

"What happened at the airport?"

Ashley could feel her eyes flutter as she thought back to the glorious moment. "I was standing at a magazine rack, drooling over this year's hottest male actors. When I looked around to see if anyone was watching me…"

"And I saw the most beautiful woman. I had to introduce myself and get her name, but Ashley ran off. Luckily for me, she happens to be on my flight heading to Key West." Sebastian stood over Ashley, grinning, his eyes fixed on her.

"Oh! Hello, Se… Sebastian" she stuttered.

Sebastian settled into the empty seat next to Ashley. He leaned across Ashley, stuck out his hand to Kerrigan. "Hi. I'm Sebastian."

Kerrigan smiled and gave Sebastian's hand a firm shake. "Good to meet you. I'm Kerrigan."

Sebastian drew his arm back and nestled into the seat. "How long will you be in Key West, Ashley?" he asked, an eyebrow raised. "Before you head back to rant and rave on Peachtree Street," he whispered.

Ashley's eyes stretched wide. She glanced at Kerrigan, who had put in earphones and shut her eyes, tuning them out. "You remember me?" Ashley asked, her head back and eyes focused on the safety pamphlet tucked into the pocket of the seat in front of her. She wondered if the pamphlet included instruction on how to avoid embarrassing moments such as this.

"How could I forget you, darlin'?" His smug grin and sarcastic tone confronted her.

"I'll be in the Keys for two weeks," she whispered back, turning away from his penetrating gaze. "I'm sorry about that night. Usually, I'm not that... that..."

"Insane." He smiled bolder now.

Ashley nodded her head in agreement. "Yes. Usually, I'm not that insane. Again, I am very sorry. I had a bad day. My dog Copper ran away and..." She stopped. Telling a man whom she had just met about her ex would make her seem crazy and desperate. "...I have signs posted, and my friend's husband is helping with the search while we're in the Keys."

"I'm sorry about your dog. I hope you find him. I'm staying at the Key West Oceanside Resort. Where are you and your friend staying?"

Ashley's lips tightened, and she frowned. Sebastian breezing past her apology raised a flag in her mind. She shrugged off the feeling. *Play nice.*

"We're staying at Kerrigan's vacation home." She bit her bottom lip, trying her best not to let something sarcastic slip past her lips. "How about you? How long will you be in the Keys?"

"Depends."

"Depends on what?" Head tilted to one side, she frowned.

"Depends on whether or not there's a reason for me to stay longer than I do normally."

Good-looking. Smart tongue. Sexy as hell. *Yep. Dangerous.* He had to go... but not yet.

"That's not an answer," she said, looking him squarely in the eyes. "Oh, I see. You're one of those men who can't give a straight answer." Pride swelled up inside Ashley. She would outdo him in a duel of sharp-tongued exchanges and send him running.

He scrunched his face, cocked his head sideways. A spark of mischief flashed in his eyes. And without warning, he threw his head back and released a gut-wrenching laugh.

Ashley jerked and tucked stray strands of hair behind her ear. *I can't believe he's laughing at me.* Heat burned her cheeks. She pursed her lips and didn't crack a smile.

"I travel to the Keys quite a bit for work, and I come and go as I please. At least six times a year." Sebastian shuffled in the seat, positioned himself closer to Ashley until lightly grazing her ear with his lips when he spoke. "I know the Keys very well. Ashley, I would love to take you out one evening, either in the Keys or back in Atlanta."

The corners of her lips twitched. A coy smile emerged. "I'll think about it."

"You do that." He reached into his pocket and retrieved his wallet. "I'll give you my card. Do you have a pen?" he asked.

"Sure." Sebastian's fingers danced against Ashley's as she handed him a pen.

His bluish-gray eyes pinned her. "Here's my cell phone number, and this is the hotel's main number. Ask for me and they'll put you through. Or, we could set up a date right now. What are you doing tomorrow evening?" Sebastian's intense eyes made her flesh tingle.

Ashley gritted her teeth. "I don't know. We haven't discussed any plans yet." She glanced at Kerrigan, who had drifted asleep. "This trip was forced on me."

"I see. So you're the desperate, single friend."

Ashley glared at him. "That's rude," she said, her tone seeded with annoyance.

"I didn't say that to be rude. I make observations. Looks like the odds are in my favor, Ashley."

"After that comment, I don't think you have any odds." She leaned away. "You're a jerk." She muttered through clenched teeth.

"No, I think the odds of me taking you out and screwing you are pretty good."

Well, damn. There it was. No pretense. Simple. Raw. Honest.

"I'm sorry. What did you say?" Ashley's voice raised high enough to shatter glass.

"You heard me, Ashley. I'm going to take you on a date. We'll enjoy a nice gourmet meal. Share a few laughs. Then I'm going to take you to my room and fuck your brains out."

Fists balled at her sides, she turned to the right. The wings of the plane sliced through thick puffy clouds reminding her they were thousands of feet in the air. Ashley lifted a few inches off the seat and glanced around at faces of potential witnesses to a midflight homicide.

Exhibiting control over her natural instinct to kill, she lowered into the seat. "Wow! Does that line actually work on other women? I've never been spoken to so..."

"Honestly." He finished her sentence. "Why get upset with me for telling the truth? I saw the way you looked at me in the gift shop. There's no point in playing games or lying to you. You did say you weren't a damsel in distress. That's what traditional dating is about—men rescuing lonely women to make them feel better about wanting to be fucked."

Ashley's temper blazed hotter now. Perspiration coated her burning skin, and heat emitted from her pores. Hands squeezed into tightly wadded fists at her sides. "Since you're breaking the rules of convention, why bother taking me out at all? Why not just invite me up to your room for the five-minute lay?" she asked.

He shook his head from side to side. "Because I don't think you have the guts. Ashley, you're a damsel in distress trying to pretend that you're not. I'm no goddamn knight, but I'll gladly rescue you if that makes you feel better about wanting ten inches of Sebastian Stone inside you." He leaned in at her retreat, then whispered more quietly, "You have my number. Call me anytime." His lips curled into a grimy smile. "I'm really going to enjoy having you."

"I don't believe this shit! First Paul and now you!" she blurted out loudly and then looked around the quiet cabin. The woman seated across from them frowned and then whispered to a man sitting next to her. Ashley frowned back and then glared at Sebastian. "Unfortunately for you, Sebastian, I'm fresh out of tolerance for losers and jerks," she snapped.

"I don't know who Paul is or what he did to you, but he has nothing to do with me. You know what I want. I haven't led you on, made false promises, or cheated on you. You'll call me." Sebastian stood. "Later, Ashley," he said with a slow, deliberate drawl and then strolled back to his seat in first class.

Still asleep with earbuds shoved in her ears, Kerrigan hadn't heard their whispered conversation. Ashley was pissed to the tenth degree. She shook Kerrigan violently until her eyes popped open.

"Kerrigan, you'll never believe what that... that ass of a man said to me. I can't believe him."

Kerrigan rubbed her sleepy eyes. "What are you talking about, Ash? Who?"

"I'm talking about Sebastian! He's the biggest asshole I've ever met."

"Obviously I missed something. Are you talking about Mr. Handsome and Dangerous from the gift shop? What happened?"

She shook her head, still in shock. "I thought our conversation was going well until he said he wanted to take me out and fuck me."

"What! He said that? Used those exact words?"

"Nearly verbatim. I can't believe I let you talk me into going on this trip."

"Ashley, forget about Sebastian." Kerrigan reached for her friend's hand.

"That creep lives in my building." She gripped her stomach. "I feel sick to my stomach. As far as I know, he could be some crazed lunatic." Ashley's leg bounced up and down as she spoke. "He could be a stalker. What if he's stalking me?"

"Don't jump to conclusions. He'll move on. He knows you're repulsed by his sleazy come-on."

Kerrigan fluffed her pillow and returned to her nap. Ashley fidgeted in her seat, stewing over Sebastian's audacious arrogance and exaggerated confidence. She pulled out her iPad and then put the tablet away. Even listening to music couldn't distract her from the thoughts floating in her head. No one had ever spoken so blatantly about sex and dating. Making matters worse, Sebastian had been right. Ashley did want him. The minute she saw him, she fantasized about his naked body. His raw sexual masculinity left her moist between the thighs. *Damn him.*

Ashley stared at the phone number scribbled on the back of Sebastian's business card. She flipped the card over to read the front. It read, *Wooster, Holman, and Stone, Inc. Sebastian Stone* had been printed on the card with no title.

She reached down into her coral-and-white-striped carry-on and pulled out her iPad to Google the company's name. Wooster, Holman, and Stone, Inc. was a real estate investment firm. A quick search on Sebastian Stone revealed his picture and title, president and chief executive officer. Ashley's stomach knotted. His high-ranking position made him believe that he could get away with treating women as objects. Infuriated and intrigued, inspiration struck her. She would teach this arrogant, entitled ass a lesson he wouldn't soon forget.

Chapter Three

Almost instantly, as though her pull had drawn him, Sebastian reappeared, hovering again. He dipped into the empty seat next to her once more. Ashley quickly shoved the iPad into her bag.

"What do you want, Sebastian?" She rolled her eyes. "I'm giving you fair warning. I've had about as much as I am willing to tolerate from you."

"Warning noted and filed away for safekeeping." He cocked his head and smirked. "Have you given my offer any more thought, Ashley? Will you go out with me?" he asked, raising a bushy brow.

"Actually, I have." She narrowed her gaze. "I'll go out with you on one condition."

"And that is?" He leaned in, his elbow rested on the slick metal armrest, and he stroked his chin.

"You promise to keep your hands to yourself unless I say otherwise."

His eyes shimmered, a victorious glint. "Yes, ma'am. We have a deal." Sebastian shifted in his seat.

"Oh, and Ashley, you will say otherwise. I'll make sure you do." The corners of his mouth slanted upward.

She huffed, releasing the tension that idled in her stiffened shoulders. "Offering full disclosure, if I was you, I wouldn't get my hopes or anything else up," Ashley batted her lashes. "Mr. Stone, I suspect you've never met a woman quite like me."

Sebastian's eyes flashed more brilliantly than before. "You're right. I've never met a woman like you, which is why I can't wait to get you alone."

"You certainly aren't lacking confidence, although you're clearly delusional."

"Thank you for the compliment."

"That wasn't a compliment, but then again, narcissists do tend to bend reality to satisfy their egos, don't they?"

He chuckled. "Luckily for you, I'm not narcissistic in bed. I'm a generous lover. Are you up for the challenge, Ashley?"

"Am I up for a challenge?" She tossed her head back, laughing blithely. "Not generally when complete disregard for common sense and good judgment are concerned. I'll agree to go out with you purely for the entertainment value. Like I said, you keep your hands to yourself. You got that, Mr. Stone?"

"Unless you say otherwise, right? That's the most important clause in our little agreement." He smiled.

"Ugh! I can't believe I've agreed to this," she replied, cupping her mouth to fight her gag reflex. "I must have lost my mind."

"You'll be surprised by what I'll have you agreeing to, Ashley." Sebastian rubbed his chin. "I believe in fate." He moved closer, gripped her with his words as his long fingers stroked her forearm. "Of the thousands of people in Atlanta, what are the chances that you and I met for the first time in front of the Carlisle and then end up on the same flight to Key West? Fate will keep thrusting us together until we work this out."

Ashley almost spewed out the sip of gin and coke that she had ingested seconds earlier. Luckily for the couple in the seats in front of her, she swallowed. A roaring laugh escaped her lips. An expectant glance met Sebastian's icicle stare. Expecting him to join her in laughter. He didn't crack a smile.

Ashley's hand flew to her chest. "It's worse than I thought. You actually believe the crap you're saying! You've got to be kidding me."

"I'm afraid I'm serious. This principle has served me well in my business dealings for many years."

"Sebastian, this is not a business transaction. If fate is the driving force, then why haven't you and I met before?"

"Maybe fate had other plans for us, preparing us separately through our individual life experiences for this day."

Ashley almost pushed the call button for help. Perhaps one business deal too many had driven Sebastian Stone crazy. She managed to keep a straight face. "Let me get this right. In your opinion, fate is a supernatural force for hookups. You think fate brought us together so that we could have sex?"

"Of course not. Sex is the perk. You and I have been fated to figure out why our paths continue to cross. Want to test fate?"

"Absolutely not. I'm not going to encourage your madness. In fact, I'm beginning to rethink this arrangement."

"Come on, darlin'. If I'm wrong, you never have to see me again." His lips curved into a confident smile.

Ashley's hand cradled her face. With a tentative pause, she considered his question. What did she have to lose? After all, the man headed a wealthy real estate investment firm. If Sebastian achieved business success following such a ridiculous philosophy about life, his success must have been pure coincidence. Putting his belief to the test might be fun, or at the very least, proving him wrong would be fun.

"And if I'm right, we'll go out. You'll have the best sex of your life with no expectations and no one to pass judgment against you. Either way, we both win. All you have to do is spend time with me in the Keys so that we can get to know each other. Are you in?"

"You're wrong, and yeah, I'm in," she replied coolly. "But no sex," she reiterated.

"There you go, darlin'. Keep telling yourself that." Sebastian's lusty eyes swept over Ashley and sent a shiver up her spine. "Now that we've gotten that out of the way, tell me about yourself. We still have an hour of flying time ahead of us."

Ashley didn't like flying. At least the nut job sitting next to her served as comic relief, distracting her phobia.

She leaned back and glanced at Kerrigan on her right. Kerrigan hadn't budged, still fast asleep. Ashley turned back to Sebastian. "What do you want to know?" she asked, cutting her eyes at him.

"What's your favorite sexual position?"

She stared at him, mouth agape. "Or how about starting with, 'What do you do for a living?' Or maybe, 'What do you do for fun?' And then there's the ever-popular, 'What's your favorite color?'" she sassed. Perhaps wallowing in her phobia wouldn't be as bad as entertaining the jerk sitting next to her.

"Okay, let's start there. Tell me what you do for a living, the sorts of things you like, and your favorite color."

"I'm glad you're agreeable." Ashley paused and rolled her eyes. "I'm in marketing, I like long walks on the beach, classic films, and reading, and my favorite color is red. Your turn."

He released a low chuckle. "I like that you're feisty." His muscled leg rubbed against hers, and Ashley shifted closer to Kerrigan. "I'm in real estate. I enjoy having sex with a beautiful woman, and my favorite color is green, as in the color of money."

"Shallow," she said.

"Honest," he replied, punctuating the word. "Since we're getting to know each other, where did you grow up?"

"Houston. What about you?"

"Same." His eyes glinted.

"Don't tell me, fate?"

"From your lips, darlin'."

Were it not for his absurdly rude and disturbing views on the attraction between men and women, and the sordid and twisted way that he talked about sex, Sebastian was almost likable. Almost.

They talked for twenty minutes. Idle chitchat that hadn't changed her opinion of his character. Soon after, awkward silence fell between them. Ashley fidgeted in her seat. Sebastian seemed content to sit there in silence and fiddle with his cell phone.

The weight of her personal drama and work stress had taken a toll on Ashley before the flight. She hadn't slept a solid eight hours in days. Like the sudden swing of a hammer, exhaustion hit. Her eyes closed.

She lay on Sebastian's bed in only her lacy bra and panties. Her hands bound above her head, tied to the headboard. Sebastian wore black slacks that hung low from the waist, and a white shirt unbuttoned down to his chest exposed hard ripples of muscle. His hands moved across her abdomen and down to her thighs. He fondled the cup of her bra, instantly unlatching the fastener. Ashley gasped. She wondered how he did that. Sebastian leaned over and nuzzled her naked breast with his mouth, drenching the firm nipple with the tip of his tongue. She moaned and writhed in delicious agony. His hand moved down further, between her thighs, cupping her sex as she moistened at his touch. A low humming thrummed in the background. The sound grew louder and louder, moved closer to her, and distracted her from the immediate pleasure that Sebastian promised.

What was that low rumbling sound? The deep tranquility soothed her anxiety as she slowly drifted back into consciousness. As she came into full cognition, Ashley saw burgundy fabric against her cheek. She had fallen asleep on Sebastian's chest. He snored softly, his head nuzzled against hers as she rested on him. Ashley didn't dare move. She stayed glued to his chest. *Shit! I had a wet dream about Sebastian.*

Sebastian relished the feel of Ashley's soft hair under his scruffy chin. She smelled heavenly. The soft, quiet moans she emanated intrigued him. He wondered what was going on in her pretty little head. Not much later, he dozed off too. When he awakened, he met her wide-eyed stare. Ashley jumped. His arms wrapped tenderly around her, held her firmly in place. He glanced down and met her nervous stare with an easy smile.

"Careful. I've got you." His voice was hoarse.

"What in the hell are you doing?" She snapped and pulled out of his embrace.

"I should be asking you that. You cozied up to me and settled in. I'm just the gracious beneficiary. Even in your unconscious state, you want me."

"You're such a pig!" She lifted her palms into the air.

"Sorry, darlin'. You were resting so peacefully and quietly. I didn't have the heart to wake you, even though you driveled a river down my shirt." He tilted his head down, scoping out the wet spot on his chest. "Then I fell asleep too."

She gasped, wincing as she slid down in her seat.

"Did you dream about me?"

"No, of course not." She jerked back, the tone of her voice escalated.

He pinned her with his eyes. "Then why were you moaning?" He raised a brow and smirked.

Ashley cringed. "What!" Lowering her face into her hands, "Oh, crap!" she muttered into her palms.

"Don't be embarrassed. I was happy to oblige."

"I'll bet you were."

"I'm much better in 4D."

She glanced around and caught the gaze of the same woman who had been ogling her earlier. Ashley rolled her eyes. "Go back to your seat in first class, Sebastian."

Ashley sat there mortified, especially since her panties were moist. She'd completely humiliated herself, having drooled all over a complete stranger, both literally and figuratively. He was the main feature in her naughty dream.

Sebastian stood, about to make his way back to his seat. The glint in his eyes and the crooked twist of his wry smile told her that he held a secret. Ashley had heard from multiple people that she talked in her sleep. Her heart raced. *Oh, crap! What did I say?*

He placed his large hand on the leather headrest, leaned in, and whispered, "I'm not the only one taking liberties with a stranger. My name sounds so good coming out of those lovely lips in the heat of passion." The smirk planted on his lips stretched into a full grin. "I'll see you later,

Ashley, in your dreams and in Key West." He gave a slight head nod and darted off.

Chapter Four

The gritty granules settled between Ashley's toes as she dug her feet into the sandy shore. Lying on the beach, hundreds of miles away from home and away from the troubles that plagued her, proved to be therapeutic. She couldn't remember a time when she felt as relaxed and at peace. The sound of the waves beating against the shoreline soothed the anxiety that haunted her.

"Hey there. You look relaxed for once." Kerrigan rolled over on her oversized beach towel and faced Ashley.

Ashley angled her head toward Kerrigan's voice. "I could get used to this lifestyle. I didn't know Key West would agree with me this much."

"Yeah, this is nice." Kerrigan sat up and planted her chin on her knees, peering down at Ashley. "Ash, did you call Sebastian?"

"And good-bye, relaxation." Ashley lifted her head up and faced Kerrigan. "Are you seriously encouraging me to call that ass of a man?"

"No. I just wondered how he knew where to find you. He's jogging toward us."

Ashley bolted up. "What!" She whipped her head around, spotted the shirtless sex god glistening in the sun, running toward them. "Crap! Come on, Kerri. Let's go. Let's go now."

"Ash, we won't get back to the house before he reaches us."

"Quick, toss that other towel to me." Ashley clambered for the towel and covered her head. "Cover your head too. Maybe he'll jog past us without stopping."

"You're ridiculous, Ash. Playing ostrich won't stop Sebastian from seeing you. Besides, he's almost here, and now he's waving."

Without warning or hesitation, Ashley leaped up. She wrapped the towel around her waist and sprinted toward the house. Her chest heaved, and her knees buckled as she reached the path that ran alongside the beach house. She landed ass up in a sand dune.

"Hmm. What a view." The thick, deep voice rang out, sending quakes rippling through Ashley's stomach.

"Ugh! Can you go away and leave me alone?" She righted her position, sat in the mound, and covered herself with the towel.

"I'm afraid I can't. We have a date tonight."

Ashley's fingers twitched. She wanted to slap that gorgeous, victorious grin off his smug face.

"Sebastian, I never agreed to go out with you tonight."

"You never disagreed either."

Her fist pounded the sand, and then she stood. The towel that had been so carefully wrapped around her fell to the earth. "This," hand mounted on her hip, "is me disagreeing. Excuse me, this conversation is over." His greedy eyes roaming her curves in the skimpy orange bikini she wore made her insides tingle.

Returning his inspection, Ashley's eyes fixed on the six-pack on his stomach, slid down past his blue trunks, and landed on golden, toned legs. *Damn, he's fine.*

She whirled around, stretched a leg forward, eager to escape. Before she could flee, a strong hand grabbed her wrist.

Sebastian pulled her toward him. "Ashley. Stop running. I promise to be on my best behavior if you'll allow me to enjoy your company this evening. I'll pick you up at seven." His pleading eyes flashed with uncertainty.

She snatched her hand out of his. "No."

He stepped back. "I thought you were up for a little fun. Don't tell me you've chickened out."

She shook her head. "Nice try, but that won't work. I'm allowed to change my mind."

"What must I do to get you to go out with me just once? Or if you prefer, I can resort to stalking you."

Ashley laughed. "You're relentless. If I go out with you once, will you leave me alone?"

His perfect white pearls gleamed at her. "See you at seven, darlin'." A triumphant grin glued to his face, he turned and jogged off.

With Sebastian out of sight, she screamed until her lungs emptied. "Ugh! I can't believe that guy. Why me? What am I supposed to do now?" she muttered, pacing back and forth along the path.

Kerrigan strolled up in time to hear the last bit of Ashley's rant.

"Ash, are you okay? What happened?"

The calm before the storm raging inside Ashley had come to an abrupt end.

"Ash, what's the matter?"

Slowly Ashley lifted her head from her chest, blinking rapidly. Nervous, uncertain eyes stared back at Kerrigan. A surge of feelings overwhelmed Ashley, and shaky legs forced her collapse to the ground. "Kerri, I can't do this. I don't know how to move on."

Ashley riffled through Kerrigan's closet, searching for the perfect outfit to wear on her evening out with the one man who knew exactly how to irritate and intrigue her. The conflicting feelings that Sebastian stirred inside Ashley made her head spin. *One night. One date. Done,* she vowed, and continued her search for just the right outfit to wear.

Racks of clothes hung along two long walls on either side of a walk-in closet larger than Ashley's entire loft apartment. She sucked in a deep breath. Her eyes glided over clothes and more clothes and shoes and bags.

"I can't believe you have this much stuff in your vacation home. Truly sickening." She poked her head out of the closet and yelled into the bedroom. Her voice reached

Kerrigan, who huddled in a corner, deep in conversation with Axel.

Kerrigan lifted her head and covered the phone's speaker. "Well, you know how Axel can be. He arranged for everything, including my wardrobe, when we stayed here for our honeymoon."

Ashley rolled her eyes. Long fingers rummaged from one garment to the next. Fabrics in an assortment of styles, patterns, and colors lined the walls. The whole experience of finding an outfit overwhelmed Ashley. "I don't want to wear anything too revealing. That would send the wrong message."

Kerrigan strutted in and pursed her lips. "Why not wear a shower curtain?"

"Ha. Funny."

"Wear what makes you comfortable. Whatever you decide to wear, you'll be beautiful."

"I'm not trying to look beautiful. Sebastian doesn't need any reason to hope." Ashley pulled out a strapless dress. Her eyes roamed the piece with caution. "This one. Simple. Elegant. Not overly stated. Yep, I'll wear this one. What do you think?" She held the dress high and twirled the hanger around for a full 360-degree assessment.

Kerrigan's eyes sparkled. "Perfect. That's a great choice. Pink looks great against your skin. Sebastian will be awestruck."

Ashley frowned, remembering the lusty look he wore when he appraised her on the beach. "On second thought, maybe this dress isn't right." She extended her arm, attempting to hang the frock back onto the rack.

Kerrigan snatched the garment out of Ashley's hand. "Wear the dress, Ashley." Laughter, like sunshine bursting through dark clouds, met Kerrigan's seething scowl.

"Who are you?" Ashley questioned, amusement edging her words. "I swear, you sound like your damn husband." She grabbed the hanger, tossed the dress over one shoulder. "All right, I'll wear the dress," Ashley said and then headed toward the closet door to make an escape.

In the solitude of her private guest suite, Ashley's hard facade faded. She leaned against the strength of a tall teak armoire. Her back level against the side of the large wardrobe, she leaned back, head pressed flat against the hard oak wood, and closed her eyes. Lying on the bed across from Ashley, the pink dress taunted her. She couldn't believe that Kerrigan had convinced her to wear such scandalous attire.

Ashley hated the feeling that settled deep in her stomach whenever she saw or thought about Sebastian Stone. *Downright pig.* His honest, yet disturbing, approach to the modern hookup repulsed Ashley. Her arms coiled around her waist, soothing the nauseous waves rippling inside her stomach. His charm, his charisma, what little he chose to display, excited her. The man played a good game, but her game would be stronger. Sebastian Stone never met a woman like Ashley Turner, and he wouldn't soon forget her or the lesson she planned to teach him.

Ashley fiddled with the doorknob, anxious fingers sliding around the globe until the latch released. The heavy wooden door opened slowly. There stood Sebastian, dressed in relaxed khaki cargo pants and a breezy cream-colored shirt. The thin linen shirt, left unbuttoned enough to expose the arc of perfection, showcased his sculpted chest. Ashley watched his eyes rove her body. He didn't attempt to mask his scope, probing her from head to sandal-covered toes.

Sebastian lingered on the front porch, both hands holding the doorjamb. "Wow! You're beautiful." The words oozed out of his mouth like sweet molasses poured over dung; the underlying taste foul despite the sugary sweetness poured on top.

Lips pursed, manicured hand pinned against one hip, and an attitude as sour as lime met Sebastian's compliment. "I thought you'd be more original," Ashley said.

Sebastian belted out a hearty laugh. "And I thought you'd be more appreciative. Obviously, sincerity and flattery doesn't work for you. Let's go, Cujo."

Mouth opened wide, Ashley stood. Speechless. "Did you call me Cujo?" Ashley asked, her voice raised and wide-eyed glare locked on Sebastian's impassioned eyes.

"Yup. Just like the 1980s movie about a rabid dog who attacked any and everybody for no good reason. Fitting, don't you think?"

"Take that back or…"

"Or what, Ashley?" Sebastian stroked his chin. His patronizing tone made Ashley's stomach twist.

He stepped back. His right foot teetered the edge of the wooden porch step. Both hands raised like a guilty man placed under arrest, Sebastian seemed to halt the tropical evening breeze.

Suddenly warm, she heaved hard breaths in the hall. Heavy legs anchored her there.

"What will you do if I don't take my words back?" he taunted, eyes flashing with mischief.

Hands raised high, his defensive posture forced his shirt sleeves up the contours of his arms, his magnificent muscular definition displayed. Ashley's eyes traced Sebastian's every movement. Her eyes glued to him as his biceps stiffened into hard steel mounds. She sucked in a deep breath.

Her dress swirled in waves of fabric around her legs as she spun around and then stomped off. Words tossed over her shoulder, "I guess I'll enjoy an evening of peace and quiet by myself. Without you," Ashley cut her eyes at Sebastian, a sidelong glance. His eyes welded to her form as the sway of her hips moved in rhythmic harmony to their dance of words.

Sebastian followed her inside, paused his steps just beyond the threshold in the foyer. "I like you, Ashley. Does every encounter between us have to be a battle of wills?"

Her back to him, Ashley waved a dismissive hand. "Take it back, Sebastian, or leave."

His footsteps tapped against the slick tile floor as he closed in. "I want to spend an evening with you. You're beautiful. Complicated. Annoying. But goddamn, you're sexy and interesting."

Ashley rounded the corner and dipped into the kitchen. "Then you should have no problem apologizing," she quipped.

"Agh! Ashley! I take it back. I'm sorry. Are you always this difficult?" Sebastian's recanted words beat against her eardrums and satisfied Ashley's temper.

Fingers curled tightly around the edge of the wall. Ashley poked her head out from the kitchen. "Difficult? I'm not difficult. I have no plans to lighten up, and I'm…" Ashley paused, frowning. "Sebastian?" she asked, peering into an empty hallway.

A warm sensation swept through her. Prickly stings radiated Ashley's spine as hot breath singed baby-fine hairs at the nape of her neck. Her shoulders stiffened.

His whisper teased her desire. "I have no plans to lighten up either, Ashley."

Sebastian pinned her in place, molding himself to her ass. His hard erection pressed between her cheeks through thin layers of cotton and linen. Heavy hands caressed Ashley's tense shoulders.

She gasped. "What in the hell are you doing?"

"If we don't leave right now, I can't be held responsible for what I do next." Ashley could hear the baleful smile in his voice. He meant every word.

She squirmed, broke free of his grasp, and darted down the hall toward the front door.

His sinister laugh, deep and filling the hall, chased behind her. "Let's just go. Sebastian, I meant what I said. I'm not having sex with you," Ashley scolded as she exited.

The thick, dank air could be sliced with a knife. Ashley hadn't realized that the humidity would loom after six o'clock in the evening. Staying cool by wearing a strapless dress made her grateful.

"What is this place?" she asked, her searching eyes poised on Sebastian's smiling face highlighted by the hazy glow of street lights cast down from above.

"This is one of my favorite spots. Casual dining. Nice outdoor ambiance. Romantic."

They approached the curb. Sebastian held out a hand, his silent offer to guide Ashley through the crowd of patrons.

Cautiously she accepted, placing her hand in his, flinching at the merger of their fleshy palms.

Sebastian's eyes softened. A smile curved the edge of his lips. "I won't bite. Unless you want me to."

Ashley knew the minutes wouldn't be long. *And there he goes again. Scum dog!*

She snatched her hand away. "Can't you treat me as a person? I'm not one of your tramps or escorts or hookers." Her escalation elicited stares from nearby diners seated at tables on the covered patio where they stood.

"Of course you're not. I would pay an escort or a hooker for her services. I have no intention of paying for yours."

His response was the straw that snapped her sanity. Ashley raised up on the tips of her toes. Her arm swung back and released like a catapult. Her palm collided with his jaw and made a loud smack. The sound echoed, and a hush fell over the patio.

She didn't know what had happened until the red fury faded away. Ashley gripped her throbbing hand as the stinging and burning sensation subsided. Sebastian's mouth fell open. He cupped his face with a hand.

He jerked back, face wrinkled. A puzzled frown painted his mug. "What the hell, Ashley?" Sebastian's voice forced Ashley into retreat. With the distance between them, she snaked tense arms around her waist. The blow she gave had been instinctual, taking her by surprise.

She glanced around. "Sebastian, you might think I'm an easy target or a worthless piece of ass, but I won't be disrespected or talked down to."

Their audience of onlookers seemed frozen in time, their stares paused on the altercation unfolding before them.

Calm. Steady. Sebastian glared at Ashley. "How quickly you forget. You insulted me first. Remember Peachtree Street? You blessed me out good and proper for no reason when I was trying to help you." The words rolled off his tongue with salty bitterness.

"So that gives you the right to treat me like trash?" She wadded tight fists at her side, resisting the urge to slap him once more. "Sebastian, this is a bad idea. You and I are combustible elements on the periodic table, and we shouldn't mix. As much as I don't mind making a scene if the moment calls for a scene, I won't do this with you. Take me home."

A wiry hand reached out, tapped Sebastian's bare forearm. "Sir, you and your date are disturbing the other guests. If you don't stop fighting, I'm afraid I'll have to ask that you leave." The waiter shifted from foot to foot. Ashley could see the fear in the waiter's bulging eyes. Sebastian possessed the power to put a man's head on a platter.

Sebastian turned slowly. A cool grimace stretched across his mouth and melted away when his gaze landed on the waiter's face. "My apologies. I'm afraid this is my fault.

I've insulted the lady and won't make that mistake again. I'll take my usual table, Blair."

The waiter had a name. Sebastian knew Blair. Still angered, Ashley frowned at both men.

"Oh! Mr. Stone, I... I'm so sorry. I didn't know... didn't recognize you. You and... and..." Blair groveled and stammered.

"This is my date, Ashley," Sebastian said, putting the waiter out of his misery. "Everything is all right, Blair." He angled his head, wrinkled his brow. Pleading eyes stared at Ashley. "Let's start fresh. I'll be on my best behavior. Or if you prefer to be alone, I can arrange for a ride back to your friend's house."

Nerves fringed, Ashley inhaled, managed her composure. "Blair, I apologize for causing a scene." She turned and faced Sebastian. "Thanks for the offer for dinner tonight. I'll walk back."

The muscles in Sebastian's downcast face tightened. He stepped forward, placed a masculine hand on her arm. "I'm sorry, Ashley. I really do like you. I don't know how to contain myself at times," he whispered softly.

For the first time since meeting Sebastian, Ashley heard a sincerity in his words. She stared silently at him for a minute, remembering that Kerrigan described how well she and Axel had been regarded when they honeymooned in the Keys. The locals knew the impressive beach-side estate and its enterprising owner, Axel Christensen. Ashley smiled and then turned to Blair. "Blair, can you point me in the direction of the Christensen house?"

Blair pointed to the left, toward a row of tiki torches lined against Croton shrubs.

A firm grip on Ashley's shoulder jolted her. "Ashley, again, I apologize. Maybe we can do this some other time when we're both ready." His tone begged her forgiveness.

She nodded her head. Instant regret gnawed at her conscience. "Sure Sebastian, I forgive you. This," Ashley waived an anxious hand between them, "wasn't meant to be. Sorry to crush your theory about fate."

The night breeze tousled her hair wildly, and her dress danced around legs at flight. Ashley whipped her head around, caught a glimpse of Sebastian's sullen stare, and darted off toward the beach. She would make the most of the spoiled evening. A walk along the shore would lighten her dampened mood.

As past experiences had illustrated, Ashley knew that entertaining Sebastian would be disastrous. Escaping his allure, even with all his fineness, had been easy, but damn her lusty hormones. Ashley wanted a taste of Sebastian Stone, and that fact she couldn't deny.

Wet sand settled between her toes and clung to Ashley's feet. She anchored herself to the beach where she sat peering at the glow of moonlit waves swelling and thrashing. The Atlantic Ocean crested on the shore at her feet. Ashley always found solace in the quiet stillness of reflection and meditation. Before long, the minutes became an hour. Her thoughts floated between her very recent encounter with the vilest man whom she had ever met, her past with Chris, and her present-day reality. When Chris died, she couldn't imagine what would become of her, but the past few years spent hopping from one man to the next wasn't how she had pictured her life.

Never one to wallow in defeat or self-pity for too long, Ashley stood, rising from the pit of despair, and dusted the sand from the folds of her dress.

"Care to share what's got you in such a melancholy state?" The thick voice jolted Ashley. She spun around to face the handsome grin planted across Sebastian's unwelcomed mug.

Ashley's hand jerked up and landed against her chest. "Where did you come from?" she bellowed with a screech. "Did you followed me?"

He took a step closer, his bare feet planted firmly in the sand. "Yes. I followed you. It's not safe for a woman to walk alone on the beach at night. I had to see that you arrived home safely."

Her eyes roved his frame gingerly. "I arrived more than an hour ago. Why are you still here? Pretty stalkerish, if you ask me."

"I didn't."

She frowned. "You didn't, what?"

"I didn't ask you. I recall what happened the last time that I asked if you needed my help. This time, I decided to take matters into my own hands." His cool, easy tone made Ashley's hand twitch. She had the urge to slap the stubble off his dimpled chin.

She shuffled past him, not offering a response.

Sebastian's long fingers wrapped around Ashley's wrist, halting her steps. She yanked away from his grip with no success. His clammy palm pressed against her pulsating vein, blood coursing faster and faster until her anger rose. "Ouch!" she yelped. "Let go of me, Sebastian."

Her demand forced creases to form at the edges of his mouth. A crooked smile. "You're the most stubborn woman I've ever met. If you're not careful, you're going to make me put you over my shoulder and haul you back to my place. You need a lesson in submission."

Ashley inhaled a deep breath and pulled back hard. Freed from his clutches, she whipped around. Their eyes met. "You kinky bastard. I told you there would be no sex, and just as sure as hell is hotter than summer in Georgia, I certainly won't role-play with you in the bedroom."

Sebastian tossed his head back and laughed. The thunder of his deep voice vibrated through Ashley's core. "That's not exactly what I meant," he defended. Entertaining her interpretation of his words, his laugh faded into a sinister grin. "Although, I do like the way you think."

Stomp. Stomp. Stomp. She quickened her pace, taking long, measured steps away from Sebastian and toward the beach house. "Go home, Sebastian," Ashley yelled over her shoulder.

A sudden burning sensation on Ashley's ankles and calves arrested her steps. Sebastian's wide gait had closed the distance between them. His less-than-graceful stride stirred up grains of sand, stinging her legs.

"What do you want?" Exasperation leaked from her lips, wilting Sebastian's grin into a frown.

"I just want to talk." He glanced around, peering at the sea swell, and then fixed his gaze on her. "A do-over. A second chance." Surrendered hands fell at his sides.

His earnest words, like a cool breeze coming from the ocean, sent a shiver up Ashley's spine. She shuddered and looped her arms across her chest to stave off the chill, and him. As if instinct had commanded, Sebastian stepped forward and placed his arms around her. The urge to resist the warmth of his embrace fled. Her head pressed against his chest. Her arms spanned his torso. Ashley surrendered to him, enjoying the feel of Sebastian's warm body against hers.

Sebastian's head angled down, he whispered, "Ashley, I'm sorry for how I've treated you. If you give me another chance, I'll make up for my behavior."

The desperation in his voice cut through her muddled thoughts. She peered up at him, her eyes wide, her vulnerability exposed. She swallowed hard. "Sebastian, this isn't the right time. I... I can't... The timing is..."

He leaned down. Gray eyes impassioned with tenderness locked on hers. "The timing is perfect," he whispered.

Slowly Sebastian's soft lips covered Ashley's, silencing her stammer. Her knees buckled. With limbs as unruly as hers, Sebastian collapsed to the earth, brought them both to their knees and clinging one to the other in a tender embrace. Her hands clawed at his chest to push him away, to pull him closer. Conflicting movements matched her feelings. Feelings that swelled and receded like ocean waves. His hardness pushed against her stomach. Ashley whimpered and moaned. Sebastian's tongue moved with expert precision, swirling inside her mouth, mixing her tattered emotions and thoughts into pure heat. He cupped her behind, molded her cheeks with skillful hands.

Passion, raw and tender, erupted. Sebastian laid back into the bed of sand and pulled Ashley onto him. The intensity of his commanding tongue and touch grew. Greedy fingers crawled up the back of her thigh and under her pink dress. Ashley reached back, covered his wandering hand with hers. His journey paused, Sebastian's fleshy palm pressed firmly against her naked flesh.

"Sebastian," she moaned, a hesitant, wanting whisper.

His desire unleashed, he rolled Ashley onto her back and forced her to the ground underneath the weight of his body. Sebastian devoured her lips, chest heaving, wild eyes locked on her. He reached down slowly, lowered her strapless dress, and exposed her breasts. Her golden-brown skin shimmered in the moonlight.

"Beautiful," he rasped.

Sebastian lowered his head. His wet tongue circled a hard nipple, forced an ache between Ashley's thighs. She wanted him. There. Tonight.

Long red fingernails tangled his thick hair as she held him to her bosom.

"Oh, yes, yes." Desire in her voice leaped into the night chill.

Sebastian pulled away. "I guess you didn't want me to do that either," he teased, his voice soft, tender.

"Mmm," she murmured back, peering up at him with hungry eyes. "Are you going to finish this?" She reached down, placed needy fingers on Sebastian's groin, pleading without shame.

"Yes." His sinewy hand raised the fabric over her bosom, and he sat up.

Sebastian's body away from hers extinguished the burning flames he ignited inside her. A frigid chill rolled through her in waves. "Sebastian, what are you doing?" she asked.

"Finishing this." A cool smile eclipsed the sensual glare that had been her captor. "I told you I wanted to make sure you arrived safely. My being here with you, like this, isn't safe. I accomplished my mission, and now I should leave."

"You can't be serious!" Ashley belted out.

"I meant what I said. I want a second chance with you."

He pushed himself to his feet. A large hand extended down to help Ashley up. She glared at him. She couldn't believe that she had allowed Sebastian Stone to bring her to the brink of desire. This game was supposed to be hers to win. Remembering her plan, and upset with how easily she had caved at his kiss, at his touch, anger welled up inside her.

Ashley jerked away from Sebastian's outstretched hand. "Fine." Shuffling to her feet, she dusted sand from her dress for the second time that evening and shook the granules out of her tousled mane. "Just go."

A smug grin greeted her. "Good night, Ashley." Sebastian lowered his head.

Ashley balled her fists at her sides, tightening each wad until her nails pressed into her fleshy palm and sent a shock of pain through frazzled nerve endings. She whirled around. Not waiting for his next move or words, she ran as fast as her legs could carry her toward the house.

Sebastian, one. Ashley, zero. She would fire the next round in their dangerous duel of desire and show that chauvinist pig exactly how unfilled desire felt.

Chapter Five

Sebastian clicked on the next tab. Scrolled to the left. His beloved Ellie stared back at him. Sebastian always loved that photo. He snapped the secret shot of her exactly two weeks to the day. Her radiance still affected him even five years after she had left him. Since his last drink and vow of sobriety three years ago, Sebastian found a new vice—his ritualistic morning cup of steaming hot java. Sometimes two cups. Sometimes more. Anxious fingers wrapped around a warm mug, lifted the rim to his lips. The sweet scent of mocha and cream teased his nostrils, and he sipped. One hard gulp and his eyes closed. He always found Ellie in his memories, and he always had memories whenever he closed his eyes, explaining countless sleepless nights, red eyes, and his general lack of focus.

A blaring ringtone startled Sebastian back to the present day. He closed the laptop, took another sip of coffee, and reached for his cell phone.

The number displayed on the screen made him cringe. He sucked in a deep breath. "Hello," he bellowed into the phone while massaging his throbbing temple.

"Stone, we have a serious problem. I need your head in the game. Do you understand how much is at stake?" The man's boisterous voice broadcast through the phone's speaker filled the tiny makeshift office in his suite.

"Stephen, I've told you one hundred times I'm working on a solution. I need a little more time." Sebastian slammed the mug down on the desk. Hot coffee splashed onto his hand, scalding him. "Shit," he mouthed silently.

"Your time is nearly up. If you can't present a plan to the board in three months, you're out and the Carlisle on Peachtree will go on the auction block."

"Damn it, Stephen! I told you I was working on a solution. Can't you buy more time? I need more than three months." Sebastian stood and ran his fingers through his hair. He paced back and forth between the fireplace mantel and the small desk.

"I've done all I can do. Hell, you've had time. More than enough time. You've had two years to pull your shit together. Everyone has been sympathetic to your situation. But business is business. You either get your head back in the game, or you're done. You have three months. Got it, Stone?"

Hard, labored breaths forced air through Sebastian's flaring nostrils. "Yeah, I got it."

The call ended. He slammed the cell phone down on the desk. Rage stewing inside him, Sebastian pulled his left arm back and catapulted the half-filled cup of coffee through the air. Soaring like a baseball aimed at an outfielder, the mug slammed into the wall, sending jagged shards of ceramic airborne. Black coffee streaked the wall and stained pristine bed linens.

"Fuck!" Sebastian yelled, startled by his action. He stepped back from the scene of the crime. He lowered his head, eyes shut. This time, Ellie didn't greet him behind closed eyelids. A minute later, like embers rising from flames, his head lifted and he erupted into side-splitting laughter. Garrett Wooster and Stephen Holman III would be in for one hell of a fight if they thought Sebastian would be forced out of the empire he had helped to build without a knock-down, drag-out brawl to the mother-fucking death.

"So what." Kerrigan turned her back to Ashley. Snickering under her breath, she pulled a carton of eggs from the refrigerator. "You and Sebastian got a little frisky. You're both adults. Have a little fun. Try something new. I recall very similar advice coming from your lips when Axel and I were dating."

Ashley tugged at her bathrobe's tie, nervous fingers seeking distraction. "Kerri, this is different. My brain knows that this guy is bad for me, but my body wants him."

Kerrigan cracked an egg along the edge of the mixing bowl set on the butcher block counter. "Ash, I don't get you. You've had more one-night stands than I care to discuss or know about. How is Sebastian any different?"

Ashley leaned forward, her elbows resting on the breakfast table. "I don't know, but he's different somehow. I don't have the upper hand when I'm around him, and that feels strange. I should hate him, especially after the way he's treated me, but I don't. I haven't been with anyone like that since…"

The words clogged in Ashley's throat like a hair trapped in a drain. Kerrigan finished her sentence. "Since Chris." She gave Ashley a warm smile and walked to the table. "Ash, liking someone is okay."

Ashley's eyes darted and then fixed to Kerrigan. "Even if he's a disgusting pig? What in the hell, Kerri? I'm screwed up."

A gentle hand covered Ashley's as Kerrigan sat beside her. "That's not true. As you said, you think there's more to Sebastian Stone than his rough exterior would have you to believe. Maybe you need to explore the possibilities."

Ashley rolled her eyes. "That's it! I'm done talking about Sebastian Stone." She pulled her hand away from Kerrigan's grasp. "Come on. I'll make the sausage and toast."

After shoveling a hearty breakfast down her throat, Ashley strolled back to her room. The room, painted in muted shades of gold and teal with wicker chairs with bold floral seat cushions, was the epitome of Key West opulence. White sheer drapes covered doors that opened to a large veranda. Solid teak furnishings in rich tones anchored hardwood floors. An Indian silk throw draped across the bed covered in crisp white linens added ornamentation. She pulled the wicker chair back and plopped down in front of the computer. Ashley's fingers flew across the keyboard. S...e...b... fifteen keystrokes later, she stared at Sebastian Stone's name in the Google search field. Page after boring page of results on Wooster, Holman, and Stone surfaced. If fate had thrust them together, then fate had better give her a sign. Ashley smacked a palm against her forehead, scolding herself for giving credence to the ridiculous notion.

As if she had conjured fate's hand, Ashley's eyes skimmed an intriguing headline on page 20 of her search. "Stone tragedy makes investors nervous. Partner in..." she read aloud. Her eyes scanned the words while the page loaded, skimming the article for a nugget. And then suddenly the site stopped loading. Redirected to a new page, an error message said technical issues were being addressed. Hands placed on the desk's edge, she shoved away. He probably had been involved in some crooked business scheme. She knew everything she needed to know about Sebastian Stone. The man was a womanizer. Nothing she read would change her opinion.

Ashley collected her thoughts, kept her composure. She walked into the living room, greeting Kerrigan with a monotone, "hey," as she shimmied past and settled into the comfort of the down seat cushion, her friend at her side.

Kerrigan frowned. "Are you all right?" Curious wrinkles creased her forehead.

"Yeah, I'm fine. Have you heard anything from Axel about finding Copper?"

She shook her head. "Sorry, Ash. Nothing yet. He's not giving up though. Axel is determined to find your little fur ball."

Ashley rolled her eyes. "No, Axel is determined to do anything for you. Thanks for getting him to help."

Ashley sank deeper into the sofa and stared blankly across the room. A small red and yellow figurine resting on a console table caught her eye. "I've never noticed that before," she remarked.

"What?" Kerrigan asked, looking in the direction of Ashley's gaze.

"That." Ashley pointed to a ceramic bird. "I've never noticed that red robin before. Where did you get that?" A hand flew to her chest to ease her harsh breaths.

"Oh, that?" Puzzled, Kerrigan's wrinkled face turned to Ashley. "That robin was one of my finds in an estate sale. I had planned to take the little bird back to my boutique to sell, but I forgot." She tilted her head. "Ash, what's this all about?"

"Uh, noth… nothing." Ashley's heart pounded hard in her chest.

"Wrong answer. Try again."

She lowered her head, nerves nearly choking her words. "Kerri, you're going to think I'm crazy." Ashley paused, looking away. "I think Chris is sending a message to me."

Silent, Kerrigan scooted closer and placed her hand over Ashley's. "I don't think you're crazy. What do you think he's saying to you?"

Ashley stood, made her way to the mirrored table. Shaky fingers enclosed the little figurine in the ball of her fist. Her back to Kerrigan, "Each anniversary, Chris gave me a red robin, just like this one," she said as she turned a hazy gaze toward her friend.

"Oh, Ash. You should take the robin." Kerrigan smiled tenderly.

The tight feeling in Ashley's chest intensified. She placed the figurine back on the table. "You don't understand." Clammy hands covered her face.

Kerrigan leaped up. "Ash, tell me. What don't I understand?"

Ashley swallowed hard. Closed her eyes. "Chris said that robins are the promise of a new beginning, new happiness." A sinking feeling anchored Ashley in place.

Kerrigan's mouth dropped open. She gasped. "Sebastian!"

Ashley's left eye popped open. A pained expression painted her scrunched face. "Oh, hell no! Sebastian Stone is not my new beginning."

Duval Street teemed with people. Tourists enjoyed evening bike rides. Yellow taxies zipped by, taking passengers to their destinations. The hustle and bustle of pedestrians perusing restaurants, bars, and shops gave Ashley relief, a distraction from thoughts crowding her head. She dipped inside a French bakery.

"Table for one," she said.

After being seated and her lunch order placed, Ashley pulled out her cell phone. Her finger hovered above Sebastian's number. Her pulse quickened, and then she quickly tucked the phone back into her handbag. Ashley glanced around the patio where she sat. Lush, green foliage surrounded and covered the area. Around her, couples huddled close together, sipped beverages, ate French pastries, and laughed.

Moments later, the garçon decked in tropical colors and shorts reappeared, placed her plate down on the tile mosaic table.

"Enjoy, mademoiselle," the tall, thin waiter said and then grinned.

"Thank you."

When Kerrigan bailed on their lunch plans, Ashley breathed a bit easier. Time alone in the tranquil ambiance of the restaurant would help clear her mind. She thought back to the article that she had discovered about Sebastian. The headline had intrigued her. She would read the story later when the site worked again.

If the pompous asshole's behavior toward women had been any indicator, he deserved business troubles. The time had come to put her plan into action. Sebastian Stone had to go down. She only needed the courage to carry through.

"Mushroom galette. Good choice." The deep timbre of his voice rolled through Ashley's gut in waves.

Jolted from thought, she lifted her face to meet Sebastian's frolicsome gaze.

Ashley took a sip of iced water, swallowed hard. "Sebastian Stone," she replied flatly with an impassive stare. She was glad that he couldn't see the baby-fine, bristled hair at the nape of her neck.

"Glad you remember my name." Ashley's mouth went dry, and she indulged in his pulsating muscles as he pulled out the chair across from her. "May I join you?" He sat without awaiting her reply.

She rolled her eyes. "Why bother asking?"

Leaning leisurely against the back of the cool wrought iron chair, he said, "I asked out of courtesy. That's the sort of thing that a gentleman does." His lips curled into a smile.

"A gentleman waits for an answer." Anger building inside, Ashley remembered the end goal, and forced a smile back at Sebastian.

Sebastian lowered his head, slowly brought a hand under his chin. He peered into her eyes. "I am corrected." He stood and then turned to walk away.

Ashley glanced around the patio. She noted the lanky waiter standing off in the distance, watching them. No one else seemed to notice their squabble.

Flames burned hot in Ashley's belly. "Fine. Fine, Sebastian." The groveled words leaked from Ashley's lips made her want to hurl. She closed her eyes. "I'd like you to stay." Shamefully she tossed her pride to the wind, watched her dignity dissipate into vapors.

Sebastian paused. Turned around. He sat again. "That's better. Not perfect, but better," he said, leaning in close.

Remember the plan. Don't mouth off. Ashley scolded herself before playing victim to his cunning.

Like a card shark at a blackjack table, Ashley pulled out a trick deck of cards. "I'm trying." She softened her tone and reached for his hand. "I'm glad you're here. Maybe we could try to go out again." Pulse quickening as lies tumbled from her lips, she watched him fall victim to the swindle.

Sebastian's eyes stretched wide. "Well. I didn't expect you to come around as easily." Radiating around him, his arrogance nearly took on an aura. "I only want to get to know you better. See where this leads."

She could smack the smug off his face. There would be no hesitation on Ashley's part. *Remember the plan.* She chanted the mantra over and over again silently.

Seven fifteen. The time on Ashley's cell phone hadn't been set ten minutes early as the time set on the other devices she owned. Sebastian was late. He hadn't even called to give her warning. Another five minutes passed. She paced the hardwood floor, walked from the foyer into the formal dining room. Suddenly a knock at the front door startled her.

Ashley twisted the doorknob. An eager Sebastian shoved the door open. Approving eyes caressed her naked shoulders, wandered up and down her curvy form. "You're beautiful." The genuineness in his tone surprised Ashley.

"You're late." She didn't mask her disapproval.

Sebastian nodded. "I'm sorry." He reached into his pocket and retrieved a shiny metal object. "I had to make sure everything was ready for our date." Reaching down, he grabbed her hand. "For you." A surge of energy bolted through her body.

Ashley snatched her hand away from his clutches and opened her fingers. The object that Sebastian had placed in her palm stared back. "A key." She frowned and then parted her lips to speak.

His index finger flattened against Ashley's lips shushed her reply. "Before you make assumptions about my gift, let me assure you that it's not what you think." A million thoughts raced through her head at once. Curiosity leading the pack of rogue questions, "This wouldn't happen to be a key to your hotel room?" she blurted out.

Amusement danced in Sebastian's eyes. "Noooo," he replied, exaggerated.

Ashley's arms coiled around her waist. "Then I suppose this is the key to your heart," she quipped with pursed lips.

He leaned against the doorframe. The amusement in his eyes spread to his shapely lips. "Noooo. I don't give away the key to my heart easily. That key must be earned." Luscious lips now grinned broadly at her. "I think you'll find that this key unlocks a place more suited to you."

Eyebrows arched, Ashley inhaled a deep breath. "Fine. I'm intrigued."

Sebastian extended his hand. "Great! Let's find out what the key opens. Shall we?" Ashley placed her hand into his. The feel of him made her chest tighten.

Sebastian paused. He faced Ashley. "I want tonight to be special for you. A guy only gets one second chance." His large hand molded to hers gave her heart palpitations.

She eyed him cautiously, watched the small creases in his brow wrinkle. Diverting his gaze, Ashley noted a rusted tin watering can that had blown onto its side. She was like that can, knocked down, a bit tarnished around the edge, but she still had a purpose to fulfill. Conceding with a smile, "All right." Eager gray eyes stayed fixed to her. "Let's go."

Chapter Six

"Push it all the way in."

"I'm trying, but…"

"Don't force it. You'll break the thing."

"Wait, wait… I think it's in. Yes, it's in!"

"Now, turn it to the right. Then push hard."

The door screeched open. Sebastian lifted Ashley's freshly manicured hand. The coral polish matched perfectly the floral print dress she wore. He always appreciated a woman who took pride in her appearance.

"That was quite a challenge," Sebastian said, taking measured steps, not wanting to get too close and not willing to get too far from Ashley. He guided her inside and then released her hand.

Ashley scanned the space. Her mouth fell open. Silence. For the first time since meeting the feisty beauty, she had nothing to say.

"Well, what do you think?" Sebastian studied her face. Watched her expression contort with emotion he couldn't place.

Still nothing.

"Ashley, say something. You always have something to say." He wondered if the surprise had been too much. After all, he had no intention of becoming serious with her, or any other woman. "I hope this isn't inappropriate. I wanted to make up for the way I treated you before."

Ashley blurted out, "Sebastian, I can't... I don't... How did...," she stammered. Her brows scrunched inward, forehead wrinkled. "Why did you bring me here? Did Kerrigan put you up to this?"

Sebastian frowned. "Uh, no. I wanted to do something nice. Did I do something wrong?"

She cupped her mouth. Spun around slowly. "This is a..." Ashley blew out a hard breath.

"This is Robin's Nest. Belongs to a buddy of mine. The entire place is ours for the evening. We'll have dinner, do a little dancing, talk. You do eat, don't you?"

She nodded. "I eat," she said, stiffly.

Sebastian narrowed his eyes. "Dance?" She didn't take a jab in response to his sarcastic questions.

"I dance too." Her whisper was barely audible.

He turned, faced Ashley. Took several steps backward. "Shall we?" he asked, his hand extended in the direction of the table in the middle of the room. The only table in the room.

Sebastian pulled out a chair covered in light blue velvety fabric as soft as Ashley's bronze shoulder. The accidental touch sent a scintillating sensation up his spine. Her delicate fingers clawed the chair's arms as she eased into the seat. Tense shoulders stiffened, refused to relax.

Sebastian's eyes glued to Ashley as he sank into a chair. Her strong, confident attitude had ensnared him like a fly caught in a web. He watched her movements, examined her expressions, tried to understand her reaction. He rubbed sweaty hands on his thighs.

Branches hung overhead captured Ashley's attention. Her gaze scanned the room again. The room, filled with greenery, mimicked a treetop. A mural of red robins and birds' nests covered the walls.

He leaned closer, resting his chin in his palm. "Do you like my surprise?" Ashley's glossy-eyed stare made Sebastian sweat.

Jolted, she whirled around in the seat. "The room is beautiful. How did you know?"

He frowned. "How did I know what?"

A hand rested at the nape of her neck. "Um, nothing. Forget what I said." Ashley twirled flyaway strands of hair around her index finger.

Sebastian didn't know what had spooked Ashley, but he intended to enjoy the evening. "Forgotten." His left hand glided across the table cloth. He smoothed out the linen. "Tell me a little about you." The tips of his fingers stroked her forearm.

She jerked away. "What do you want to know?" The tips of his fingers kneaded his throbbing temples.

Leaning back in the chair, Sebastian folded bulky arms across his chest. "You live in Atlanta. You vacation in the Keys. You don't put up with anyone's crap. I like that about you." His voice strained. "What else?"

Ashley inhaled and then released a deep breath. "Well," she said, her shoulders loosening. "That's a loaded question. Where do I start?"

He had to take control, otherwise his head might explode. "Start at the beginning. Where did you grow up? What do you do for a living? What is your life's aspiration?"

She sneered behind a perfect grin. "I was born in Houston. I'm a marketing account manager. When I grow up, I want to..." Ashley paused, stared past him blankly.

Her stare turned cold. Of all emotions, Sebastian recognized sadness.

His lips pursed. "When you grow up, you want to what?"

She shifted in her seat. Her round brown eyes held a far-off gaze. "I don't know." She shook her head. "Honestly, I don't know anymore." The haze seemed to dissipate. Ashley met Sebastian's stare.

He spoke softly. "Did you ever?"

Ashley crossed a toned, curvy leg over the other. "Did I ever?"

Sebastian's eyes scaled her frame. "Did you ever know what you wanted?" He yearned to trail those mocha legs with his lips.

Her shoulders tightened again. "I suppose I did. Things are different now." She rushed her words like a gust in a windstorm.

Her hasty response told him she desired to breeze past this topic.

Sebastian slid his chair closer. Leaned in. "How are things different?"

An exasperated sigh escaped her luscious lips. "Does it really matter? We're just hanging out. This isn't going anywhere. Let's keep the conversation on the surface, not too deep."

Sebastian's hand gripped the back of his neck and massaged the knot. He fired back. "I want to get deep into you. Really deep."

Both hands wrapped the edge of the table. Ashley pushed back and then stopped. "I'm sure you do." Her sneer faded into a coy smile. "Your turn. Tell me something about you that doesn't involve your sex drive."

He chuckled. "Ashley, I'm sorry. I find you incredibly sexy. I say and do stupid things around you. I don't..."

Cutting him off, Ashley snapped, "Save the bullshit and stop skirting the subject."

His eyebrows jolted up. "Well, damn. You're not a woman to anger." He wondered how her feistiness would translate under the sheets.

Ashley shook her head. "If this is going to be a one-sided conversation, you can take me home."

Sebastian shuffled to his feet. He stood in front of a window overlooking a tropical garden. "Ashley, talking about myself isn't easy," he said, his hands planted in his pockets. "I'm a Texan, born and raised. Deep down, I'm a good person. I don't mean to be an asshole. There used to be a time when I knew exactly what I wanted. Things are different for me too. I'm still trying to figure out how to be happy."

Ashley's chair scuffed the tile floor as she scooted away from the table. She joined him at the window. Stood at his side.

Sebastian peered down at her with surprise, eyes widened. "Hey." A tentative smile paused on his lips. He peered down into hypnotizing brown irises.

Candor stared him in the face. Ashley placed a small hand on his shoulder. "We're all trying to find our own version of happiness. Work on not being such an asshole first."

A wide grin stretched his lips thin. Sebastian's left hand stroked Ashley's cheek. He stepped closer. Leaned down. "I'm sorry," he whispered, an inch from her ear. Whispered words that forced a gasp from her.

Slowly his lips soldered her tender flesh. From the ball of her shoulder, his lips traveled to her neck. Her skin smelled so good.

She lifted her chin, exposing her neck. His tongue swirled and licked, sucked her tender flesh. Her salty sweetness tantalized his taste buds and made his head swim. Inch by inch, a trail of kisses led his lips to hers.

He devoured her lips. She fed him more. Their tongues collided in passionate rage. Greedy fingers traced her spine. His hand rested at the small of her back and then cupped a voluptuous ass cheek.

"Ahhh," she moaned.

Sebastian pegged Ashley to the wood-paneled wall. His large masculine body commanded her to his will. She groped his shoulder with one hand. The other hand inched down his chest, passed his stomach, and stilled on his groin.

His right hand hoisted her leg high. He fiddled with his belt buckle, unzipped his pants. Her foot hooked around his thigh. His stiff cock rested at her heat.

A single finger glided up her leg, found the end of her dress. His hand dipped beneath the floral fabric. He massaged her thigh, worked his way up between her legs. Anxious fingers pushed aside the passion-soaked thong. He buried his fingers between her soft, fleshy folds, eager to dip into her sweet spot.

Breathless, Ashley panted wildly. "Sebastian, what are you doing?"

Teeth sunk deep into her neck. He smiled and then lifted his face to hers. "What you've wanted me to do since the day we first met."

Her small hands strained against him. "Stop. We can't do this here."

He captured her wrists. Stared into her eyes. Buried his face in her bosom.

Shit! Lost in the moment, lost in Ashley, Sebastian forgot where he was. He hadn't been with a woman in months. That tight, curvy body made his testosterone boil. He needed Ashley. He wanted Ashley.

Heart racing, Sebastian pried hot lips away from Ashley's breast. "You're right. Not like this. Can you give me a moment?" He peeled himself away and walked down the narrow hallway toward the restroom. Glancing back, he watched Ashley nibble her bottom lip. A pained expression erased her look of passion. She wanted him too.

Ashley stood at the opposite end of the room. The smell of impending sex emanated, their hot musky scents lingered in the intimate space. Her eyes darted around. Red robins painted in the mural scene covered every wall and haunted her. She gasped for air, forcing away the panic that threatened to attack. Sebastian's surprise had been either an act of fate or irony. Tears stalled behind cold eyes too stubborn to leak.

She felt his presence drawing near, pulling her to him. Ashley turned. Every breath in her body had been forced out. Her chest pounded hard. Moonlight streamed in from the picture window, illuminating Sebastian's heavy steps. His cocky swagger, his lustful gaze, captivated her as he approached. She hoped she could carry out the plan.

His gray eyes pierced her, locked her in place, motionless. "Ashley? Ashley?" Worry etched across Sebastian's face forced her back into the moment.

Had he been calling her name for long? She couldn't remember a time when she had been under any man's spell. She blinked rapidly, wouldn't look him in the eyes. Ashley steadied herself against the wall. "Ouch. It hurts. Oh, my ankle," she groaned.

Sebastian's lips pressed thin. He crouched down, lifted her right foot, and examined her ankle. "Hmm. Looks fine to me. Exactly how did you injure yourself in the three minutes that I stepped away?"

Ashley's eyes darted from side to side, avoiding his stare. "I… um… I don't know. I… I…" she stammered. "My ankle just hurts. I… I saw you heading this way, and I took a step, and, well… oh, the pain. I think we should leave now."

Sebastian narrowed his eyes into a squint and looked up at Ashley. "All right. We'll leave now." He stood and swooped her into the cradle of his arms. "Do you have all your things?"

"My handbag," she said, pointing to the chair. Being in his powerful arms had her nearly hyperventilating.

Sebastian eased her down into the passenger seat. Clinging to him, Ashley's hands glided over his sculpted muscled arms. She ignored the tingling sensation that flowed through her core.

He rounded the Jeep Wrangler and hopped into the driver's seat. A crooked smile emerged. "An evening in won't be so bad."

Ashley jolted forward. Turned to face him. "No, please. I don't want to inconvenience you. Take me home. We can go out some other time."

He leaned back casually. "There's no inconvenience." He smiled. "I mean other than my wasted effort and money I put into planning this evening." He glanced at her and then started the engine. "Would you look at the time? I think you'll need to spend the night."

A hard lump formed in Ashley's throat. Rendered speechless for a moment, she took a deep breath and ignored the nervous energy rattling her body. "My ankle really hurts. I should go home and nurse it."

Sebastian reached over and squeezed her hand. "Nonsense. I feel terrible. You're going back to my place." Fire flashed in his eyes. "I'll take care of you, all night."

Ashley swallowed the lump. "Kerri will worry."

He stayed focused on the road ahead. "Then call her and tell her not to worry. You're in expert hands."

Sebastian turned the Jeep left and stopped at a traffic light.

"Sebastian, I'm afraid to be alone with you," Ashley blurted out. She closed her eyes and blew out a hard breath. She hadn't meant to say that aloud.

He leaned his head back against the tan leather headrest. "Ah, finally. The truth. Is that the reason you faked a sprained ankle?"

"I… I didn't fake a sprained ankle."

"Of course you didn't." Sebastian's tone softened. "You have nothing to be afraid of. We're both adults. We both know what we want. What's wrong with that? Let's have fun while we're here. I swear you'll never have to see me again after this trip."

Her elbow positioned on the door panel, Ashley rested her chin in her palm. She stared at a group of people waiting to cross the road. Tourists wearing flip-flops, tacky floral shirts, and bright neon colors walked up and down Duval Street. "We both live in the Carlisle building. I'm sure we'll run into each other at some point," she said.

"I moved out about two months ago. Problem solved," he fired back.

"Oh. You did? Where… never mind."

Sebastian grinned. "I don't mind telling you where I've moved. I bought a house in Inman Park."

She let out a loud sigh. "There are probably hundreds of beautiful women in the Keys. A good-looking guy like you should have no problem finding a date who's DTF."

"Thanks for the compliment, I think. What is DTF?"

She huffed. "You're kidding, right? Everyone knows what DTF stands for."

Sebastian shook his head. "Not everyone."

Ashley rolled her eyes. "It means 'down to fuck.' Like I said, you should have no problem finding a date who's DTF."

"Weren't you DTF?" he asked.

The vehicle turned down a familiar road. Ashley frowned. "Haven't we already discussed this subject? I won't have this conversation again."

Sebastian cleared his throat. "You sure seemed DTF at Robin's Nest," he said under his breath.

Her chest tightened. She turned away. Silent for a moment. "Nothing happened."

The Jeep came to a near halt on North Roosevelt Boulevard. The sign in front of the building read Key West Oceanside Resort and Villas. Ashley remembered the name of the hotel where Sebastian had been staying. She sneaked a sidelong glance at him. Did he really think she would spend the night with him?

Inspiration struck. Ashley raised slouched shoulders. Poked out her chest, boobs thrust forward. Her plan to teach him a lesson took a dark turn. Since Sebastian had been fixated on getting her into bed, she would give him what he wanted. *What the hell! I am DTF.*

He glanced at her. "I'm attracted to you. Sure, I could chase other women, but you're interesting to me. You're witty. Strong. Bold. Annoying."

"I'm not annoying."

Sebastian chuckled. "Yeah, you are." The SUV continued down the street.

Ten minutes later, the Jeep came to a stop in front of the Christensen house. Sebastian strutted to the vehicle's passenger side and opened the door. "Be ready tomorrow night at eight." He extended his hand and helped her climb out of the Jeep.

Ashley shook her head, frowning. "Sebastian, I shouldn't." She climbed down from the vehicle and walked briskly toward the house and away from him.

"Looks like that ankle is feeling better already. Tomorrow, Ashley. Eight o'clock."

Chapter Seven

A rerun of a late-night talk show greeted Ashley when she waltzed into the living room. Kerrigan sat coiled up on the sofa. A bowl of popcorn rested in her lap. "How was your date with Sebastian?" she asked.

Ashley breezed past her friend, yelling over her shoulder, "That man is the biggest asshole I've ever met. He has some nerve. The evening was a huge disappointment." She disappeared into the guestroom.

Seconds later, Ashley stomped back into the living room, fists balled up and propped on her hips. "I've let Sebastian Stone get the upper hand for the last time. He's obnoxious, arrogant, and…"

Kerrigan sat up, swung her feet down to the tile floor. She interrupted Ashley. "And hot as hell. You're pissed because all those things about him turn you on."

Ashley's mouth fell open. "Uh, whatever!" She stomped off and headed to the kitchen. The scent of burned popcorn overwhelmed Ashley. She pinched her nose.

Kerrigan followed. "Come on, Ash. Is he really that bad?"

Ashley threw her hands up in the air. "He's the worst."

Gathering the silk tie around her waist, Kerrigan tightened her robe. She sat at the kitchen bar, elbows rested on the granite countertop. "I've seen you handle far worse than Sebastian. What's this really about? Something happened."

Ashley joined Kerrigan at the bar and buried her face in her hands. "Yes, shomthin hoppened," she said, muffled words uttered into her clammy palms.

"What? Tell me!" Kerrigan nearly bolted from her seat.

Ashley rocked back and forth, shifting in her seat and tumbling her hands. The uneven barstool wobbled, clobbered the tile floor beneath with a loud tap, tap, tap. "He took me to a place called Robin's Nest. Red robins were on the walls, on table linens. Everywhere."

Kerrigan's eyes grew wide. "Really?" She squealed.

Recalling the evening, Ashley shook her head. "We made out. We went too far."

She cupped her mouth. Her hand fell away, eyes wide. "Ash, you didn't have sex with him in a restaurant, did you?"

Her fist struck the countertop with a loud thud. "Hell no!" she belted out. Ashley lowered her voice, slowed her pace. "Almost," she conceded, guilt tinting her words. "He rented the entire restaurant. The room was beautiful. No one has ever done that for me before. You should have seen the place. That part was very…"

"Romantic." Kerrigan finished her sentence. "Ash, Sebastian doesn't sound like a bad guy. Why are you fighting him?"

Like a hot-air balloon deflating, Ashley let out a long sigh. "Sebastian has been very clear that he only wants one thing from me. His obnoxious outbursts are a constant reminder." Tears burning inside her eyes broke free. Ashley sniffled and wiped her runny nose. "I'm not like you, Kerri. A man looks at you and he sees a lifetime. A man looks at me and he sees the next thirty minutes." Ashley tossed her head back, released a snort-cry-laugh. "I mean the next ten minutes."

Kerrigan grabbed a handful of tissues and placed them in Ashley's hand. "I still believe there's more to Sebastian Stone than you realize. He likes you."

Dabbing her damp eyes, Ashley leaped down from the stool. She jutted out her behind. "He likes this," she pointed to her backside.

Kerrigan swatted at Ashley's rear end. "He's a man. That's what men like, at first. Show him that there's more to you than your body or your booty."

Cool water cascaded down rigid shoulders, rushed over Ashley's arm, and trickled down to her toes. Easing away tension and heat, even the tight knot in her belly loosened. Tonight she shortened her time in a relaxing shower. Within an hour, Sebastian expected her to be ready.

The evening promised to be less eventful, she hoped. Imagining him outdoing the Robin's Nest date, impossible.

She pulled her hair back into a long, thick ponytail. Lightly applied makeup, mascara, and a hint of lip gloss would be the extent of her beauty regimen. Sebastian didn't say where he was taking her that evening. A knock at the bedroom door interrupted her thoughts.

Kerrigan poked her head inside. "Hey, Sebastian is here. Are you almost ready?"

Ashley glanced at herself in the mirror a final time. Hand on her hip. "This is as ready as it gets tonight. What do you think?" She spun around, flashing a smile as brilliant as the moon shone down on the sparkling the sea.

Kerrigan smiled back. "I think you look great, just like you always do." She turned to head out. "I'll let Sebastian know you'll be ready soon."

Sebastian was sitting on the sofa when Ashley strolled into the living room. He bolted to his feet the moment she approached.

Standing an inch away, "Wow!" he greeted her. His gray eyes sparkled brilliantly. "You look amazing."

Sebastian's compliment forced a grin on Ashley's tight face. "Thank you." She noted how his jeans hung from his waist, the way the muscles in his arms flexed and pulsed as he moved. *Damn, the man is hot.* Not hot in the kind of way that left her slightly warm and flustered. Sebastian was the kind of hot that made her break into a cold sweat, tingle from the inside out, and draw her knees together tight. He was the kind of hot that made her look away for fear of eyes that would betray the sensuous thoughts floating in her head.

Thoughts that turned to physical manifestations like the drool pooling at the parting of her lips ready to ooze down her chin.

She swallowed hard. Her lips became a quivering line. "Are you... you ready?" she asked, stammering and anxious to get their evening started. She whirled around and raced toward the front door.

Sebastian reached out, fingers coiled around her wrist. "Hold on a minute." His palm seared her skin, giving Ashley a heat flash. Her eyes glided up from their joined flesh, met his wanting gaze. His hand that had been hidden behind his back emerged. "This is for you." He held out a single yellow rose.

Her eyes stretched wide. Ashley's words caught in her throat. "Sebastian." She paused and then turned away from his imposing stare.

He pulled Ashley to him. Towering from behind, he leaned down, whispered in her ear. "A simple 'thank you' would be nice." His hot, minty breath singed the hairs at the nape of her neck.

She turned to face him. "Thank you," she replied softly, batting surrendered eyes. Ashley yanked her arm away. She retreated to the door and shuffled down the walkway toward Sebastian's Jeep.

Sebastian trailed Ashley's hurried steps, his heavy feet crushing and crunching fallen palm fronds beneath his shoes. "I'm glad to see you've made a full recovery." The I-know-you-were-lying smile in his voice made Ashley's insides tingle.

Sebastian raced ahead and opened the passenger door. Ashley climbed inside. He strolled around and crawled into the driver's seat. The Jeep rolled onto the street. Sebastian's heavy gaze landed on her. "Where are we going this evening, Sebastian?" Her icy tone lowered the temperature in the vehicle.

He cut a sidelong glance at her. Didn't say a word. Ashley squirmed.

She looked him squarely in the eye. "Where are you taking me?" Her tone was more insistent than before.

Sebastian's hands wrapped the steering wheel. "I'm afraid if I tell you where we're going you'll come up with a thousand reasons to escape."

Ashley laughed. "I won't. I swear." There would be no escaping this date.

The Jeep rounded the corner. An art gallery caught Ashley's eye. She whipped her head around. Tropical foliage and plants in brightly colored acrylics and watercolors stained canvases displayed in the picture window of the Moss Studio and Gallery.

Sebastian pulled the Jeep into a parking spot and turned the engine off. "Let's go." He jumped out and jogged to the passenger side of the vehicle.

The door opened. Sebastian guided Ashley out with a steady hand, clutching her small hand tightly. "This way." Despite her protesting tug, he kept a firm grip and led her to the front door. "I thought we could explore our creative ambitions tonight."

A deep breath released, a heavy weight lifted from Ashley's shoulders. There would be no sexual tension between the two in this atmosphere. Sebastian held the door open. Ashley walked inside. The gallery was larger than its roadside appearance. Canvas art mounted the walls, leaned against easels, and hung overhead on a thin wire.

Ashley whirled around. A light tapping sound drew her attention. A woman wearing a smock smeared in a rainbow of paint colors sauntered from a room in the back of the gallery. "May I help you?" Her brow wrinkled.

Sebastian stepped forward, grinned at the pretty blond. His outstretched hand collided with the woman's hand. "Miss Kennedy, I'm Sebastian Stone."

The woman was quite attractive. Scratch that. She was flat-out gorgeous.

Sebastian squeezed Ashley's hand. "And this is my lovely date, Ashley."

Does he sense my jealousy?

The woman's pale green eyes locked on Sebastian's fingers entwined with Ashley's. Snatching her hand from his grip, Ashley reached out. "Hello, Miss Kennedy."

She smiled. "Nice to meet you both. The studio is all yours." Small, frail hands untied the sash behind her waist and lifted the smock over her head. "Will anyone else be joining you?"

Playing the perfect gentleman, "No, ma'am," he replied. "This special evening is for Ashley and me. Is everything else, uh, set up?"

Like a cat chasing a shiny moving object, Ashley's head turned from side to side, listening and watching their exchange. If Sebastian found Miss Kennedy attractive, he should be awarded an Oscar for acting as though he had no interest.

"Yes. Everything else is ready." Miss Kennedy headed to the back of the gallery. "I'll leave through the back door. You'll exit through the back door too. Lock the bottom. I'll send someone to lock the deadbolt after you're gone. When you're done, place your brushes here." She pointed at a ceramic bowl set on a cabinet at the rear corner of the room. "Have a great evening," she said and dashed out into the night.

Ashley admired Sebastian's date-planning skills. Even though his intentions weren't pure or genuine, he made her feel special.

"Why are you doing this?" she asked softly. Her right hand massaged her chin.

"Because I like you. Because I want to get to know you better. I have something to show you." Ashley placed her hand in Sebastian's open palm. His touch always made her tingle inside. "This way."

Sebastian led them to a metal spiral staircase that ascended to the loft above.

He nodded. "After you."

Ashley smirked and glance back, looking down at Sebastian. "Thank you. Don't you dare look up my dress," she said.

Sebastian chuckled. "Don't worry. I'll be too close to look up your dress."

The warmth of his body pressed against her. His stealthy swagger synchronized with Ashley's steps as they glided in unison up the spiraled treads.

They reached the loft. Ashley froze. Her mouth dropped open. A wall of glass doors framed a breathtaking view of the ocean and a magnificent sun setting at the horizon.

Sebastian advanced. He didn't say a word. She spun around to face him, mere inches between them. "Sebastian, I... I..." She closed her eyes. Shook her head, at a loss for words.

Tender lips melted into hers and jolted Ashley. She whimpered into his kiss, eyes shut tight. Sebastian's left hand held her in place, drew her nearer to him. She reached up. Her fingers tangled thick hair at his nape. Eager hands captured her wrists, commanded them to his will.

"I'm in control tonight, baby," Sebastian murmured. He held her hands against his chest. Her tender breasts pressed into him, igniting an inferno.

Feverish kisses blazed the crook of her neck. Her heart pounded hard, as though it would burst. "Ahhh, Sebastian." Ashley exhaled a breathy release. She couldn't help the moan that escaped her.

His skillful hands eased the stretchy fabric of her strapless dress down. He unsnapped her bra. "Baby, you belong to me tonight."

His deep bravado thundered through her core. Ashley couldn't object even if she wanted to.

Strong hands covered her chocolate mounds, molded the fleshy peaks. Sebastian dipped his head low. His tongue swirled around her erect nipples, tasting the sweet, succulent morsels. Ashley moaned. "I want you."

Sebastian pushed Ashley against the wall, pinned her arms above her head. His senses abandoned, unrestrained erotic energy coursed through his veins. He wanted her. Wanted to be inside her. Her smooth velvety skin, her soft feminine aroma, and her tight, curvy body called to his masculine desire. The look in those big brown eyes revealed she wanted him back. *Damn, she's beautiful.* Blood rushed to his cock. His chest heaved with uneven breaths. "Then I'm going to give you what you want," he said, releasing her hands. "I'm going to make you scream."

The room began to spin around them. She clung to his shoulders, her grip clamping down hard. "Yes, Sebastian. Make me scream," she panted breathlessly.

His hands slithered along her inner thigh until he reached her thong. Needy fingers dipped under the fabric and found her slick wet folds. A surge of sexual heat flowed through his body and his temperature rose. His cock throbbed with an ache. Sebastian stroked her vigorously. Ashley moaned at his touch. He ripped the lacy nuisance from her flesh. The flimsy wadded fabric crumpled in his fist, disappeared in his hand. He pitched the shredded panties over his shoulder.

His eyes locked on hers. He lifted a hand to his nostrils, and then inhaled. "Mmm," he groaned, savoring the delicate scent that lingered on his fingertips. His heart hammered. His hard cock twitched. He slid a damp finger into his mouth and closed his eyes. His tongue swirled around the digit relishing her tangy flavor. "Mmm," he groaned again. She tasted like sex. And she belonged to him for the taking. Her sweet essence, like an *appeteaser* taunted his sexual appetite, and he was ready for the main course.

Sebastian lifted Ashley on top of a nearby cabinet. She released a small whimper. He crouched down slowly while stroking her sumptuous thighs. His shoulders wedged between her silky legs and his knees hit the floor. Anxious hands gripped her ankles and spread her legs wide. God, she was perfect. His cock pressed firmly against the metal zipper of his annoying jeans.

Her small hands braced him again, nails digging into his shoulders as his tongue found her center and stroked her tender flesh. His tongue whirled around, gliding over her soft pearl. His fingers fondled her wetness as he spread her lips to taste her honey. She trembled as he devoured all of her. Slowly, he eased a wet finger into her warm center.

"Ahhh," she moaned.

"You like this?" He broke into a light sweat.

"Yes," she rasped and arched her back, thrusting her round naked bosom forward.

Her feminine heat provoked his natural impulses. "This?" he asked, inserting another finger.

"Ahhh, Sebastian. Yes!"

"So sweet," he murmured. "Mmm, I'm going to fucking break you."

A sharp pang shot through his groin. The thick heat between them stifled his breathing. Taking harsh, ragged breaths, he snatched himself up from the floor and stepped between her gaping legs. He clawed at the small round buttons, couldn't strip open his shirt fast enough. A few buttons popped off and bounced on the floor. Ashley's jittery fingers fumbled with the buttons on the lower half of his shirt until his shirt hung open.

He leaned forward and covered a nipple with his mouth. Heat rolled through his chest. The chocolate morsel beaded under the stroke of his circling tongue. Another pang, sharper than the one before, shot through his groin and Sebastian stepped back.

"You ready to scream, darlin'?"

"Yes!"

He fiddled with the leather strap at his waist, unbuckled his belt, and then unzipped his jeans. The rugged twilled cotton fell to his ankles. Yanking furiously at the elastic band, briefs pooled to his ankles, joining his jeans.

Ashley's eyes widened. "Damn," she said, gawking at Sebastian's erection. Hungry brown eyes coasted up his washboard stomach to meet his lusty gaze.

Sebastian leaned down, kissed her, nibbling and sucking her bottom lip. "Think you can handle this?" he asked, a touch of danger and a dare edging his question.

"Yes," Ashley whimpered, hoping she was right as she watched him stuffed himself into the condom that appeared too snug for his swollen penis. Every inch of her burned. She would burst into flames at any moment. "I can handle it."

A slow, sexy smiled crawled across his lips. "I'm about to give you everything you want, baby."

Sebastian held his cock, ready to guide himself into her wet opening.

Ripped out of the moment, Ashley bolted forward. "Did you hear that?" Her heart leaped in her chest.

Heavy lids covered Sebastian's lustful gaze. "Did I hear what?" He whispered the question.

Sebastian leaned forward. The tip of his cock surged between her moist folds.

Ashley's back arched. Her walls ached with desire. "Ahhh, yes. I want you so bad." She tossed her head back against the wall.

"Yoo-hoo!" A man's cheery voice rang out from the gallery below. Then silence. Then footsteps. Clack. Clack. Clack. The sound drew louder with every step.

"Shit!" Sebastian stumbled back, nearly crashed to the floor. He clung on to the wall to right his position and then yanked up his pants to his waist. His throbbing erection prevented the zipper from closing. Nervous fingers fumbled to button his shirt.

"Get dressed, baby. Quickly." Sebastian faced the stairs. "I'll cover you," he whispered, shielding her view of the staircase.

The footsteps grew louder, nearer as the intruder ascended the staircase. Frantic, Ashley leaped down from the cabinet, raised her dress over her naked bosoms. Her eyes scoured the floor, hunting for the evidence of their impropriety, her destroyed panties. She remembered seeing them sail over the rail. "Oh, shit." Smoothing the rumpled dress with her clammy palms, she slid on her sandals. The visitor appeared with not a millisecond left to spare.

A bald head peaked over the staircase's top riser. Then two bushy brows and a pair of dark, beady eyes. The man's face came into view. "Well, hello, folks." The gruff voice greeted them, his tone salty and brows raised. He paused, scanned the room, and then frowned. Glaring eyes rolled up Sebastian's six-foot-plus frame. His stare idled on Sebastian's shirt, misaligned buttons and holes fastened together out of sequence.

"Either you dressed blindfolded before you arrived or you just got dressed in a hurry." The man walked closer to them, placed both hands on his hips.

He glanced at Ashley, pursed his lips. "I suppose these belong to you," he said, opening his left fist, his hand raised high. Red lacy thongs dangled in the air from disfigured fingers.

Ashley glowered at him, her cheeks warming. She could cram the four-foot dwarf into the trash bin she had seen in the corner.

Sebastian snatched the panties out of the man's hand. "I'll take those." Stuffing them into his back pocket, he placed a protective arm around Ashley's shoulders.

"This isn't a whorehouse. I'm sure Miss Kennedy wouldn't approve of your behavior."

A hand mounted Ashley's hip. She struggled to break free of Sebastian's hold.

He squeezed her shoulder. "I've got this, baby," Sebastian whispered into her ear.

Before she could protest, Sebastian had jacked the man up against the wall. He held the scrawny imp at least a foot off the floor by the jugular. "You don't want to fuck with me," Sebastian warned. Fire flashed in Sebastian's eyes. Ashley moved back. "I don't appreciate you coming into my place, interrupting my date, and insulting my lady. Get the hell out!" Sebastian released the man. The man crumbled to the floor, nearly passed out.

The man held his throat and gasped hoarsely for air. He scrambled away from Sebastian and to his feet. "I'm sorry. Miss… Miss Kennedy," he rasped. Sebastian's larynx-crushing chokehold made speaking difficult for the man. "Miss Kennedy asked me to stop by… make sure you had everything you needed."

Ashley didn't imagine that Sebastian could get so mad. One minute he was ready to pound into her until the cabinet broke. The next minute, he was ready to pound the man's face into dust. She had already been turned on by Sebastian's ostensible swagger. Coming to her defense had earned him some major points. Tonight proved one thing only. The hunger they shared had to be satisfied.

Chapter Eight

Sebastian's firm grasp fused Ashley's hand to the console between them. He regarded her with a sullen expression, his lips tugged into a frown. "I'm sorry." He spoke softly, stared straight ahead, and waited for the light to turn green. "I wanted this evening to be special. I owe you that at the very least." A melancholy tune, Sam Smith's "Safe With Me" piped through the stereo and matched his mood.

Ashley saw a different side of Sebastian tonight. A side that she liked. A side that intrigued her.

"Sebastian, maybe you're trying too hard. You don't have to arrange elaborate dates. You're very thoughtful and your plans are great, but truthfully," she paused, flexing her fingers. "This is temporary."

Sebastian raised his brow. He glanced at Ashley. "You think I should be more spontaneous?"

Ashley bit down on her bottom lip, remembering the taste of Sebastian's sweet, salty lips. "Oh, I don't think spontaneity is a problem for you." Sebastian's chuckle made her stomach flip-flop.

He pursed his lips. "I can't take all the credit for my actions." His eyes darkened. "We can't keep our hands away from each other." The glint in his eye indicated Sebastian shared as vivid a memory of the evening as she did.

"I'm just saying every date doesn't have to be staged."

"All right. No plans. You want to hang out with me? See where the night takes us?"

"Sure. I'd love to see what happens when Casanova lets spontaneity guide him."

"Fine." He twisted his lips, and turned the steering wheel hard to the left. The Jeep made a U-turn. "We haven't eaten. Are you hungry?"

"Well, I didn't get this curvy figure by eating air pie," she said.

Sebastian huffed. "No, I suppose you didn't." He shot Ashley a sidelong glance.

She winced. "That was rude. I'm sorry."

He shook his head. "No apology needed. I like your plainspoken honesty. I like that you speak your mind. And I especially like your curvy figure. No, air pie will not do."

Ashley laughed. Being herself felt like being unshackled.

Sebastian pulled the Jeep into the parking lot. "I imagine people never wonder where they stand with you." His dimpled grin her tonic, Ashley's slumped shoulders lifted.

"Honesty is my gift to the world," she raised convicted hands, shrugged her shoulders, and released a sigh. "And my personal burden."

Fine lines creased the edges of his eyes. He cupped his chin. "You should never see your strength as a weakness.

I admire your outspokenness." He stared at her in puzzlement. "Beautiful independence," he muttered under his breath. "That's the way I see you."

"Beautiful independence?" She frowned.

Sebastian placed a hand on the door handle. "You're strong. Independent. You can take care of yourself. I like that about you."

Ashley smiled. Most men cowered at her confidence and didn't have an appreciation for her quick tongue. Before she could respond, he jumped out the Jeep and slammed the door.

Despite his gruff exterior, Sebastian was chivalrous, opening doors and pulling out chairs. The sort of behavior that made a woman feel like a woman. Even a strong, independent woman like herself wanted a man like him. *Mr. Chivalrous.*

The passenger door opened. He held out a hand. "I hope you like hot dogs and chips."

A man pumping gas into a sporty red convertible eyed them as she hooked arms with Sebastian.

Ashley laughed aloud. "Convenience-store store grub. My favorite."

He winked. "Not staged. Not elaborate," he said with a cocky smile.

"Perfect!"

"Oh, but there's more. Come on." He gave a gentle nudge. "Our dinner awaits."

"I can't wait to find out what else you haven't planned." She walked through the door. He followed behind.

Sebastian's arm settled across her shoulders. "That makes two of us. I'm making this up on the spur, so anything goes." Unwittingly, Ashley leaned into him.

A new feeling emerged. A feeling she hadn't felt before. A feeling she didn't think was possible. Safe. Safe to be her. Sebastian's strength and self-assuredness didn't come at the expense of stifling hers. Not having to temper her temperament freed Ashley, felt as natural as the erratic pitter-patter of palpitations in her chest and clammy palms whenever Sebastian held her close.

Sebastian looked too good. He leaned against the black Jeep, his muscular arm extended. Calm. Commanding. Confident. Once Ashley broke through his rough exterior, she learned that there had been more to Sebastian Stone. Beyond his disturbing beliefs about dating and interactions between men and women, she liked him. She already determined him desirable, which didn't have anything to do with his personality. Being likeable put Sebastian into a new category. As far as she was concerned, liking Sebastian Stone could be very good or very bad.

Sebastian set out a large blanket. They lounged seaside, side by side. Ashley lay propped up by an elbow. Sebastian leaned forward, rested his forearms on bent knees. He stared at the waves rolling to shore.

He met Ashley's gaze. "That's when I decided to try my hand at commercial real estate investing," he said.

Ashley covered her mouth to contain her laughter. "I didn't mean to laugh. I just can't believe you said that to the judge." She laughed again, clutching her side.

"Yeah, well neither could the judge. I'm a smartass. What can I say?" He turned back to the ocean. "I guess I never belonged in the courtroom. I'm much more suited to buying and selling and property management than I am to courtroom decorum." He popped the last piece of his hot dog into his mouth.

Ashley frowned. "So were you disbarred?"

"No. I wasn't disbarred. I decided that practicing law wasn't for me. I stumbled my way into investing. When I turned twenty-five, I inherited a distressed property as part of my trust. My options were to sell the property at a loss or turn it into a profitable venture. I discovered I had a knack for taking broken things and fixing them to make money."

"You're brave."

"I'm not brave. I didn't have a job. I needed money."

"What did your family think? That must have been a difficult conversation with mom and dad."

Sebastian froze. His jaw set tight. He stared blankly into the night. "I don't really have much family left. My parents were killed when I was seven. I barely remember them," he stated flatly, emotionless. The callous way he talked about his dead parents surprised Ashley.

She winced. "Oh, I'm so sorry. I didn't mean to…"

"Stop apologizing. You didn't kill them. There's nothing to be sorry about." A frosty stare bore into Ashley. She righted herself to stave off the chill. "That's life. People die, Ashley." She recognized the bitter, angry bite in his tone.

She joined him in reflection, staring at the open sea. "We're born, and then we die. If we're lucky, we find love in the middle."

"You believe that crap, about love?" he asked.

"I used to. The older I've gotten and the more life has happened to me, I realized that we're just carnal beings. Love is the excuse some people use because they want regular sex."

The sound of crashing waves amplified in the silence. Sebastian planted an elbow on his knee. His temple rested on a white-knuckled fist. "Hmm, your insight isn't much different than my own beliefs. Spoken from experience?"

Arms folded across her bosom, Ashley regarded Sebastian with a reluctant glance. "Some." She exhaled a deep breath to release the tightening in her chest.

He studied her for a moment, deep sunken lines forming across his brow. "Yeah, I guess there's no point in getting too personal," he said as though he had contemplated deeper conversation.

She fastened her lips shut and then swallowed. Meeting his eyes, "Exactly," she said.

Like a caterpillar transformed into a butterfly, Sebastian's mood morphed from somber to rollicking. Arms outstretched, he tossed his head back. "That's what I like about you. You don't want a relationship. You're not trying to manipulate the situation or pressure me. You're confident, independent. That's sexy as hell." Sebastian moved closer. His finger traced the curve of her shoulder to the crook of her neck.

His words slammed into her brain like a jackhammer to concrete. Ashley's darting eyes avoided his. "Yep, I don't want or expect anything from you."

Sebastian had come to a very different conclusion than was her reality. She did want a relationship. She just didn't know how to move on to a healthy relationship after Chris. To open that can of worms for debate with Sebastian—wasted effort. Two weeks from now, she planned to be back in Atlanta. Only God knew where Sebastian Stone planned to be.

His smile reached the stars. "You're perfect." He leaped to his feet and extended his hand. "We don't have a minute to waste. Time is running out. Let's go back to my place. I'll take you to the house in the morning."

Ashley didn't budge. She frowned, looking up at him. "Hold on a minute, Sebastian. I think you misunderstood. I don't want a relationship with you. That doesn't mean I don't have respect for myself."

Sebastian squatted beside her, whispered into her ear. "Did you feel less respected when I almost screwed you at Robin's Nest or when my cock went inside you at the art gallery tonight?"

Her chest heaved. She ignored the rolling sensations in her stomach. She resisted the danger of his scent, swirling around her like a whirlwind in the ocean breeze.

"We both have our reasons for not wanting to get involved. We have incredible chemistry. There are only a few days left. You'll never see me again. Aren't you at all curious?"

She deliberately ignored his question. "Sebastian, don't ruin the evening. I'm not going to your place." Sebastian had no idea how right he was. Ashley wanted to feel all of him swell inside her like the waves at their feet. But there was the matter of the cat. And everyone knows what curiosity did to that poor little creature.

"I don't know why you women torture yourselves. It's only sex. We all want it. We all need it. There's no reason to feel guilty for wanting sex."

"This isn't about guilt."

"Oh, I see. This is about control. You'll sleep with me under your own conditions, not mine. Am I right?"

"No!" she exclaimed, although Sebastian had pegged the truth. To protect her heart, sex had to be on her terms. "Your fixation with sex is disturbing."

He leaned away. Studied her face. A slow smirk appeared. "You can't handle sex without strings. I scare you because you like me," he said.

Any thoughts she had that might redeem her opinion of Sebastian fled in an instant. Ashley raised her hands in defeat. "I'm not a robot. In general, I tend to have some interest in the men I invite into my bed." The man, regardless of the situation that left him wounded, was hopeless. Her plan to teach him a lesson was on, with a vengeance.

Sebastian settled down beside Ashley. Obvious frustration at their dissonance, tense fingers roiled through his hair. "I realize that I come across like an asshole. Maybe I am. The truth is I'm not good at meeting new people, especially women."

"Really? I would have never guessed," she said and then rolled her eyes.

"I deserve that, and more. My life is complex. I'm complex. I'm not a man you want around for the long haul." His comment revealed kinks in his armor.

Ashley jerked her head back. "I don't want or expect anything from you."

"Ah, but Ashley, everybody wants something. Everyone has a motive."

"Is that the reason you work so hard to keep people away? You think people want something from you."

He stared at her with empty, heartless eyes. "Maybe. What's your reason?"

"My reason?" she asked. "I don't push people away. I'm not the asshole in this equation."

"Aren't you? One minute, you've got your hands all over me. The next, you're acting as though nothing ever happened. You're like fire and ice. Soon you'll reach your boiling point."

"Then if I was you, I'd be careful. Boiling water burns, and it evaporates, like any thought I might have about seeing you again could disappear."

The pad of his thumb swiped across his upper lip. "I have nothing to worry about. Desire like we have doesn't vanish into thin air. Are you going to answer my question, or are we going to continue this childish game. I have all night. Why do you push people away?"

She clasped her hands tightly to avoid the mishap that would be her open hand smacked against his cheek. "You're complex. I'm complicated."

He squinted at Ashley. Raised her chin. Stared into her eyes. "You're afraid that you might get too close. Too involved. Hurt."

She swallowed hard. Her determination gave her strength. "No more than you are."

"Possibly," he conceded. He stared back at the sea. "Two tortured souls united on Peachtree Street, who just happen to find themselves thrown together in Key West. Don't you wonder why?"

Ashley rolled her eyes and shrugged her shoulders. "Our meeting was merely a coincidence. And who says I'm a tortured soul?"

He didn't answer her question with words at first. His raised brow said what he thought. But just to make his thoughts clear, "Keep telling lies to yourself."

A buzzing sound drew Ashley's attention. Sebastian retrieved his phone from a pocket. Glaring at the number, he winced. "Excuse me a moment. I have to take this call." He stood and walked several feet away.

Heavy steps, head hung low, and eyes downcast, Sebastian paced back and forth.

"Look Stephen, I told you I'll have it," she heard him say. His gait quickened. He stopped. "No! Are you fucking kidding me? I'm not going to make a decision about that right now. I need to research the options." He glanced at Ashley and then turned away. "When is it? A week! We agreed to three months!" His stride, taken with long, broad stokes, matched his fiery words. "Fine. I'll be there with a plan." Sebastian disconnected the call. After fiddling with his phone for a few seconds, he headed back toward Ashley.

He plopped down. Folded his legs. Didn't look at her. His mood had changed. "You're smart not to get mixed up with me. People in my life end up hurt or worse."

Had his comment been about his shady business dealings or something else? She didn't have the guts to ask.

Her heart hammered in her chest. Words stuck in her throat. "What were you like as a child?" she asked. Her change of subject seemed a welcome distraction for Sebastian.

"Lonely. Scared. Sad. Death is hard, especially for children." He spoke in clipped sentences, distanced and disinterested in the conversation.

She nodded in agreement. "I can't imagine how difficult that must have been for you."

"Well, I grew up. I got over their deaths. What was your childhood like?" Sebastian's one question that showed interest in something other than sex forced Ashley's eyes to widen.

"I'm an only child, raised by a single parent. I never knew my father. I had a good life, though. My mother worked two jobs and provided everything I needed. Who raised you?"

"I lived with my grandmother until she became ill. Then my older brother took over the job. Apparently I was a surprise to my parents who already had two grown children when I came along. At twenty-three, my brother put his life on hold to care for me."

"Do you stay in contact with him?"

Sebastian's tone softened. His contentious behavior subsided. "I do. He lives in London. I stalk him and his family during the holidays."

Ashley leaned back on her elbows, laughing. "I always wanted a brother or sister. It's nice that you get to spend time with him."

"Or depressing," he chuckled. "I'm always intruding on his family time."

"I understand," she said. "I'm intruding on my best friend right now. I feel so guilty."

Sebastian glance at her. "Aren't you on vacation? Why do you feel guilty?"

The cool night breeze swept across the ocean, sending shivers through her body. "This isn't really a vacation. Kerri sort of forced me here for my own good. She's a newlywed, new mom, new business owner. For two weeks, she's being a really good friend, and I feel guilty for taking her away from her life."

"Hmm," he murmured. "She certainly has a lot of 'new' in her life."

"Yeah, that's another story entirely."

He inched closer. "Come here." He patted his chest. "You're cold. Let me keep you warm." The muscles in her face pulled tight. Ashley's lips twisted, left brow arched up. Sebastian frowned and jerked his head back. "Don't give me that look. I'll behave."

Ashley nuzzled up to Sebastian. She surrendered her skepticism, yielded to his beckoning embrace.

"Your being forced here on vacation, is that topic off-limits?" Sebastian's fingers danced along her arm, a feather-light caress waltzing in repeated pattern across her skin.

Ashley closed her eyes, delighting in the tickle of his trace. "Yes, that topic is off-limits."

"Hmm," he murmured again. "You don't have to tell me. I can guess."

They talked all night long, amicably, no mention of sex. Ashley learned that Sebastian played recreational soccer on the weekends. His love of the arts had led him to purchase several galleries.

"Why did you buy the Moss Studio?" she asked.

"The gallery is a special place for me. Don't ask." He shook his head, tightening his hold.

"I used to dance. Ballet. I stopped years ago though." *Like everything else in my life, when Chris died.* "Don't ask."

Sebastian gave her a gentle squeeze. "Have you ever considered dancing again?"

Her cheek pressed into his shirt. She shook her head.

"You should. You have a great body. And I mean that in a very nonsexual sort of way. You have a beautiful dancer's body. Like artwork."

"As the owner of a few art galleries, I suppose you are an art expert."

His lips touched her forehead, the feel of genuine affection. "Only fine art, baby. And you are definitely that."

The sun began to peek above the horizon, bursting through the clouds. The early morning rays streaked across the aureate sea. Ashley had never noticed the bright gold strands highlighted in his darker tresses. Their date had been filled with the unexpected and new discoveries.

Sebastian walked her to the front door. She fumbled with the key. He held out his hand. "Here, let me," he said.

The door opened and Ashley stood at the threshold. Her fingers wrapped the frame. "Thank you for a pleasantly surprising evening. I did have a good time."

"I'm glad. I'd like to take you out again." He paused and looked away. His gaze fixed on the lush landscape. "I have some business to handle. I won't see you until Friday."

She shrugged heavy shoulders. "You don't owe me an explanation. I understand."

"Our time is running out. I hate to lose four days with you." Sebastian leaned closer, pressed his lips into the crook of her neck. "I want you, Ashley," he rasped.

Ashley rolled her neck to the side. She closed her eyes. Breathed him in. "Make it happen," she muttered.

Sebastian tilted her chin. Impassioned eyes met her apprehension. "I'm going to give you the best night of your life." His questioning brows squeezed together. "Ashley, I don't want to hurt you or lead you on. Are you sure you can handle this? I only have one night to give." At least he had been thoughtful enough to consider her feelings, the asshole.

Snapped out of her intoxication, Ashley blinked hard twice. "Of course." She scoffed at his concern, marked by her frown and twisted smirk. Inside, the pang in her chest spread to her stomach. "Sebastian, don't screw up. This is your last chance."

His brutal honesty didn't make the reality any easier to absorb. To Sebastian, Ashley had been nothing more than a conquest, an easy lay. Their desire, a temporary affliction.

Ashley watched him drive off. She sprinted to the guestroom. Slammed the door shut. She leaned against the wood grain and closed her eyes. Soon Sebastian would become a faded memory like everything in her life that held any significance.

Chapter Nine

Kerrigan stumbled into the kitchen. She whirled past and plopped into the seat opposite Ashley at the breakfast table. "Ash, you didn't come home last night," Kerrigan chimed, a wide grin plastered on her naturally rose-colored lips. "That's good, right?" She paused, scrunched her face into a frown. "Why do you look pissed?"

Ashley's shoulders twitched, a limp shrug. "There's nothing to tell. Sebastian is like every man I date. He wants sex." Anger burned in her belly, the mere thought made her temperature rise.

Kerrigan lifted a glass, gulped a large swig of orange juice. "But you already knew that about Sebastian. What changed?"

Ashley gave a dismissive wave. "Nothing changed. I'm tired."

She pierced Ashley with a penetrating gaze. "No. Something's different." Suddenly her mouth fell open. "Oh, Ash. You really do like him. I'm sorry. I know you were hoping for better."

Ashley rolled her eyes. "Yep, my mistake. I let my guard down. Then he reminded me. To men, I'm only a piece of ass." She turned her face, nodded her head.

Kerrigan's jaw clenched. She reached out. Lean arms encircled Ashley, engulfing her in a comforting hug. Ashley yanked out of Kerrigan's hold. She shoved her plate away and stood.

"Kerri, I'm sorry. I was up all night running my mouth. This is exhaustion talking. I'll be back to normal after a few hours of sleep." She crossed her arms over her chest and bolted for the exit.

At the sound of chair legs scraping the tile floor like tongs of a fork dragged across a chalkboard, a shiver skirted up Ashley's spine and she winced. Kerrigan's footsteps amplified as she drew closer to Ashley.

"Ash, forget what Sebastian thinks or says or does. You are worth gold. Don't let him reduce you to feeling less than your worth. You deserve better." Her voice trailed Ashley's steps. "I mean it, Ash. You are worth gold."

Ashley spun around. She rolled her eyes. "Thanks for the pep talk. Right now, I feel like I'm worth about ten karat gold or that gold-plated stuff that wears away." She trudged off toward her room and yelled down the hallway. "Or maybe that gold-tone stainless-steel crap that rusts and turns skin green. I'm going to bed."

In the sanctuary of the guestroom, Ashley unloaded. First, a firing of angry curses filled the air. She paced the floor, ranting. "That asshole! I can't believe him!" Her arms flailed, throwing air punches. "Damn jerk! Fucking damn jerk! Oh, he's going to get what's coming to him. I'm going to serve his ass to him on a platter and watch him eat it. Ugh!"

Then, a river of emotions flooded her insides. She collapsed to the floor in a heap, muttering incoherently. "What's wrong with me? I'm a good person. I'm pretty, smart. Where are the normal men?" Sobering after several minutes, she gathered her composure.

Finally, calm and rationale found her huddled in a corner. She closed her eyes and leaned against the cool wall. Of all the men on planet earth, why did she have to be attracted to this man? She reached up, snatched a pen and notepad from the nearby desk. Hurried fingers scribbled fiercely. The list noted the three items she needed to carry out her plan. Shopping tomorrow would be fun.

Sebastian shuffled along the sidewalk. Despite the lack of sleep the night before, his brisk pace hastened with each stride, nearly to a jog. He ran on adrenaline and his usual three cups of coffee. The presentation that had been his all-nighter lay at the bottom of his jeans pocket between a gum wrapper and two pennies.

"Hi," he said, handing the flash drive to a young copy-center employee. "I need twenty color copies of a sixty-page presentation. Can the copies be ready later this afternoon?"

The wide-eyed girl gawked at him. She placed the flash drive into a plastic pouch. "Here." She shoved a form across the counter. "Fill this out. Your job should be done by tomorrow morning."

Sebastian frowned. "I need the copies this afternoon. I have to mail them tonight. Can I pay for rush service and get the copies by five?"

She rolled her eyes. "Probably not."

He pointed overhead. "Your sign says you offer same-day service at an additional cost."

She smacked her lips. "Sir, we don't make guarantees on same-day rush jobs." Miss Null and Void stared blankly. Her lackluster personality nudged him to the edge.

Sebastian glanced at her badge. "Lisa," he said, placing both hands on the counter. "Let me tell you how this is going to work." His glare locked on her like a missile. "I pay you money. You do the work. No questions asked." Sebastian retrieved a pen from the counter and scribbled on the form. "Otherwise, I'll have to speak with your boss and tell him or her about your horrible attitude and general lack of interest in making a sale." His irritated voice raised. The girl flinched.

A hand with long purple fingernails snatched the completed form from Sebastian's fingers. "I can have your copies ready at six o'clock," the snarky voice said.

He eased back. Pocketed his hands. "Six o'clock will be fine. What's the total?"

She typed a series of keystrokes into a computer. "One hundred and eighty dollars plus tax. Will you need them bound? Binding costs extra."

"That's fine. The extra cost is not a problem. I'll be back at seven."

Sebastian bolted for the exit. The vibration in his right pocket slowed his steps to a crawl. He pulled out his cell phone and glanced at the caller's number. "Stephen," he muttered under his breath. He punched the talk button. "What can I do for you, Stephen?" He didn't hide his annoyance.

"I'm checking on your progress. The meeting is at seven on Monday morning. Is your proposal ready?"

Sebastian lowered his voice as a man and woman passed him on the sidewalk. "Yes. I'm having copies made now. They'll ship tonight, in plenty of time for the meeting."

Stephen didn't say a word. "Hello. Stephen?" Sebastian asked.

Breaking the silence, "Uh, yeah. That's great news, Stone. Why are you shipping the presentations? You do know there's a hurricane headed straight for the Keys, don't you? Shouldn't you get an earlier flight out?"

Sebastian unlocked the door and climbed into the driver's seat. "Yes. Of course, I know about the storm, but I'm not changing my plans. I'm leaving Saturday morning as planned."

"Stone, that's cutting it awfully close. You should try to get an earlier flight out. There must be flights leaving tomorrow. I'll have Judith change your arrangements."

Sebastian inhaled a deep breath. He couldn't wait to see Ashley on Friday. The mere thought of her aroused him. "Stephen, that won't be necessary. I'm leaving Saturday morning. The presentations will ship tomorrow. I'll have them sent to Judith."

Stephen huffed. "If you screw this up, I can't protect you."

A knot formed in Sebastian's stomach. "I never asked for your protection. I'll see you bright and early on Monday."

"Seven o'clock, Monday. Later, Stone."

"Good-bye, Stephen."

The call disconnected. Sebastian's hands came down hard on the leather steering wheel. He gripped the wheel tightly. Another vibration. He glanced at the incoming call. A smile washed away his angry scowl.

"Hey, man! What's going on?" Weeks had passed since Sebastian last talked to his best buddy Daniel.

"I thought I'd better check on you. I figured you must be getting so much action that you forgot my number," Daniel joked.

Sebastian chuckled. "No action yet, but not for lack of trying."

"I'm surprised. You've been there for more than a week. Nothing?"

He huffed. "Daniel, man. There's this woman, Ashley. I met her a few months ago in Atlanta under interesting circumstances. Ran into her again at the airport. We happened to be on the same flight to Key West. I've taken her out a few times. I like her."

"You like her, but... I sense your hesitation."

"But, she's different. Different than my usual type."

"Different can be good."

"Different is definitely good. She's got edge, which I like."

"She a blond?"

"Nope. Darker."

"Oh yeah, dude. Blondes are fun, but brunettes are wild. I'm jealous."

"No, she's not brunette. She's black."

The phone went silent. "You mean she's black as in Goth or she's black as in soul sista?"

Sebastian hadn't ever considered how to describe Ashley. Being interested in a black woman had only ever been a notion, not that he had ever given the idea serious consideration. He started the engine and put the vehicle into reverse. "I mean she's black as in African American." He swiveled around to glance at his rear left and then right. The Jeep reversed out of the parking space.

"Wow! I didn't think they liked us."

Sebastian rolled his eyes. "They? Who in the hell is they?"

"Man, you know exactly what I mean, black women.

He shook his head. "They," he said making air quotes, "don't like you."

"I'm not trying to be insensitive or insulting. I've seen many attractive black women who I haven't had the courage to ask out. I wish I had your balls."

Sebastian pulled out onto Duval Street. "I know you wish you had my balls." He chuckled. "Ashley is an intelligent, beautiful woman. I didn't have to think twice about asking her out. We had an instant attraction… chemistry."

"You know I'm not a racist jerk, but I must admit, this news is shocking. I never knew you were interested in exotic women."

Sebastian glanced at the clock on the dashboard. He still had time to run one more errand. "I never knew I'd be interested in any woman. I wish the circumstances were different. I would have liked to get to know her better."

"Why don't you continue to see her? She lives in Atlanta, right?"

"She does, but I… I don't know." Sebastian paused. "I haven't had this much fun in years. I'll see her Friday night. Maybe I'll throw it out there. Maybe."

"Sebastian, this is good. Hearing you talk about a woman is very good. If you do the deed, you have to let me know what that's like." He heard Daniel's smile.

Sebastian pulled into the parking lot. The Flower Pot had the best selection of flowers in the Keys. "I plan to do the deed, and I absolutely will not share those details with you when it happens."

"You really like this woman, huh?"

"I think I do. I like her. She's interesting and she doesn't hold back." Sebastian slammed the door. "By the way, I need a favor. I need your help to find something. I'll e-mail you details later. Can you help?"

"Sure, man. Whatever you need. I'll look for your e-mail."

"Awesome. I've got to run. The big date is Friday."

Sebastian leaned against the front of the Jeep. One foot settled on the bumper. Busy fingers scrolled the address book. His chest tightened. His nerves hadn't bothered him until now. The phone rang.

"Hello," Ashley said, slightly hesitant. Normally she didn't answer calls from unknown numbers. Seeing the Atlanta area code gave her chills.

His velvety smooth voice satisfied her secret desire. "Hello, beautiful," Sebastian said. His husky voice quaked through her core.

Ashley's pulse raced. She guided the rickety shopping cart down an empty aisle. Good thing no one could witness her gushing like a silly pubescent teen. "Hi, Sebastian," she managed calmly. The cart rattled loudly as she strolled down the aisle.

"I've missed seeing you, talking to you. What are you doing?"

Her fingers curled around the basket's handle until her hands ached. Would she have the nerve to go through with her plan once he had her?

"I've been thinking," she said, her voice softening to a whisper. Ashley leaned down on the shopping cart handle. "Let's leave things between us as they are. Besides, a storm is coming. Kerri thinks we should leave early."

As though he found his courage in her weakness, "That's not good enough for me," he said, his tone marked with renewed confidence. "I want to see you again. I don't care that a hurricane is coming. Let her leave. You can stay with me."

She wanted to see him again, too. She stood up straight, put the cart in motion again. "Okay. Friday?"

"Yes, Friday. I want you all day." His voice lowered to a seductive growl. "And all night."

Ashley swallowed hard, fell silent. She should have been angry. To him, she had been a two-week booty call. Damn her for finding his desire for her sexy. With her plan, she could get what she wanted. She found her nerve and voice again. "What time?"

"I'll pick you up at two o'clock. I have a special day planned for us. We'll spend the evening at my place." She heard the smile in Sebastian's voice.

Her hand slipped. Bottles of lubricant slid off the top shelf and crashed to the floor. "All right. I'll see you at two on Friday."

"Ashley, are you okay? Don't you dare hurt that ankle again before I get my hands on you."

Desire tempered her fury. Bitterness would fuel her revenge later. Right now, Ashley focused on cleaning up the mess she had made. "Uh, everything is fine. I've got to finish my shopping."

"See you Friday," he said.

Ashley shoved the phone into her handbag. She squatted. There must have been a thousand bottles of lube on that shelf, now scattered across the entire floor. She stood, drove the cart to the end of the aisle in search of someone who worked at the small grocery store for help.

She wheeled the cart to the right. "Oh, crap! I'm sorry," she squealed, almost making a handsome young clerk aisle kill. "There's a huge mess on aisle sex." Ashley cringed. A wave of heat rolled through her belly. "I mean aisle six."

The clerk frowned and then headed in the direction of her destruction. Ashley followed and stood next to the endcap where gallons of water were on sale. He hopscotched down the aisle, carefully stepping from foot to foot to avoid the plastic bottles. A small gathering of shoppers and other store employees assembled at both ends of the aisle. He glanced back at Ashley, his face turning red. "Did you get enough K-Y Jelly or need anything else?" he asked, barely containing his laughter. Snickers came from the onlookers.

Ashley wished shrink-ray technology existed. She could shrink herself to two inches in height and duck for cover under a shelving unit. What the hell, she thought. "Yep." She held up one of the tiny bottles. "I'm going to get everything I need Friday night. Thanks for the help."

An odd sound came from her handbag. Ashley peered inside her purse. Light illuminated the leather cave. She reached in and lifted the cell phone to her ear. Piercing laughter assaulted her eardrums.

"Sebastian?" she asked. Her heart hammered through her chest wall.

"Yes, baby. You will get what you need Friday night," he choked out through his laughter.

Ashley let out a loud sigh and hit the end button, disconnecting the call. She tossed the phone back into her handbag.

"Give me that," she said, snatching another bottle of lubricant from the grocery store clerk. *Fuck it!* "Where are your handcuffs, whips and chains?" She asked, without cracking a smile. The young man turned a shade of red that she had never seen on a human being. Crayola could call the color nuclear red.

Sebastian   Stone   had   better   be   worth   her embarrassment.

A beach towel tumbled aimlessly like a weed. He watched the rag float down the shoreline until it vanished from his sight. The cool early morning breeze invigorated him after his jog. Sebastian shuffled sand under his feet and stared out at the open sea. His thoughts wafted from the Monday morning board meeting to his date planned with Ashley. For the first time in years, he looked forward to something and life seemed less mundane. Maybe Daniel had been right. Seeing Ashley in Atlanta might be good for him.

Sebastian whipped out his phone and sent a text message.

Today is the big date. I plan to ask her to continue seeing me back in Atlanta.

He sent the message. Waited. Paced. Without fail, his friend replied.

Good move. Finally using those huge balls of yours? Seriously, have fun.

Sebastian respected his friend's advice and opinion. Daniel had been married and divorced twice and recently started dating again. Sebastian, on the other hand, had dated Ellie since high school. He thought they would grow old together. Finding himself again, without her, had been the most difficult period in his thirty-five years.

Another text from Daniel came in.

I know you. Stop feeling guilty. Do what you must. Be happy. Live.

Sebastian smiled and then rolled his eyes. He fired back a response.

Don't know if you're the devil or an angel on my shoulder. In either case, get the fuck off.

A reply from Daniel took seconds.

I'm both, fucker. Leave me alone and go get laid.

He smiled and headed back to his room, excitement and energy flowed through him.

Sebastian prepared everything for their date. The special gift he ordered would arrive for Ashley this morning. Tonight no one would interrupt them. He wouldn't let her make excuses. He wouldn't make any excuses himself. She would be all his.

He sat at a desk in his room. The presentation that he spent hours to create and practiced at least one hundred times stared back at him on the laptop. He had crafted a winning proposal, and the Board would be crazy if they didn't approve his plan. An opportunity to buy six foreclosed properties and turned them into revenue engines would get their attention and secure his future. He leaned back, rested his hands behind his head. Fire that flowed through his veins hadn't been there in five years. He smiled, exhaled a breath. Sebastian found his way back, on all fronts.

Chapter Ten

The doorbell rang, the chime echoing throughout the house. Kerrigan hurried to the foyer. She peeled back a sheer curtain, peeking through the narrow sidelight window. A refugee from an eighties punk-rock band sporting a spiky Mohawk held a large white box in his arms.

"I have a package for Ashley Turner," the delivery man droned, his voice barely penetrating the wooden door.

Kerrigan turned and smiled at Ashley. "Ash, I bet that's a gift from Sebastian." The giddiness in her voice made Ashley's eyes roll like marbles.

Ashley opened the door and pried the box from the man's tattooed arms. "Here you are," she said, handing him a ten-dollar tip. "Thank you."

Ashley scuffled with the box, setting the large square object on the breakfast table in the kitchen.

"Use this." Kerrigan held out a box cutter to slice through the meticulously sealed package.

Ashley eased into a chair. She took the blade and set it aside. With bare hands, she ripped off the tape.

"Or, maybe not." Kerrigan laughed. "Should I worry about Sebastian tonight?" she teased.

"Definitely," Ashley quipped back, lips twisted into a sly grin.

Impatient hands peeled away the last remnants of the stubborn tape. Ashley lifted the lid slowly. Carefully. She folded back layers of tissue paper to reveal the treasure.

Her mouth dropped open. "Oh, wow!" She lifted the dress from the box, held the garment up high. "This is gorgeous. Sebastian must have spent a small fortune."

Kerrigan's eyes caressed the sleek, backless gown. "That satin will hug your curves like a glove. Sebastian has good taste."

Ashley's heart leaped into her throat. Kerrigan's eager hands riffled through the box while Ashley's nerves paralyzed her motionless and speechless.

Pinched fingers held up what appeared to be a torture device used for asphyxiation. "I need to wash my hands," Kerrigan joked, her eyes stretching wide. "With bleach," she added, tossing the scanty lingerie made more of string than fabric, and crotchless thongs, onto the table.

Ashley swallowed hard. "Damn," she blurted out. "I think we might kill each other tonight." She leaned over and raised the straps of a small overnight bag. Handing the bag to Kerrigan, "Take a look," Ashley said, her sultry expression marked by a wink.

Kerrigan unzipped the bag and stuck her hand inside. "What in the hell?" Metal handcuffs dangled from her fingertips before she placed them on the table next to the fetish threads. "What else is in that bag, or dare I ask?"

"A few toys, condoms, lube." She laughed, remembering the incident at the grocery store and the nuclear-red store clerk. "The usual stuff."

Kerrigan blushed. "The usual stuff for you, not for me."

Ashley stood, wagged her index finger at Kerrigan. "Your husband needs to be kept satisfied. I could teach you a thing or two."

"What you teach me might land me in prison or worse."

"But you'd thank me," Ashley warbled, the cadence of her words rising in sing-song fashion.

A wedge of paper caught Ashley's eye. She pulled a note from the box. "What's this?" She unfolded the small piece of paper. Her eyes scanned the letter word for word, line by line.

Ashley,

I've never felt physical desire like I have for you. I want you to enjoy the special evening I have planned for us. This gift is one that I hope will always remind you of our special night and the memories we created. I can't wait to see you. I can't wait to touch you. Years from now, no matter where you are and no matter where I am, we'll always have Key West. Two strangers, two lovers for just one night.

Sebastian

Silenced again, Ashley blinked several times and then dashed down the hallway.

The note floated to the floor, and Kerrigan trailed Ashley's sprint. Ashley slammed the guest bedroom door and twisted the lock behind her. Shriveling to the floor she heaved hard and heavy, her chest swelling as though her sternum would burst. She couldn't breathe. She couldn't think. She couldn't feel.

"Ash, open the door," Kerrigan's words fell on numb brain cells, not comprehending her words.

"What?" Ashley bawled. "I need a minute."

Kerrigan's voice shrank. "Ash, why are you upset? What's wrong?"

"He's messing with my head!" she yelled at the top of her lungs. Ashley bellowed from the pit of her belly, festering rage fueled her release. How dare he write her such an eloquent note! Clearly, Sebastian didn't understand the concept of the one-night stand.

Kerrigan's words pierced the lower half of the door. Tap. Tap. Tap. She rapped lightly on the wooden barrier. "Ash, you don't have to go out with him." Ashley knew her friend would camp in the hall until she came out of the room.

Five minutes later, the door cracked open. Ashley planted her toes in the lush carpet lining the hall. She huddled next to Kerrigan. The mark of pinned-up emotions marred her stone face. "I'm going out with him," she said, slouched over, her posture matching her disposition. Kerrigan would never approve of her plan. Rolling her eyes, "Can you help me get ready?" Ashley asked, her lifeless glare hiding the secret behind swollen eyes.

Kerrigan lifted her gaze, eyebrows scrunched together. "Are you okay? You're not about to do something crazy, are you?"

Her head tilted to the left. She shrugged. "I'm going to give Sebastian what he's been asking for." Wilted of interest in a debate, Ashley told a partial truth. "Come on. Help me squeeze into that 'fuck me' dress."

Like cogs turning with precision to display the exact hour, the doorbell rang the moment Ashley waltzed into the living room. Sebastian's burly silhouette was visible through the sidelight. Prickly stings traveled her spine. Her feet welded to the floor. She froze. Kerrigan rounded the corner. One look at Ashley, and she came to a halt.

A soft hand reached for Ashley's. "Ash, Sebastian's here. Are you sure you want to do this? I can tell him to go away."

Fists balled at her sides. Her knuckles grazed the hem of the taut, black dress that fit more like a second skin than evening attire. Anger ironed her lips flat. Ashley had never been more certain of a thing. "I'm ready." She glanced down at her smooth, glistening legs. Her knees unlocked and she moved toward the door. She reached for the knob, twisted her hand. The door opened and there stood Sebastian.

The hazy moonlight bounced off the contours of his arms, rippling of sinew and muscle. His musky aroma tantalized her nostrils, made her dizzy. Her eyes scaled his form, taking measure of thick, sturdy thighs wrapped in black dress slacks. A neatly pressed shirt conformed to his hulking chest. His square jaw set tight. Those smoky gray eyes devoured her. Exchanged desire traded in twilight. She wanted him bad.

"Wow!" Sebastian spoke first. "You're gorgeous." His sweeping gaze settled on her, locked her eyes to his.

Ashley flexed her foot, twisted her ankle. The heel of her platform stiletto pivoted. "Thank you." Her insides rolled.

His freshly cut hair gave him a youthful glow accentuated by a wide, boyish grin. "Nice shoes," he said, his thick mane tousled by anxious hands. Damn, he looked good.

"They're borrowed," she replied, glancing down at Kerrigan's four-inch black stilts.

Sebastian stepped forward. Close. "Mmm," he groaned, tilting his head down. His breath warmed her cheek. "You smell great. Jasmine?"

She twirled a stray hair around her manicured finger. "No. Laundry."

Behind him, a palm frond floated to the step on the porch.

His arm curled around her waist, pulled her to him. "What?" Sebastian whispered, his hand guided her chin, brought her avoiding stare center.

Her eyelids fluttered at the speed of light. A small hand flattened against his chest. "Laundry. The fragrance I'm wearing is called Laundry." Ashley's pulse raced, in sync with his.

The corner of Sebastian's mouth twitched. "Ironic." A full grin spread across his lips and met her puzzled expression. "Because tonight, you and I are going to soil my bed sheets."

Candle flames danced, flickered amber and gold light, casting distorted shadows across a stark-white dinner plate. Ashley's hands twisted. Her eyes darted from one end of the outdoor patio to the other side. She had never seen such beauty. The tropical sanctuary of orchids, bleeding hearts, and a variety of other exotic flowers surrounded them. The pungent aroma of ginger blossoms drifted on the cool breeze. Lights strung overhead added elegant charm to the ocean view just beyond the patio.

Sebastian's guiding hand gently nudged Ashley toward the table. "I wasn't sure what you'd like. I spent most of the day at a friend's house making several dishes."

Her head jerked back, surprised. "Really? You cook?" Sebastian didn't strike her as the type who would or could prepare a meal. The amused glint in his eyes affirmed her question. "Impressive." She gave an approving nod.

As though he had intercepted her next thought, "I'm quite domesticated. I do my own laundry, put down the toilet seat when I'm done," he teased, pulling out a bamboo chair for her.

She pursed her lips and sank into the comfort of the seat. "Someone trained you well," Ashley quipped.

His left hand lingered on the back of her chair. Sebastian leaned down, placed his right hand on the table. His deep timber whispered into her ear. "I'm housebroken, but don't mistake that to mean that I'm tame." The thick vein in his neck pulsed hard. Instantly, she warmed, despite the chill rolling off the shore.

Ashley glanced at him. Light bounced off the silver Burberry watch banding his wrist. "I'd never make such a mistake."

His expression morphed into a dangerous half smirk, the silent warning a guaranteed promise of the night to come.

Sebastian shifted away, took his place at her side. All man and muscle crammed into a small seat, and so close to her, Ashley broke into a light sweat. She scooted her chair to the left, creating a pronounced chasm between them. Her knees locked together. She wasn't tame either. Sebastian would be wrong to think otherwise.

Her eyes roamed the feast spread out in front of them. He had made more food than two people could possibly eat in a setting.

Ashley frowned. "Why so much food? Is someone else joining us tonight?"

His eyes twinkled once again. "Yes, there is a lot of food." His tone darkened, matching the storm brewing behind seductive eyes. "You'll need lots of energy tonight. All night. Now, eat up."

Sebastian's heat rolled off his body in waves. His piercing gray eyes laser-focused on Ashley. Usually she had complete control in situations involving men. Usually a man sitting across from her would be a bundle of nerves sporting sweaty palms and donning a racing heart. A knot at the pit of her belly settled like a fifty-pound weight. For the first time in a long time—heck, if ever—vulnerability found her. She didn't like the feeling.

Ashley blanketed her lap with a cloth napkin. Sebastian followed, repeating the motion. He dished out small servings of the feast for them both. Spearing a crab-and-shrimp-stuffed mushroom, he brought the fork to Ashley's tempted taste buds.

Her eyes stretched wide, tasting the sample. The savory flavor exploded on her taste buds. "Hmm," she moaned. "This is great."

He smiled and raised an eyebrow. His surprise seemed genuine. "Glad you approve."

Sebastian scooped a spoonful of seafood soufflé. "Open wide," he said, pausing the morsel at her lips.

Ashley obeyed. Bursting with flavor, an infusion of pepper, onion, scallops, lobster, and shrimp seasoned with spices and lightly misted with citrus melted on her tongue. Her left hand cupped her mouth. "Oh my goodness. This. Is. Heaven," she mumbled, her mouth filled with the delicious seafood medley.

"Darlin', I haven't taken you to heaven yet, but I'm glad you like the food."

Ashley rolled her eyes and then swallowed. "You sure do a lot of smack talking."

Sebastian's spoon clanked against the square plate as he set it down. He pushed back from the table. Head cocked to one side, he stroked the light stubble on his chin. "Enough with the insults and sarcasm." His voice remained calm and low. "I can see right through you. You're afraid."

That feeling swelled in her belly with a vengeance. "I'm not afraid of you," she snapped, twisting in her seat.

His brow wrinkled, pegging her with a serious stare that burned a hole through her defense. "Yes, you are." He sprung to his feet.

Her wide eyes traveled up his length as he stood. She swallowed the lump that had formed in her throat. "What are you doing, Sebastian?"

He held out a confident hand. "Taking charge." Dark mischief flashed in his eyes. "Give me your hand."

She shook her head from side to side. "No." She wasn't a freaking marionette to be pulled and jerked around as he pleased, when he wanted.

Sebastian didn't say another word. He turned his back to her and strolled through the sliding glass doors. The door slid closed with a bang, and a shiver skittered up her spine. He left her alone on the patio. Ashley closed her eyes and rubbed her forehead, meeting the crossroads in her mind for the one hundredth time. Consequences of their intemperate passion terrified her. She could never admit the truth, even to herself. She liked Sebastian, and sleeping with him would leave her vulnerable to feeling. No man made her feel, or penetrated her shield, since...

Exactly seventeen minutes later, after mulling over her plan again, Ashley stood. She had nibbled on her food during her musing. Sebastian abandoned his plate of food when he left. Ashley shook her head. He was a grown man, and one whom she didn't know very well. Being concerned for his well-being was irrational and infuriated her.

She stared at the plate for another minute, tapping her toe against the wood planks. Ashley turned toward the sliding glass door, expecting Sebastian to walk out at any moment. She pushed away from the table with brute force. "Ugh," she huffed and snatched the plate from the table. Ashley kicked her heels to the side. Long strides and the heavy stomp of angry feet led her to the glass door.

Sebastian leaned against the small kitchen counter, arms folded across his solid chest. Head cocked to one side with an arched brow, "You knew what you were getting into when you came here tonight," he said softly. He stalked toward Ashley.

She lowered her head. "I know." She handed him the plate of food as a peace offering. "I thought you might want to eat something before..." Her words trailed off.

Sebastian arched a brow, like he was either surprised by her thoughtfulness or shocked that she gave in to their desire. "Thank you, but I'm not hungry for food," he said, easing the plate from Ashley's clinging fingers. He set the dish on the counter. "I want to treat you the way a man should treat a woman." Fire flashed in his eyes, and his voice growled seductively.

Ashley's head spun, and she faltered. "I'm sorry. I'm okay." She flushed as his hands spanned her waist to keep her steady on flat feet.

Sebastian's eyes seemed to laugh at her despite the hard lines in his face. "Come with me." He held out a hand.

This time she accepted his offer. "Where are we going?" She didn't need to ask. Heavily lidded eyes and the bulge growing in his slacks answered the question.

He squeezed her fingers in his large hand. "Where do you think we're going?" he asked.

She swallowed hard as they passed the threshold to his bedroom. Her eyes roamed the space, an ode to classic Key West character and charm. White sheers draped the canopy covering the bed blanketed by an aquamarine duvet. Across from the foot of the mattress, another set of glass doors framed a breathtaking ocean view of the private beach. The hurricane brewing in the Atlantic felt mythic in view of the calm, peaceful waves.

The spotless room appeared untouched by its occupant. Sebastian's scent permeated the air, the only evidence that he had lived there for almost two weeks.

Releasing her hand, "You look tense. Have a seat," he said, motioning to the heavy oak bed. "Would you care for a glass of water? Might help you relax." Not giving her a chance to respond, "And, don't tell me that you're not nervous."

This was crazy. Being around a man never made her anxious until Sebastian. In fact, she had been the aggressor on an occasion or four. "I'm fine," she said coolly. "I'll take that glass of water, please. Or something stronger."

Sebastian sauntered to a built-in minibar and began filling a glass. "You know," he began, giving a slight glance over his right shoulder, "maybe when we get back to Atlanta…"

Ashley bounced to her feet, her erect index finger meeting his words with immediate opposition. "Sebastian, let's get one thing clear. I'll give you tonight," she spouted, her neck prepared to roll. A deep breath prevented the full-on verbal assault she'd become quite adept at delivering on command. "But I won't become your regular booty call. You will not have access to me whenever you want. This is only one night of sex. No strings, remember?" She sucked in her belly, tempering the tremble that threatened to overtake her body.

Sebastian turned back to his task, pouring the next glass of water. "I was only going to say maybe when we get back to Atlanta the weather will be nicer than when we left." His voice remained even.

Sinking back into the plush mattress, "Oh," she muttered, feeling insignificant and small, like discarded shipping popcorn. He wanted the gift at the apex of her thighs. The rest of her he could do without.

Sebastian stood in front of her, his masculine glory exhibited as his unbuttoned shirt hung open. Slacks set low on his waist. He placed the glasses of water on the wicker nightstand. Ashley's eyes roamed his sculpted strength. She sucked in her bottom lip. As though she were a rag doll, he whisked her into his arms. Square-tipped fingernails dented his biceps through the cotton fibers of his black shirt sleeves.

Hot lips grazed her neck as he whispered. "Are you wearing the other gift underneath?" The bulge in his pants grew larger, pressing into her stomach.

Ashley's knuckles ached, her tight grip clenching his arm. Her eyes lifted to his wanton leer. "I am."

Sebastian's hand dipped under her dress. His fingers sank into her cheeks, grabbing as much flesh as he could grip. "I love your ass." He lifted the dress just above her waist. Ashley poured into his waiting hands. "Darlin', you're already wet for me."

Starting in her core, the intensity built, spreading in all directions and igniting every cell in her body. Tonight she faced a moment of truth, a confrontation between her raging hormones and the feelings she denied. Whether or not she dared to accept the truth, Ashley wanted to be more than Sebastian Stone's last night in Key West.

Chapter Eleven

Sebastian's tongue swept into Ashley's mouth, mingling their unique minty flavors into one. One hand inside her panties massaged her swollen clitoris. Responding to the sensations of his caress, she curled her fingers around his biceps, clenching and releasing them in rhythm to the circling motion. His other hand held her close, cradling her crown and tangling her hair.

Slowly Sebastian brought their burgeoning passion to a still. He pried lips from hers and unfolded his body from around Ashley. "Do you want to keep the dress?"

She frowned. Her fingers relaxed, and she came down from tippy-toes. "I don't have many occasions to wear something like this." She panted between breaths. "Why? Do you want to recycle the dress for your next conquest?"

He deserved that. He knew how he treated her, from the beginning, had been wrong. "No darlin', I don't have any other conquests lined up. I just wanted to know if I should rip the dress off or be gentle."

Smiling, she rolled her eyes. "There's something sexy as hell about a man who takes control."

Sebastian chuckled. "You're my kind of woman," he said, releasing her from his hold. "Don't move. I'll be right back."

Flat palms flush on either side of the bathroom mirror, Sebastian leaned in close and stared at his reflected grimace. His right hand fisted and then pounded the wall without making a sound. "Maybe when we get back to Atlanta, the weather will be nicer than when we left," he muttered to himself quietly. Anger filled him at how easily he caved at Ashley's tirade when what he intended to say was maybe they could continue to see each other. He would have to work hard to convince her to give him a chance. Sebastian tore away one of the square gold packets and stuffed the condom into his pocket. Time for his hard work to commence.

Sebastian strutted into the room. Ashley had settled back against the oak headboard, one leg slightly bent, the other stretched out straight atop a contrasting white sheet.

"Thought I'd spare you the agony," she said.

His feet failed him. Sebastian stopped where he stood. White clearly shone around the circumference of dilated pupils set in gray irises. His admiring gawk caressed every square inch of silky smooth brown skin. "You're naked." He approached. Took slow, calculated steps, ensuring his balance. A confident hand unbuckled the leather belt encircling his waist and then dipped into the safety of his pocket.

Ashley scanned his shirtless torso. "And you're halfway there." She arched her back. Her bosoms thrust forward. "I guess you'll have to exert that barbaric energy in some other way."

"I guess so," he said, the growl of his voice deep and husky.

Black slacks fell to his ankles. He kicked the annoyance to the side. Shed off equally irritating briefs, a toss sent the underwear airborne, flying across the room and landing next to a white wicker chifforobe.

Gravity was no match for his desire. Her eyes ensnared by the one-eyed beast, Ashley swallowed the lump in her throat.

Sebastian crawled onto the bed, grabbed her ankles, and spread her legs wide. He rolled the condom onto his thick shaft. "You're more beautiful each time I see you." He planted his hips into the cradle of her thighs. His head tilted down, and his lips found hers.

Guiding himself, he slid into her. Fast. Hard. Deep.

"Ahhh," she gasped, accepting all of him.

Sebastian anchored her feet at the side of her head. He slammed into her over and over, stretching her to his magnificent size. Thrusting and grinding his hips hard, he pounded into her until tremors took hold of her movements.

"Oh, Sebastian," she moaned, breathy and barely above a whisper. Her fingers clawed his back with each thrust. The fire burning inside him seared her insides, the feeling sensational and amazing.

After filling her completely, Sebastian eased his assault to a slow grind.

Ashley's eyes rolled back. Every inch of her tingled, edging toward complete rapture as he tapped mercilessly at her sweet spot. "Ahhh," she moaned.

"Baby, not yet." He slid out of her and rolled onto his back. "Can we talk?"

She mounted him, her legs straddling his broad hips. "I don't want to talk." Slowly she lowered herself onto his rod, pressing him deep inside until she was filled again. Ashley moaned. Sebastian gripped her thighs, arched his hips high, thrusting into her hard, repeatedly. She moaned louder. Edging toward release, "Yes. Yes. Yes," she screamed.

"Slow," he commanded. "We have all night."

Small hands placed on his heaving chest subdued the beast. He yielded to her control. She folded herself down, captured his bottom lip between her teeth. His hands caressed her thighs, roamed freely to her backside. Large fingers sank beneath her mounds, gripping hard. He raised her up and brought her down, his giant cock reaching her end with each exertion.

"Ahhh, Sebastian, yes," she cried out.

She bore down, swirling her hips, grinding him hard. Around and around and around.

A whirlpool of ecstasy at the joining, "Oh, baby," Sebastian groaned. Sweat drenched his forehead.

His fingers found her aching button. Vigorous attention to her clitoris at his expert touch controlled her. "Oh, Sebastian. Just like that. Don't stop," she screamed.

Her body quaked with tremors. Ripples of pleasure rolled in waves, tingled inside her from her curled toes and exited limp, weak hands. She collapsed her head, nestled on his chest. He coiled strong arms around her back, caressing her tenderly as she stabilized. A hand placed under her chin lifted her face to his.

His eyes centered, and longing focused only on her. He captured her plump lips, sucking them tenderly. He tasted so good, like peppermint. Invading her mouth, his tongue circled hers. His arms tightened around her waist, securing their melded bodies.

Without warning, he flipped her onto her back again, her legs spread wide, his cock still buried deep inside. "I'm going to take you to heaven."

Fierce pumps into her made Ashley wail. Sebastian hammered her like he had something to prove. Thrusting his hips high, he slammed into her over, and over again. Commanding hands banded her ankles and anchored them to the headboard, giving him full penetration into her.

Her eyes rolled back, and she lost hesitation. She gave generously, pushing back against his thrusts. Sensation became her. Sebastian pounded her hard. Her feet arched. Her legs trembled. Her insides ached. His large body pinned her beneath him, subjecting her to the delicious brute force of his relentless pounding. Harder. Faster. Deeper. Repeated. The sensations compounded inside her, left her destroyed.

"Oh, Sebastian," she whimpered. "No more."

"I can't stop. I haven't even started yet, darlin'."

He raised himself, resting on his shins. He clutched her inner thighs and slammed into her with full force until all his cock disappeared into her.

The musk of hot sex made her dizzy. "Ahhh!" Ashley screamed, her head thrashing from side to side.

He repeated the motion. Her body convulsed. A single tear leaked from the corner of one eye and trailed her cheek.

Sebastian paused a moment. "Did that hurt?"

"Yes," she whimpered.

"I'm sorry," he said, stroking her cheek. "I'll stop."

"No, please don't stop," she begged, apprehension clinging to her words. The hurt she felt wasn't physical pain. The hurt she felt was pain in the emptiness of her soul.

"You sure?"

"Sure," she panted heavy breaths.

"Now you're about to get fucked."

In and out, he slammed his thick cock into her. Harder. Deeper. Faster. Again and again. Her hands roamed his chest. He grabbed her wrists. Raised them above her head. Continued his pounding.

Sebastian's attention focused on her, gazing at her with unsure eyes.

"Don't stop," she screamed as loud as exhausted lungs would allow. "Ahhh. Oh, Sebastian. Ahhh!" Her nails pierced his back and drew blood.

"Are you okay?"

Her necked rolled slowly to the left and then to the right. "Yes. Yes," she whispered lifelessly.

"Good. My turn," Sebastian said.

He turned her over. Raised her hips high. Her ass saluted the air. He slid inside her, taking her from behind.

His cock felt larger in this position, every inch of him clenched by her insides. "Oh, Sebastian. You're going to kill me."

"I won't kill you." He leaned over and kissed her ear. "Ready?"

She grabbed a fist full of sheet. "Okay," she said and bit down on a pillow.

He pounded her hard. She whimpered with each thrust. He hammered into her harder. Her body trembled again, her knees near collapse. He continued his deep thrusts, stroking her breasts and fucking her hard. Finding his release, "Yeah, baby," Sebastian groaned.

Another wave of ecstasy sailed over her in slow motion. Ashley fell forward. Her skin tingling with pure sensation. She uttered words that fell from her lips on instinct. He crashed down beside her, pulled her to him, and tilted her face up to meet his.

He inhaled a deep breath and then released. "Hey." His broad smile withered into a line and then descended into a frown. His brow scrunched, "What's wrong? You okay?" he asked, concern marking his face.

Dazed, Ashley nodded. "I'm… I'm…" she stuttered, breathless. "I'm fine."

A slow, sexy smile resumed its position. "You've never had that much man inside you before, have you? You liked it."

Ashley's eyes widened in mocked horror. "Shut up, Sebastian," she muttered.

Tenderly Sebastian stroked her cheek. He spoke softly. "I'm sorry. You told me not to stop. I didn't mean to hurt you. I'll be gentler the next time."

Ashley's heart pounded. The next time? She barely could handle a single one-night stand with this man. Her heart couldn't handle another night of the best mind-blowing sex she had ever known and then just walk away. Well, not without being hauled off in a little white coat afterward.

She peered at him, desperate not to show her vulnerability. "You didn't hurt me. It was okay."

Sebastian jerked up. "Okay?" His voice raised. "Just okay?"

Ashley couldn't move. She lay there, looking up at him. Ashley shrugged sore, achy shoulders. "It was good," she said, deliberately conveying no conviction in her words. She hoped her eyes didn't give her away.

Sebastian leaned over her, pinned her beneath him. "Really? Just good? Obviously, I've screwed you senseless." He must have sensed her anxiety or seen the terror in her eyes. He leaned down, captured her willing lips, and then whispered softly, "Oh yeah, baby." His eyes called her bluff. "We just made magic. At least I'm not afraid to admit that tonight was the best sex I've ever had. The best sex that either of us have ever had."

Ashley didn't argue. She swallowed hard. Spoke softly. "And what makes you so sure that the same is true for me?"

He smiled that sexy, cocky grin. "Because I made you cry. Those were tears of joy, not to mention the fact that you said so."

"What?" Ashley avoided his amused stare. Her eyes fixed on a spot in the plaster of the ceiling. "What did I say?"

He ran his finger along her hairline down to her chin. "You said 'I've never felt so good. Don't ever stop.'"

Ashley closed her eyes. She remembered her words. "Sebastian, what I said was spoken in the heat of the moment. Nothing more."

He tilted her chin. Brought her eyes back to his. "Not true. Stop lying to yourself." His lips captured hers, a tender, sensual kiss. Sebastian pulled back. "Do you know what I think?"

Her head spun. The last thing she could do was think. She closed her eyes to stop the spinning. "What?" she rasped, under his spell.

"I think I'd like to see you again. In Atlanta."

"I've been alone my whole life. It's my destiny. You can't run away from destiny," Ashley glanced at the flickering candles across from the bed. Sebastian must have lit them after round three.

His dimpled chin relaxed in his palm as he hovered over her. "There are some things you can't fight, darlin', like the passion burning between us that comes as natural as air and breathing."

"Sebastian, this is as far as I can go with you." She stiffened. The constricted feeling in her chest had spread through her entire body.

He straightened himself, assuming a more assertive posture. "Look, I'm not saying I want a relationship. We have amazing sexual chemistry, and letting that go to waste would be a shame."

Her heart ached to pump with excitement, her veins longed to course with adrenaline. Her stomach already did that jittery fluttering thing that felt like motion sickness. But Sebastian only wanted sex. "I don't think you'll have a problem finding sexual chemistry with another willing partner." *Another woman here in my place.* Her stomach flip-flopped.

He frowned. "I saw your reaction at Robin's Nest. I don't know what the experience meant for you, but for me there was a purpose." An earnest thoughtfulness wrinkled his face. "When I lived at the Carlisle, a robin visited me every day. It was odd. In my research, I learned that the robin is a symbol of new beginnings. A robin flies into your life on the wings of change."

His words pierced her hammering heart. She turned away to hide her anxiety. "So." Her flippant tone socked him in the gut like a full-force punch.

"Ashley." The tremor in his voice called her attention to serious gray eyes. "I saw you from my balcony that evening because the robin led me there, led me to you. You were in distress and I thought my purpose was to help you. Turns out, it's the other way around."

The clock on the nightstand read two o'clock in the morning. Normally she would have passed out by now, but energy like Red Bull mainlined through her system buzzed in her veins. "Sebastian, let's not read into signs and tea leaves."

He shrugged his shoulders. "I believe we are given clues to finding happiness if we pay attention. Maybe I'm crazy, but I can't get rid of the feeling that you and I are meant to share more than one night."

"You told me everything I need to know when you proposed sex with no strings."

He gazed at the ocean, his forehead wrinkled, eyes squinted. "You're like the sea. Dynamic. Beautiful. Turbulent. There's more to your depths than the surface swells. I want to explore all of you." He sat fully upright, knees bent, his gaze forward. "Ashley, I'm sorry for my behavior." His chin dropped to his chest. "I'm sorry for how I've treated you. I want to be a better man. I want a try at more than sex without strings."

She had purposefully cultivated meaningless, hopeless relationships to avoid feeling. Keeping Sebastian around would definitely evoke emotion. She could already feel herself inching toward heartbreak.

Like armor, a quick tongue shielded her. "You know what they say about leopards and zebras."

"What? They can't change their spots or stripes," he replied with an assured grin.

"Close. They can't change what they are. Haven't you heard the story of the leopard and zebra?"

Sebastian shook his head. "No. Why don't you tell me?"

"Sure," she said, her head cocked to one side and then shrugged. "A leopard was admiring a herd of zebra. He went to the zebra and told them how much he loved their stripes. They were flattered. Probably a little arrogant. The zebra said they admired the leopard's speed. Do you follow?"

He frowned. "I follow so far. Go on," he said.

An eyebrow perked and Ashley pursed her lips. "Well, they agreed to live together so they could learn from each other. Weeks passed. The zebra didn't run any faster and the leopard's spots didn't change. The leopard became angry. One by one, he lured them away. Ate the entire herd. Too bad the zebra didn't learn to run faster. Of course, the leopard never got those coveted stripes."

"So, the leopard tricked the zebra? Was that his plan all along?"

"Maybe not intentionally at first."

"And you think I'm the leopard, that I will trick you, consume you?"

"Maybe not intentionally at first," she repeated. Ashley's eyes fixed stern on his. "Wanting can be dangerous. Some things are better left as they are."

Sebastian shifted his position, tilted his head, eyes fixed into a serious stare. "Which are you, the leopard or the zebra?"

Ashley glared at Sebastian as though fault lay with him for the raw passion flowing through her insides. "Does it matter? In the end, neither got what they wanted."

Sebastian leaned down, whispering, "Hmm, the night isn't over yet. I still have time to change your mind." His hand parted her thighs and massaged her swollen button.

She peered at him, anxiety building in waves. "My mind isn't easily changed," she said.

"Then the loss will be mine. For now, I'm going to enjoy trying my hardest."

What was she thinking? How did she let Sebastian sweet-talk her onto the beach at that hour? Since meeting the man, much thinking on her part hadn't occurred. She lay on the cool, wet sand, staring past him, up into the starry sky. The ocean waves soothed her anxiety.

He entered her slow, took his time. Wispy kisses tickled her neck. His tender touch caressed her in a way she had never felt before, the sensations reaching her heart.

The way he touched her felt different. She peeled her eyes open. "What are you doing?" she asked. Her heart thundered inside.

The hazy look in his soft gaze said he knew. Knew what he was doing. Knew what she meant, without elaboration.

He reared up to a slight hover, determined eyes never leaving hers. "Taking my time. Making love to you." His brows pressed together, defining an unspoken statement that said more than his words allowed.

Swallowing a breath, she pressed a sand-dusted hand to his chest. Anything to add some distance. Separation. "Why are you doing this?" Her voice cracked.

Sebastian's head tilted. His lips pursed. She could almost see the wheels in his mind spinning like a slick, oiled can on smooth metal. And then the spinning stopped. "Because that's what people in our condition do."

She didn't remember him pulling her into the ocean. His words became an elixir, his touch became the tonic, and she was drunk.

"I… I can't swim," she said, still intoxicated from his spell, legs shaking beneath her.

His sexy grin and a soft chuckle forced a shiver up her spine. Sebastian pulled her to his warmth. "I didn't bring you out here to swim," he said, lust in his eyes.

She turned away. Chris always said she should never cry. And since Chris, tears became a menace that she could subdue at will.

A thumb traced her jawline, gently bringing her gaze to him. "What's behind those tears?"

His words hammered her brain. She had been careful with her emotions for so long. Even numb to them. How did a moment of indiscretion tempt her to abandon the rules?

She blinked, eyes fluttering against the tears leaking from wet sockets. "The salt is stinging my eyes," she lied.

He said nothing for a while. "Hmmm. Salt, huh? Close your eyes," he whispered. "I have a remedy for salty eyes."

His lips found hers. Like a fierce hunger possessed him, passion overtook his controlled movements. His arms snaked around her waist and held her close. His tongue moved like a cobra being charmed by an enchanting melody. A melody that was her. Unhinged, she surrendered, meeting his kiss with matched desire.

He hoisted her up. Her legs wrapped his waist. She clung to his shoulders, bobbing in the shallow waters surrounding their passion. Sebastian eased into her once more. Her heightened senses now aware of his soft, swirling thrusts. Deep and intense. She felt the build, like fireworks bursting from cannons. Couldn't stop the feeling even if she tried.

Like the waves crashing around them under the moonlit ocean, a flood of emotion and sensation crashed into her. Her fingers curled, piercing nails dug into his muscled biceps. "Sebastian." Her soft moan screamed of something more, like an echo of his sentiments. Sentiments that almost whispered of love.

Her body convulsed, shuddering. Ecstasy pulsed through her veins and seeped through every pore. She buried her head in his chest.

Sebastian followed, holding her tight against his body as he found his release.

"How are your eyes now?" he asked.

"Better," she whispered back.

He squeezed tighter. "And the rest of you?"

"The rest of me is fine too," she lied.

Never had she felt farther away from being fine than in that moment, with him.

Sebastian groaned. "Ahhh! Baby." His release complemented Ashley's. She let out a scream, "Sebastian. Yes!"

In the dimly lit room, sweat glistened, drenching limp and tired bodies. She dismounted him and stood beside the bed on quivering legs. Ashley reached for his robe and flung the terrycloth around heavy shoulders.

Glancing at the clock, she noted the time was a quarter after four. The sun would make an appearance, rising above the horizon just after six that morning. "Be right back." She hoisted her overnight bag onto her shoulder.

"You going to leave me here, like this?" he questioned.

She flashed a smile. "I'm not done with you yet, Mr. Stone," she teased, knowing full well there wasn't an ounce of energy left in either of them for another round. "I just need a minute."

The bathroom door closed, making a soft click. She twisted the button on the knob. Behind the sanctuary of solitude, she unleashed a fury of emotion. She turned on the shower to drown any accidental cries that might escape her lips. Wobbly legs collapsed beneath her and brought Ashley down, seated on the edge of the tub. Hunched over, she buried her face in her palms. After the roiling waves had subsided inside, she turned the handle. The faucet came to a full roar.

Steam quickly filled the room. Water flowed over her tender skin, washing away the scent of ocean and sex and anxiety. He had said he wanted to see her in Atlanta. Maybe she didn't have to go through with her plan after all. Maybe she should give him a chance. Maybe she wouldn't be a zebra this time. Her dilemma demanded a decision, a decision that needed to be made soon.

Minutes later, she toweled herself dry and pulled her wet hair into a ponytail. Inhaling a deep breath, a sense of peace fell over her. She landed on the right choice. Ashley rummaged the bag for her cell phone. *Crap!* She left the phone in the room. She didn't want to explain calling off the cab ride she had scheduled for a five o'clock pickup. Panic set in, and then, as though the thing had miraculously appeared, she spotted Sebastian's phone on the counter in the corner. Most likely, his phone would be locked. Taking a chance, she glided her finger across the glass screen. Success.

She browsed the name of the cab company and found the number. Javier would be there in twenty minutes. Suddenly, the phone buzzed, jarring her. She ignored the sound until the phone vibrated again.

She knew violating his privacy was wrong, but damn her curiosity. A finger hovered over the text message. Her conscience tugged in both directions at the same time. *Press it. Don't press it.* Giving into the pesky itch of temptation, she tapped the message. Just a light tap. Ashley closed her eyes. Nervous about her invasion, her leg bounced up and down, scared about what lie on the other side of that click.

Just then, his voice rang out. "Hurry up, darlin'. I'm losing my strength." The phone leaped into the air from jolted fingers. She scrambled to prevent the crash to the hard tile floor.

Fumbling, she caught the phone and glanced at the screen. Not a scratch. "I'll be right out, Sebastian," she managed to say on shaky vocal chords.

Her fingers pressed the precise sequence of buttons to display the incoming text message.

She breathed hard. Hurt burned behind angry eyes. Rage built in her core. She read the words again. There was no mistaking the meaning of the message. There was no mistaking his intent. The message from Daniel was clear:

Hey man, I got your e-mail. I'll start the search. BTW, did you bang that ebony chick yet? Can't wait for details.

Ashley strolled back into the room. The bag tossed behind her shoulder was lighter than the weight growing in her belly. An eerie calm had settled over her despite her discovery. Her eyes raked his naked body. Sebastian was all man and muscle. She moistened at the mere sight of him, angering her all the more.

His gray eyes sparkled with mischief. "What took so long, darlin'?"

Ashley didn't answer, only scowled at him, her stare unwavering through swollen eyes.

Sebastian's smile faded. "You don't look okay. Is something wrong?" His eyes scaled her, did a double take. "Why are you dressed?"

Her scathing glare withered his confidence, squelched his euphoria. Her stone face without a smile. Inside raged a swirling tempest as wild and fierce as the storm threatening the peninsula.

"Uncuff me, baby." He yelled out. "We can talk about whatever's wrong."

She reached the door and whirled around. "Fuck you, asshole. Fuck. You." Hurt behind her words revealed itself, and her brown watery eyes glistened tears that refused to be shed.

His eyes scaled her frame, found her deadpan stare. "Ashley? What... what happened?" His panicked voice boomed. A plethora of sour emotions marred her face, made his chest ache.

Sebastian jiggled his arms frantically. "What the hell happened?" he screamed.

Sobered of their rapture, his intoxication wafted.

Ashley stood in the open doorway, glaring. "You got what you wanted. Now go tell that," she said. The markings of her soul were revealed, and his heart sank.

Her markings were spotted like the leopard. Sebastian struggled against the cuffs again. "We can talk about whatever's wrong," he pleaded.

She didn't say another word. A single tear streaked her cheek. She stepped into the hall. The door slammed shut.

Sebastian had met revenge, and from the evil he saw in her eyes, she frightened him.

Chapter Twelve

Ashley plopped into the seat. Like a fugitive on the run, her heart pounded hard in her chest. If Sebastian strolled down the aisle at that very moment, she would die. The anxiety gnawing her insides would subside as soon as the plane reached an altitude higher than ground level. She rested her head against the slick leather seat and closed her eyes. Soon, her adventures in the Keys, including Sebastian Stone, would be a distant memory.

His sultry eyes. His tender lips. His expert touch. Ashley paused a hand on her heaving chest. Vivid images of their bodies thrusting and merging together flashed through her mind. The feeling lingered in every cell. She locked her knees together.

The plane began to move, and she exhaled a breath.

"Flight attendants, prepare for takeoff," the pilot announced.

The plane taxied to the runway. She made her escape on the last flight out. Another exhaled breath. Being with

Sebastian rocked her to the core. Last night was a mistake, the beginning of an obsession.

Flight attendants and beverage carts moved up and down the aisles.

"Miss, would you like a drink?" A platinum-blond flight attendant stood nearby.

Ashley glance at the assortment of drinks on her tray. "Yes!" She hadn't meant to sound as eager or loud as she did. "I'll take the strongest drink you have." Ashley handed a twenty-dollar bill to the flight attendant. "Here. Keep the change."

The woman's questioning eyes focused on her task. "Coming right up."

Ten minutes had passed. Ashley placed the iPad on the tray next to the empty cup. She thrummed her fingers on the cold hard plastic. A hesitant tap clicked on the saved article link. The article she had intended to read about Sebastian Stone before the site went down. The little wheel at the corner of the browser window spun. Words and images began to appear. Now, thousands of miles in the air and away from him, she had nothing better to do. She read the headline again.

Stone tragedy makes investors nervous; partner in rehab.

Nausea rolled through her belly as she scrolled down the page.

The sudden and tragic death of Ellie Stone, late wife of Sebastian Stone, president and chief executive officer of commercial real estate investment firm Wooster, Holman, and Stone (WHS), made investors nervous. Stone, who admitted publicly to developing a drinking problem following his wife's alleged suicide in March, has spearheaded ten of the firm's largest mergers and acquisitions and brokered deals with at least half a dozen fortune 500 companies to relocate their corporate headquarters. Stone played a strategic role in taking the company public in 2010. In a statement, Angela Whitman, spokesperson for WHS said, "The board is saddened by the sudden passing of Ellie Stone. Our deepest sympathies go out to the Stone family during this difficult time. Mr. Stone is receiving the best possible treatment for his addiction and recovery. The board remains fully prepared to act in the best interest of its shareholders."

The constricted feeling in her chest spread like an inkblot on porous paper. Her heart, as black and hard as obsidian, crumbled. She stared blankly at the screen, not able to believe what she had read. She had made a horrible mistake. Suddenly, in a lapse of control, salty tears stung her eyes and burned her cheeks. She wept quietly, taking shallow breaths between sobs.

Sebastian wasn't a saint, but he hadn't been involved in shady business dealings. He was a man battered and broken by life, her equal in pain and suffering. She remembered the text message that had made her upset. If Sebastian were anything like her, he would do whatever he could in an attempt to avoid getting too close to another woman, including reducing women to mere objects. A talent she also acquired regarding men.

She wept quietly, taking shallow breaths between sobs.

A hand came down on her shoulder. "Miss, are you all right? Can I get you anything?" the flight attendant asked and then handed her a tissue.

"Thank you," she said, sobbing harder. "I'm sorry. Excuse me." Ashley leaped up and dashed toward the back of the plane.

She shoved her way past a woman blocking the aisle and locked herself up in the small restroom.

Fate, if the thing existed, had been cruel to bring two injured souls together in a bond of grief for lovers long gone.

She splashed water on her face, staring into the mirror at red eyes and puffy cheeks.

Guilt. It festered deep in her belly. Replaced the memory of their passion.

Her chest felt heavy, like the walls caved in on her heart. What had she done? Ashley raked her hair, pulled her head back. The walls of the sky vessel closed in, suffocating her. Both hands covered her face in shame and horror. Had she destroyed a good man?

"Help! Somebody, help!" Sebastian yelled as loud as his voice would carry. "I'm trapped!" He heard voices in the hallway, on the other side of the door. "I'm in here. Hurry!"

The knob jiggled. Seconds later, two women and a man stood at the threshold, gaping at him.

"¡Ay dios mío!" a petite Hispanic woman with thick curly hair exclaimed, immediately shielding her eyes with her forearm. After the initial shock, she seemed quite comfortable to fix her eyes on him, particularly below the waist.

Sebastian couldn't believe Ashley left him cuffed to the headboard in the nude. "I need help. My girlfriend locked me up. We had a disagreement, and she left me here." His tongue slipped, calling Ashley his girlfriend. She would never earn that title. Not after this.

"Uh, I'll go see if we have… um, maybe a key or something to cut off those handcuffs." The man, whose arm covered his face, must have been a maintenance worker. He fled on winged feet, shutting the door behind him.

The woman, whom the others referred to as Maria, walked closer. "My English no very good. Understand?" she asked.

"Si. I understand. My español isn't very good either, so we're even."

Eyes as black as her hair wandered down below Sebastian's waist again. Maria blushed.

"Maria?" His voice forced her attention to his face. What was the point? She didn't understand him anyway. *Oh, what the hell!* He'd try anything at this point. "My wrists hurt. Can you adjust the cuffs?"

She stared blankly. Didn't answer his question. She didn't understand him.

"Sir, why you locked up?" Wrinkled lines formed across her forehead, as she struggled to find the right words. "Um, how long?"

Sebastian shook his head. "That's a great question, Maria. I don't know why I'm locked up. I've been screaming for help for the past four hours. I missed my flight. I need to go to the airport to catch the next flight out."

Maria shook her head. "No es good, sir. Flights cancelados," she said in Spanglish.

Another woman, standing in the doorway, spoke up. "That's right. All flights are canceled due to the storm. Hurricane Alba will arrive early, making landfall tomorrow morning," she said, walking toward them. She reached down and draped a blanket across his waist. "I'm Isadora." At least she didn't seem content to ogle his naked body.

"Isadora, Maria. I'm Sebastian Stone. I'd shake your hands, but, well, as you can see, they're a little occupied."

Both women shook their heads. Maria blushed. Isadora did not.

"Yes, Mr. Stone. I know who you are. We are going room to room, evacuating guests to the shelter. Since no one can leave the Keys…" Isadora said.

He cut her off. "So, it's true? All flights are canceled?" Sebastian's voice raised. "How am I going to get back to Atlanta?"

Isadora pointed at him, wagging her finger. "Mr. Stone, this is a serious storm. We have to leave the hotel. Well, as soon as we find something to break open those handcuffs." Her stare landed on his cuffed wrists.

Still shackled, agitated and losing patience, Sebastian scuffled against the headboard. "I need a phone. Can you get a phone?" He asked.

Isadora shook her head again, and the maintenance man returned, bursting through the door in a bustle. "Sir, all circuits are busy and have been for the past couple of hours," she said.

Banging his head back against the headboard, "Ugh!" he released an exasperated sigh.

Charles, as the man's name tag stated, rushed to the bed and began testing the lock, using a makeshift device. He met Sebastian's curious stare. "My brother's a locksmith."

Sebastian watched Charles and then turned back to Isadora, pleading. "You don't understand. I have a presentation to make on Monday in Atlanta. I need to be there."

Both hands placed on her hips, "No, sir, you don't understand. You're not going anywhere for at least another three days."

"Mr. Stone," Maria said, pulling his attention away from the photographs mounted on the wall. "You eat now." She motioned to a table where a steaming hot bowl of soup awaited.

Sebastian found her kind eyes. "Thank you, Maria. You have a lovely family. I'm grateful for your generosity." He glanced around the tiny room. Maria lived in a small two-bedroom house with her three teenaged children.

"Si, Mr. Stone." She turned to a tall, lanky boy whose black eyes were just like hers. She mumbled something in Spanish.

Roberto, Maria's eldest son, acted as her translator. "Mom says she couldn't leave you to roam the streets, and the shelters are full."

Sebastian stretched his legs under the table. He rubbed the swollen welts on his wrists left by the handcuffs and then pulled out his cell phone. He couldn't make sense of what happened. The look in Ashley's eyes as she left him there haunted him. She was hurt, devastated. He thought they had reached a new plateau considering the night they shared. At least for him, the evening had been spectacular.

Sebastian hit send on his text message to Stephen.

All flights out are canceled. I will miss the meeting. I need you to buy more time.

A few hours later, the hurricane made landfall.

Roberto, who appeared to be about fourteen, stared at him with wonder. The boy sat across from Sebastian. "What's Atlanta like? I bet you don't get storms like this, do you?"

Inside, candlelight and the aroma of homemade chicken noodle soup had been comforting. Outside, the wind howled, beating fiercely against the metal storm shutters. The eerie sound reminded Sebastian that despite the peaceful calm of Maria's house, outside raged a monster.

He smiled at the boy. "No, Roberto, we sure don't get weather like this in Atlanta."

"That must be great," Roberto said, "To never have to worry about putting up storm shutters. I hate putting them up."

Sebastian frowned. That should have been a task for a man, not a boy. "Where is your father?"

He rolled his eyes and shrugged his shoulders. "Don't know. Don't care. My parents immigrated to the U.S. when I was five. He left us a couple of years later."

Sebastian stared at Maria's peaceful face. Despite whatever hardship she endured, she didn't shrink away from life as he did. She seemed to have risen above despair. Even now, she willingly took in a stranger, a formerly naked and bound man, and extended open arms.

"Please let your mother know that I would like to repay her kindness."

Roberto relayed the message as Sebastian scribbled on a piece of paper.

Maria's face lit up, her one-hundred-watt smile brightening the room. "No, sir. You no pay."

Sebastian leaned across the table and handed her a check. "I hope this covers my stay and helps you a bit."

Maria's eyes doubled in size. She handed the check to Roberto, whose expression matched hers. He said something to her in Spanish and tears cradled in her eyes. "Thank you, Mr. Stone. Gracias. God bless you."

For Sebastian, writing a check for ten thousand dollars equated to most people writing a check for five hundred dollars. Sebastian was glad to give her the money, but more importantly, Maria and her family would be able to put the money to good use.

He smiled. Maria inspired him. "You are a kind and courageous woman. The world needs more people like you."

Roberto translated Sebastian's sentiment. Maria smiled back and replied in Spanish. "Mom says she isn't courageous. She is simply being there for those who needed her," Roberto repeated in English.

He thought of Ashley again, remembered the pain he saw inside her. She needed him. Whatever he did to anger her, he would find out. Whatever the problem, he would find a resolution. Whatever his infraction, he would right the wrong. He could be a better man. He could be the man Ashley needed.

Stephen glanced at Sebastian's text message again.

All flights out are canceled. I will miss the meeting. I need you to buy more time.

He snickered and deleted the message and then strutted into the boardroom.

The meeting was called to order and the agenda read. When the time came for discussion about the Carlisle building, Stephen spoke out first.

He glanced around the room. "Gentlemen, Sebastian has been in charge of this project for five years, and to date, there has been no progress. When I spoke to him last week, he assured me of his attendance so you can imagine my surprise not to see him here this morning." He squirmed in his seat and cleared his throat. "For the past twelve months, I've monitored the books closely. The Carlisle continues to operate in the red, a trend we simply can no longer afford. I've urged Sebastian to take this matter seriously, given him ample time and opportunity to propose a plan for the future of the property. He has yet to produce a plan."

"Get to the point, Stephen," Garrett, a founding partner of the firm, spoke up.

Stephen glanced at the faces around the long table. "I strongly encourage the board to consider Sebastian's effectiveness in his role. His behaviors are obstructive and costly."

Garrett raised a brow. "Exactly what are you suggesting?" he asked, challenging Stephen.

Stephen leaned in, his forearms pressed against the table's edge. "A vote. I'm in favor of Sebastian's dismissal as president and CEO," Stephen replied.

"For the record, I will be on the opposing end of such a vote. Sebastian helped grow this company from its infancy to nearly $800 million in annual revenues. He took WHS public. I believe his personal struggles are behind him and he is fully committed to the future of our business."

Stephen clasped his sweaty palms. "Garrett, I respectfully disagree. Sebastian's absence today is evidence that his priority lies elsewhere." Using the most commanding tone he could muster, "It's our job as the ruling board to supervise the CEO. Let's be honest. He would have been fired long ago if he were anyone else. We. Have. A. Responsibility."

Garrett pleaded, his glare locked on Stephen. "This is wrong. I do not support this motion." His voice soared, bouncing off every hard surface in the room. "Sebastian's wife committed suicide, for God's sake."

Stephen brought down a firm fist, banging the table. "Speaking plainly, the man's a drunk. Sadly, I don't see him

making any effort to change his behavior in the near term."
Stephen relaxed his tone and caught the eyes of each person
seated at the table. "The future of this company rests with the
board. Sebastian doesn't own a majority share. He is a
liability. Are you willing to take a risk on Sebastian Stone at
the expense of our shareholders? I don't have to tell you what
an angry mob we will face, from the media to investors, if we
don't do the responsible thing, if we don't turn this company
around."

Garrett stood. "Sebastian built this company," he
yelled. "You all live in fancy houses and drive ridiculously
expensive cars because of him." Stephen didn't move or
glance back as Garrett stalked past him. The door slammed as
he exited the room. Two other board members rose and
followed Garrett.

Stephen smiled. "Gentleman. Anne. Please turn your
attention to the screen. I'd like to share my proposal, and
then we can vote on the other matter." He could almost taste
victory. Sebastian had created a brilliant proposal. Stephen
had made alternative preparations in case Sebastian flaked on
the meeting. He had taken a day to review Sebastian's
proposal and had created his own version.

The presentation ended. "I am seeking the board's
approval to move forward."

"Stephen, the proposal is good, really good. However,
I am concerned about the size of investment needed to pull
this off," Anne said. Head nods followed her comment.
"And, quite frankly, only Sebastian has the experience to pull
something of this scale off."

"It's bad debt. I'm hesitant to throw good money after bad. I say we count our losses and sell to the highest bidder," another member spoke out. More heads nodded.

Sweaty beads of moisture formed across Stephen's forehead. His plan to oust Sebastian needed to be salvaged, even if he didn't come out the hero with the winning proposal. Otherwise, Sebastian would have his head when he returned and learned what Stephen attempted to do.

"Understandable." Stephen remained calm, trying to reassure the board that his interest lie with the company. "I'm in favor of selling if the majority agrees." Every hand raised in the room. "Now, the other issue at hand. I motion a vote to dismiss Sebastian Stone from his position on the board and his position as WHS CEO."

Chapter Thirteen

The plane had barely landed before Ashley dialed the number. No one answered when she called the Key West Oceanside Resort. Panic seized her. She did the only thing that seemed logical at the time. She called her best friend.

Kerrigan answered immediately. "Hey, Ash. You're back?"

Her voice low, defeated, "Yes. Kerri," she said and then paused. "I'm a horrible human being. I've done something terrible." She imagined Kerrigan's sweet face riddled with shock and disappointment. "Can you meet me at my apartment in an hour?"

Kerrigan had left Key West the day before Ashley, the afternoon of her last date with Sebastian. Hours and hours of scheming, she kept Kerrigan in the dark. Ashley's devious secret plot, locked away tight behind lips sealed like vault, never passed her lips.

Ashley always needed to be the strong, confident, and assertive one. Now in her weakness, Ashley needed

Kerrigan's strength. She waited on pins and needles for a reply.

"Of course. I'll leave in twenty minutes."

"Thank you, Kerri. I'll see you soon."

Ashley lay on her sofa, legs propped up on the armrest. She had thrown out her defiled mattress before the trip and hadn't replaced the soiled love nest yet. She stared at the gaping empty space in her loft that matched the emptiness in her heart.

Kerrigan, who arrived ten minutes prior, hoisted her heels on the sofa table, the way she'd always done during girls' night, watching chick flicks and talking about their lives and men. Her soft voice soothed Ashley. "Ash, what's all this talk about you being a terrible human being?" She rested her head back into the sofa.

"I did something terrible to Sebastian." She eased into the truth. "He… he made me angry and I… I don't know why," she stammered. Her hand covered her forehead "I'm tired of men stepping all over me, treating me like I don't have worth or feelings or dignity." She grabbed fists full of hair at either side of her head, tossing her head back.

"I know you two got off to a bumpy start, but I thought things with Sebastian improved."

"That's just it. Things did improve, considerably until I…" Ashley prolonged her confession. She didn't want to divulge what she had done.

"I'm sure whatever you did isn't as bad as you think. Exactly, what happened?"

Ashley released a loud sigh. "I did something awful to Sebastian our last night in the Keys." She paused to exhale a deep breath. "I handcuffed him to the bed. Early the next morning, I got on the plane knowing he was trapped to that bed, and I left him there, naked." She hung her head in shame, bracing for a lecture and Kerrigan's horrified stare that would make her feel as tall as a blade of grass.

To her surprise, Kerrigan burst into a roaring laugh. She leaped up from the sofa, clutching her sides. "You're joking, right?" She couldn't stop laughing. "He was naked? Imagine the hotel staff when they found him naked and handcuffed to that bed!" Suddenly, her laughter stopped. "Oh, no! The hurricane! He's okay, isn't he?"

"I don't know. I tried to call the hotel six different times, but no one answered."

Kerrigan kneeled down beside Ashley, gently stroking her friend's arm. "Ash, I'm sure he's all right. The lines are probably busy or down. We'll try again in the morning, okay?"

"Okay. Thank you, but there's more." Ashley sat up, reached for her tablet sitting on the sofa table. She swallowed hard, handing the iPad to Kerrigan. "I read this article on the plane, on the way back to Atlanta."

Kerrigan's eyes scanned the article about Sebastian's wife and his drinking problem. She let out a gasp. Ashley's stomach knotted. "Ash, this explains everything, his behavior." She shook her head, her forehead wrinkling. "You didn't know about this. Maybe if you explain your situation, he'd understand. The similarities…"

Ashley interrupted. "Similarities? Chris didn't commit suicide," she defended. She stifled her sob, fighting an emotional outburst. "There were no witnesses to confirm the accident was caused by him or that it was intentional. The only conclusive evidence was the kid whose blood alcohol level was twice the legal limit." She hated that look on Kerrigan's face, that poor-little-broken-Ashley-pity-face. Despite the argument that Chris had with his brother hours before the wreck, Ashley refused to believe that he went through with the threat to kill himself.

Kerrigan didn't debate her. She never did. "I know. I know," was all she ever said, and Ashley appreciated her kindness.

Kerrigan stayed with her throughout the night. Ashley didn't sleep. She watched the hours tick past, minute after minute. If anything happened to Sebastian, she'd never forgive herself.

As soon as the clock read nine o'clock the next morning, Ashley headed to the bathroom for privacy. Kerrigan slept peacefully. She dialed the hotel's number. Still no answer.

Later that day, after having made at least two dozen or more attempts to call the hotel, she gave up. The news reported no casualties in the Keys, only minimal damage from hurricane Alba. By nine o'clock that evening, exhaustion became her enemy, having not slept in over twenty-four hours. Guilt and determination won, not allowing her rest. She called a final time.

"Hello, Key West Oceanside Resort and Villas."

Adrenaline jolted her fully conscious. "Hi, I'm looking for the guest in room 114. His name is Sebastian Stone."

She pressed her ear against the phone, listening. Waited through a long pause on the other end of the phone. Her pulse quickened. A shiver slithered up her spine.

"Please hold a moment. Let me check our records."

Precisely at the two-minute mark, Ashley lowered the phone, checking that the call didn't drop. Sixteen seconds later, the woman returned. "I'm sorry. The gentleman has already checked out."

A gust of air rushed from her lungs. "Mr. Stone checked out? He's not there?" She waited with eager anticipation for the woman to repeat her words.

"Yes, miss. Mr. Stone is no longer here."

"Oh, thank you! Thank you! Thank you!"

Before Sebastian left Key West, he checked out Maria's home, making sure of a sound structure. On the flight back, Sebastian couldn't stop thinking about Ashley and what she did to him. Why? He couldn't make sense of her actions. He'd let some time pass between them before confronting her. At a minimum, he wanted an explanation. She owed him that. And he owed one to her.

Sebastian glanced at his cell phone's blank face. He wanted to explain his situation to Stephen. Odd. He called Stephen three times in the past couple of hours and received no answer or returned call. Stephen always returned his calls immediately.

Right now, Sebastian wanted to place both bare feet on his newly refinished hardwood floors. He had just pulled into his driveway when an incoming call announced through his car's speakers caught him off guard.

"Hello?"

"Sebastian, this is Garrett. Where have you been? I've been trying to call you for the past two days."

"You know I went to the Keys. Hurricane Alba arrived earlier than expected. I was trapped. I'm pulling into my garage now. What's wrong? You sound panicked."

Garrett sighed. "I am panicked. You really should have been at the board meeting." He paused, took a deep breath. "That snake Stephen convinced the board to vote for your dismissal."

Sebastian stood at the entry door to his home. His body was numb. His lips pressed into a flat line. "What happened, Garrett? Was there a vote?"

A slow, long sigh echoed in his ear. "Yes. The board voted." Garrett spoke softly. "Sebastian, where are you?"

"Are you fucking kidding me?" Sebastian's voice elevated to a near yell. "That asshole convinced the board to fire me! Garrett, don't tell me I've been fired?" Silence. More silence. Sebastian's hand fell from the doorknob. "Garrett?"

"Sebastian, please don't do anything rash. Of course, I voted against the motion. So did Walters and Smith."

Sebastian braced himself, placing his right palm on the wall. He lowered his head, eyes fixed to the concrete floor. "What about Anne? Did she vote to have me fired, too?"

Garrett hesitated. "I believe she did vote for your dismissal, but I don't know for certain."

A rush of anger flowed through Sebastian's insides. Every one-night stand seemed to count against him. "She's been after me since I broke it off. She shamelessly threw herself at me." His hand covered his forehead. "This is fucked up."

"You'll get a healthy severance agreement, healthcare for three years, your other benefits…"

Cutting him off, "Spare me the goddamn details. I created that shit agreement. I know how this works," Sebastian said, releasing a labored breath. "Listen, Garrett, I want you to know I appreciate your standing up for me, but I'm not going down without a fight."

"You let me know what I can do."

"Thank you, Garrett. If we end up sparring in the courtroom, don't take it personally." Inside his home, he paced the hall. "You and I, we built this company from nothing. I won't let some junior-level, pencil-dick asshole waltz in and steal everything I've worked so hard for," Sebastian yelled.

"You know I'm on your side." Garrett fell silent for a few seconds before speaking again. "Sebastian, I'm worried about you. Why did you miss the board meeting? You're not drinking again, are you?"

Sebastian let out a hoarse laugh. "No, I'm not drinking again. I met someone, the first woman I've really liked since…" he paused, not finishing the statement. "I missed that meeting because she screwed me over and left me trapped in the Keys until the hurricane passed."

Garrett spoke softly. "I'm sorry, Sebastian."

"There's nothing for you to be sorry about. Ashley Turner will be sorry."

Their conversation ended. Sebastian sat at the edge of the sofa. Leaned forward, his forearms pressed against his thighs. The contents of his stomach churned, the sick feeling urging him to find consolation. Every manner of thought passed through his mind.

He could see her just as plainly as the Waterford crystal set before him on the sofa table. Ellie's soft gaze, the way her amber hair shined on a summer's day. All good memories of happier times before... He opened his eyes, rejoining the present. Neither the past nor the current moment had brought memories he cared to think about now. A deep breath didn't offer recovery. His hand clamped down. Achy fingers curled the bottle of Evan Williams 23.

The liquid splashed against the sides of the glass until reaching the rim. Just one sip, he thought, eying the tumbler filled with bourbon. Sebastian lifted the glass to his lips. The toasty, charred oak scent singed his nostrils. Eighteen months. Seven weeks. Sixteen days. He glanced at the clock hung above an antique cabinet. Both the large and small hands pointed to the number twelve. He imagined the hands of the clocks rotating in reverse, counterclockwise. If he sipped, he would undo the vow he had made and upheld for all that time. The vow of sobriety.

Courage or strength, whatever the source, found him there on the sofa that evening. Sebastian stood. Eyed the welts around his wrists. Eyed the liquid swishing around in the glass he gripped in his hand. He remembered cleaning up the mess made after hurling a half-full coffee mug at the hotel room wall. His pitch arm lowered. Instead, he found himself standing over the kitchen sink. A pang struck his chest as gravity sucked the expensive bourbon down the drain, much like the direction of his life.

The clock displayed the time. Three o'clock in the morning. Sebastian kicked the blanket to the floor. A cool sweat coated his skin. He turned to face the other side of the room. Tiny springs prevented his eyelids from shutting. He counted each minute, each second. Restless tossing was his companion that night. This time when he glanced at the clock, the hour displayed said five fifteen. Still his mind raced. Thoughts carried over into the dawning of a new day.

Previous thoughts about becoming a better man were a distant memory. Precisely at five minutes after six that morning, a plan was born. A plan to rise victorious. A plan for revenge.

A surprise greeted her when the elevator doors parted and she stepped into the lobby. Men wearing hard hats and holding clipboards huddled in discussion. Work crews dismantled the lobby, ridding the space of the old rickety concierge desk. Two men consulted with a woman who wore a killer suit and the exact pair of Valentino T-strap pumps Ashley stalked for months. Glancing around, she noted fancy architectural renderings and signs mounted on easels.

She stepped over and around debris strewn across the floor and made her way to one of the signs. Studying the poster, she was impressed to learn that the renovations called for significant improvements. A hard tug on the usually jammed door to the leasing office revealed an unrecognizable space. A pretty woman with long, straight red hair welcomed her.

"Good morning, I'm Cassie. How may I help you?"

Cassie was new, her warm smile and friendly handshake a welcome change compared to Mrs. Cranston's sneer and usual greeting of, "Yeah, what do you want?" or her typical response to maintenance requests that went something like, "Well, did you pay your rent on time?"

"Hi, my name is Ashley. I live in the building. I wanted to find out what I needed to do to break my lease, but…" Ashley glanced around the office, stunned. A fresh coat of paint, new floors, and office furnishings from this century did wonders for the space.

Cassie held out a hand, motioning Ashley to have a seat. "Well, Ashley, I certainly understand your concern considering the prior management company." Cassie gave the most professional eye roll she had ever seen. "You just missed our new owner. He left a few minutes before you arrived. I'm sure you've seen the construction happening over the past couple of weeks."

Ashley frowned. "Well, no. I... I've been out of town." The truth was she'd been trudging up nine flights of stairs and sneaking through the back alley, like a criminal lurking in the shadows. A month since her return from Key West, she couldn't get that night, or Sebastian Stone, off her mind. She regretted carrying out her plan to humiliate him. The damage done, she gave him reason to hold a grudge. Thus the reason for her back-alley antics.

Cassie didn't miss a beat. "Then isn't this a nice welcome-home surprise? I'm sure you haven't opened your welcome letter yet."

Ashley shook her head. She vaguely remembered the letter slipped under her door. She'd tossed the envelope into her junk-mail basket on the kitchen counter.

"Everything I'm going to share with you is inside that mailing." Ashley's lips twisted into a smile. "I'd love to tell you about the exciting changes coming and the really fantastic discounts available to current residents. Do you have a few minutes?"

By the end of their conversation, not only did Ashley decide to stay at the Carlisle for the remainder of her lease, but she also signed a twenty-four-month contract. Somehow, she forgot her reason for wanting to move in the first place, worries about Sebastian muffled.

She could move into a newly renovated luxury apartment double the size of her current space, complete with all new stainless-steel appliances and hardwoods, while paying her current rate for the next two years. When Cassie said her new apartment would be ready in six months, Ashley signed the dotted line.

The faces around the conference table were drained of life. The Monday morning meeting always dragged on too long. When Kerrigan married their boss Axel and then left the company to start her own business, Ashley was promoted to Kerrigan's former account manager position. Ambitious,

Ashley wanted to take the next step to senior account manager.

Axel cracked his knuckles. "All right. Last item of business. We have a new client, and I need to assign someone to the account. The account is…"

Before he could finish, "I'd like this account," Ashley said, nearly bouncing out of her seat with excitement.

She ignored a few eye rolls and gestures from the usual suspects in the room. Megan shifted in her seat, faking a cough. Ryan rolled his eyes and cleared his throat, shoving a finger to the bridge of his nose to push up thick-ass coke-bottle lens. Ashley straightened her posture, waiting for Axel's reaction.

He smiled and gave an affirming head nod. "Very good. Thank you, Ashley. This will be good for your growth. The job is a big one and will last for the next 18 months. I'll give you details later this week."

"Thank you."

Axel leaned in close and whispered. "I'm sorry we still haven't been able to find Copper."

"I appreciate your help. Copper will turn up. This isn't his first escape."

Ashley forced a smile. Copper was going to be found. Until then, she would throw all her energy and effort into the account and land the promotion. An added bonus, the project would keep her thoughts off Sebastian and what might have been.

Sebastian peeled off his jacket. Prickly hairs on his forearm stood on end, the crisp morning air the culprit. His jog slowed to a complete stop. Hands placed on both knees, he waited until his heart rate returned to normal. He collapsed onto the green metal park bench.

Across from where he rested, an attractive woman wearing a gray tracksuit and whose hair had been pulled up into a ponytail caught his eye. Eyes averted, his head fell to his chin. The thought of his stolen glance being found out made his stomach ache. Instead, he ignored her and tied the laces on his right shoe. Before he could finish the task, his phone buzzed in his pocket.

Sebastian glanced at the number. He leaned back and relaxed against the backrest, his foot colliding with the earth, twigs crunching beneath his Nikes with a loud crunch. "Hello," he said, still winded.

"Hey, man. I haven't heard from you in weeks. How's it going?" Daniel asked, sounding as he usually did, without a care in the world.

He leaned forward, resting sweaty forearms on his knees. "I don't know where to begin. So much has happened since we last spoke."

"I bet it has," Daniel said, a smile clinging to his words. "You never replied to my text. Did you ever bang that black chick?"

The ache in his stomach ignited, flared into a burning sensation. "Why do you have to refer to her that way?" Sebastian tried to shrug off the warm feeling in his gut.

"Sorry! I didn't know you'd be offended."

"When the only reference you make is about the color of Ashley's skin, yeah, that's offensive."

"Sorry. I didn't mean anything by it. Well, did you bang her?"

"Yeah, I did. Turned out to be the worst mistake I've ever made. I mean, the sex was amazing. The aftermath…" He paused, nodding his head. He told Daniel the entire story, from being trapped in the Keys to losing his job. Sebastian omitted the fact that, despite his seething anger, he couldn't stop fantasizing about that night or thinking about Ashley. "She's going to wish she never fucked me over."

"Damn!" Daniel said. "That's rough. What are you planning to do for work? You gonna fight back?"

The woman across from him jogged off. "Why fight back? I don't want to spend the next year and a half or more in a courtroom broadcast to every home in America. The best revenge is success. I built that company, and I can build another one. In fact, I already have irons in the fire. Stephen Holman is in for a world of trouble, all his own doing."

"My friend, I'm glad you're confident and not defeated. Word of caution, may I?"

"Sure. What?" He tuned in attentively.

"Let go of your anger. I mean with that woman. Move on. You're Goliath. She's nobody. With her attitude and actions, undoubtedly she'll bring a reign of terror to herself without your aiding or abetting. You don't need anger rotting your soul."

A hearty laugh burst from his lips. "Hmm. You're right. She has brought a reign of terror to herself, and his name is Sebastian Stone. She just doesn't know it yet. No one tramples on me. No one."

Daniel grew silent. Sebastian knew what that meant. Daniel didn't approve, but the choice wasn't Daniel's to make. He would have his revenge on Ashley. And his revenge would be sweet.

"Right or wrong, that poor girl had her reasons for what she did to you. I'm your friend and you know I love you, man, but I've seen how you treat women since..." Daniel paused. He knew where to draw the line. He didn't dare say Ellie's name. "All I'm saying is that you should dig deep and own up to any actions that may have caused her to do what she did. Forget about revenge. Revenge isn't worth the cost."

Sebastian rolled his eyes. Cocked his head to the side. "Thank you, righteous sir. I'll consider myself advised."

"But you won't listen, will you?"

"Probably not. Well, I've got to go. I have an appointment later this afternoon, and I have some errands to run first. Later, man."

Ashley sat in the executive suite lobby, waiting for Axel to invite her inside. She eagerly awaited details on her new client and the project she volunteered to take. She waited for nearly fifteen minutes. Brenda didn't know how much longer Axel and his guest would be.

Brenda's phone rang. "Yes. Yes, sir. I'll let her know."

Ashley knew that Axel called to invite her into his office. She stood and headed toward the large oak double doors. Brenda nodded. Nervous excitement flowed in her veins. Ashley couldn't wait to hear the project details.

She pushed open the large doors, lifting her gaze across the room to the conference table. Those eyes. Those eyes stared at her. Angry bluish-gray eyes leered at her from the other side of the table.

A searing pang gripped her insides, made her instantly nauseous. Ashley's stomach twisted and knotted as heat spread through every limb and steam rose from every pore.

Axel frowned. "Ashley, please come on over. I'd like to introduce you to our new client and your new account."

She walked the plank, heading for certain death. That's what seeing Sebastian Stone's foreboding grin felt like as she lined one foot in front of the other. Somehow she found her way to the table and managed to collapse into one of the chairs, her actions like thrusting her head into a guillotine and awaiting the blade to drop.

Chapter Fourteen

Ashley's porcelain mask, the one smart brown girls wore to hide their emotions, shattered the instant Sebastian's eyes found hers. She had never been more grateful for her rich mocha pigmentation.

Leaned across the table. Hand extended. He made the first move. "Hello, Miss Turner." The brevity of his three words, though professional and unassuming, held an undercurrent of hostility matched to the fire blazing behind a searing gaze.

Her head pounded. Her chest tightened. She stared at him, motionless. Speechless.

"Miss Turner," he snapped, the boom of his voice jostling her. "You look as though you've seen a ghost." He jeered, an unmasked chortle exposing his satisfaction. "I don't believe we've met, have we? Stone. Sebastian Stone." He tilted his head to the side, and smiled. His patronizing tone as hard as his surname made her flinch. His proffered hand, like being courted by the grim reaper.

A long blink. She inhaled and then released a breath. Her heaving chest returned to a steady calm. Peeling her eyes open slowly, she won the fight. She picked up the porcelain pieces and reassembled the mask. Game face on.

She reached out and took his hand, giving him a firm shake in return. "Mr. Stone. Pleasure to meet you." His eyes bore a hole into her soul, and she fought the urge to cower.

Axel folded his arms across his chest, silenced in the crosshairs. His eyes darted back and forth between them. She could almost see the cogs in Axel's mind turning.

Sebastian held her hand, squeezing her fingers until she grimaced. "Oh, no. The pleasure is all mine. Please, call me Sebastian." She tried to pry her hand away, but he squeezed tighter. "I asked to work with you specifically. Your reputation precedes you, Miss Turner. May I call you Ashley?"

She nodded, granting permission at his request and remained quiet, resisting the pain of his grip.

"Ashley, I need an aggressive marketing plan, and your savvy comes highly recommended. I want a bold thinker on my team who can get results. Don't worry, I won't handcuff or shackle your creativity. I need someone who can weather the storm. I understand that person is you. Am I wrong?" Sebastian relinquished his grip.

Ashley pulled her throbbing hand away. She met his scowl with fluttering eyes. "That's me." Inside, her stomach flip-flopped and her heart hammered in her chest.

"I thought so. Knowing your promotion rests on the success of this project, I know you'll do whatever is necessary to get the job done. One account goes sour, and your whole career is up in smoke." He shook his head and sighed as though he gave a damn. "This is a big account for A.C. Advertising. Three million dollars is riding on your shoulders. You have a tough job. No pressure, right?" He chuckled.

Fuck that porcelain mask. By this time, Ashley was upset. No longer able to hide her emotions, she lowered her head to regain composure.

Axel cleared his throat. He studied her for a moment and then turned his attention to Sebastian. "Sebastian, I can assure you Ashley is the right person for the account. She always gets the job done."

Sebastian smiled and relaxed in his seat. "So, I've been told. Well, I'm eager to get started. Renovations to the Carlisle have already begun, and I need a marketing plan. Yesterday."

Ashley's head shot up. "The Carlisle?" The words choked in her throat, barely came out. She glanced at Axel and then at Sebastian.

"Oh, didn't you know?" Ashley met Sebastian's smug gaze. The Carlisle is the project you'll be managing. I own the building. There's a major renovation going on. Is this a problem for you?"

Ashley bit her bottom lip. She swallowed hard. "No. Um, no! Of course not. No problem," she stammered, trying to mask the faint quaver in her voice with an invisible confidence and a wax smile.

Axel narrowed his eyes and fixed his gaze on her. Axel chimed in. "Ashley, don't you live in that building?"

"Yes, I do. I learned about the construction earlier this week."

Sebastian shook his head. "But construction has been going on for weeks. You sound surprised to hear about the renovation." Sebastian puckered his lips. "I guess, in all fairness, some residents don't use the main entrance at the front of the building."

Ashley nodded in affirmation.

Sebastian jerked his head back, mocking surprise. "Don't tell me. You're one of those tenants who prefers alley rats and the stench of a pissy stairwell?"

"I take the stairs on occasion." Ashley said, without making eye contact with either of the men. If Sebastian thought he could goad her into making a scene by insulting her, he would need a new strategy. She'd dealt with every sort of client, from a sexist jerk who seemed more interested in the contents of her blouse than her work to an asshole who spewed racially insensitive remarks throughout an entire meeting.

Sebastian gasped. "I'm shocked!" He shrugged his shoulders. "I guess it's a matter of comfort, I suppose."

Ashley kept her head down, salty puddles pooled in her eyes, threatening to spill. "Excuse me," she muttered, her lips pulled taut. "I need to use the ladies room." She couldn't escape the office fast enough. Not waiting for a response, she stood and headed for her rescue.

"Great. Then it's settled." Sebastian called out as she sprinted toward the massive doors to exit. "I'll be in touch, Ashley. I'm looking forward to working with you."

She ran down the hall and ducked into the restroom. Sebastian had been cruel and relentless. He wanted blood.

Ashley refused to shed tears, blinking damp eyes until the moisture retreated. She knew what she had to do.

Later that night when Ashley arrived home, she decided to walk through the main entrance. There was no point to hiding in the shadows. Apparently Sebastian had been watching. At least she knew his plan of attack would take place on the corporate battlefield.

Ashley mashed the elevator's call button with her knuckle and the doors opened. She stepped inside, kept her head hung, eyes to the ground. Releasing a yawn, she jabbed the illuminated number nine. The doors began to close when a hand reached in, forced the doors to part. She lifted tired eyes. There stood Sebastian.

Ashley gasped and stepped back into the corner. His impassive stare chilled her. He followed her retreat, his scowling mug within inches of her face. She swallowed hard, stared into cold, expressionless eyes that once held warmth and passion.

Instinctively Ashley's arms rose in defense. A sinewy hand took hold of her left wrist and pinned her arm to the cool, reflective surface beside her head. His other hand held her right arm steady at her side. Her heart beat like a drum. She turned away from his menacing stare, staring at the mirrored back wall.

His breath brushed her cheek as he spoke. "Surprised to see me today, darlin'?" Thin lips pressed against her neck, grazed her supple flesh.

Her mouth dropped open, teary eyes fastened to the ceiling. She wanted to scream, but no sound came out.

She fought the panic. "I'm sorry. Tell me what you want."

He glared at her. Rage burned behind his eyes. "I own this building, and I own your job, yet you think you have something to offer me." The eerie sound of his voice forced a whimper. He leaned in, whispered in her ear, "I. Own. You."

Her chest heaved. Her heartbeat echoed in the small car. Boom. Boom. Boom. Boom. Amplified terror. Ashley's eyes shut. "Please don't hurt me. Don't hit me. I'm sorry," she cowered.

The fingers tightly wrapped around her wrists released. Sebastian's overpowering presence dissipated like vapors into thin air. With a scuffling gait, he distanced himself. His back molded to the wall on the opposite side of the elevator. Slowly Ashley opened her eyes.

Sebastian ran both hands through his hair. "Ashley, I'm not going to hit you." He stared at her, lips sagging into a frown.

"What?" She blinked rapidly, peering at him through the defense of shielded arms covering her face. She lowered her defense, eyes stretched wide, eyebrows raised.

"You begged me not to hit you," he said. Sebastian realized at that moment he had gone too far. He had only meant to unnerve her.

The doors opened, and Ashley whizzed past him. He ran after her, heavy steps overtaking her hasty tread. Sebastian eclipsed her doorway at the other end of the hall.

Arms folded across his heaving chest, he blocked her entry. "I'm furious about what you did to me." Sebastian's baritone bounced off the walls. Ashley's eyes darted to the left and right, seeking an alternate escape. Sebastian's tone softened. He stepped to the side, granting her access. "But I'd never hit you or any woman," he said. To Sebastian, there was nothing worse than a man who hit a woman. "I didn't mean to frighten you in that way."

Ashley's arms encircled her waist. She turned her face down, refusing to find his eyes.

"What you did to me…" he started.

Her eyes centered on him. "What I did to you was wrong. Sebastian, I'm sorry." Her remorse streaked down her cheeks in irrepressible waves.

His jaw set tight, clenched. He watched the lines of her sullen face contort. Tears washed her face in shame. Her tears, the anecdote to his rage. His jaw loosened. "You have no idea how much pain and trouble your little stunt has caused me." Seeing Ashley again, like this, should have infuriated him. He should have felt anything other than the lusty hunger that pumped through his veins, awakening his arousal.

Giving in to an overwhelming urge to feel her body constrained by his, Sebastian stepped behind her and weaved his arms around her waist. He held her close, persuading her surrender. "I promise, I'm not here to hurt you," he whispered softly. "We need to talk."

Ashley breathed ragged breaths, inhaling and exhaling hard and deep as she nestled into the strength of Sebastian's embrace. The feeling, an undeniable need. The tremors that controlled her impulses refused to subside.

"I'm not going to hurt you," he repeated.

Sebastian allowed her to push away from him. Ashley turned to face the door. Moist, clumsy fingers fiddled with slippery keys. His steady hand covered hers, helped to guide the key into the lock, and they twisted the knob together.

Whether by choice or inability, neither moved. Entwined fingers lingered on the knob for what seemed an eternity. Shallow breaths tickled her nape. The deep rumble of his breaths pearled her nipples. Sebastian's erection pressed against her backside. Even now, their bodies responded to each other despite better judgment.

She shrugged unsure shoulders. "Would you like to come inside?" she asked.

His voice, low and husky, "Yes," he said, without hesitation. A hand positioned at the small of her waist nudged Ashley inside.

"I've got the door." The tenor and command of his voice called to a deep yearning inside her, awakening feminine desire and primal lust. A surge of moisture readied at the crest of her thighs.

Sebastian turned to face her, unveiled. Her longing eyes scaled his face, climbed past his dimpled chin to his well-defined philtrum and landed squarely on his impassioned stare. Cloudy eyes roved her frame, caressed her soft, sensual curves, taking her in, one savory inch at a time. There was no mistaking the look he gave or the intent behind his stare. Sebastian wanted to fuck her, and Ashley wanted to let him fuck her.

He broke the charged electricity flowing between them. "All right. Let's talk." Veiled again, his hard, chiseled mug and icy stare beckoned a response and snatched her out of her lusty stupor and into the reality of the present.

Ashley swallowed hard. "Right."

Sebastian planted himself on the sofa. His large masculine frame dwarfed her furnishings. She took her place on the chair next to him and wiped her clammy palms on the cushion at her side. She exhaled a breath. "I'm sorry for what I did to you. You said I caused you pain and trouble. Please let me know what I can do to fix what I've done."

He tossed his head back. A chuckle emanated from the pit of his gut. "Darlin' there's nothing you can do to get my job back." He leaned forward, forearms on his thighs, baring a sneer. "My entire career and everything I've worked to accomplish these past sixteen years is gone thanks to you." Sebastian's sunken eyes narrowed. Hard lines in his face stiffened. His arctic glare locked to her and chilled her solid.

Ashley's foot tapped the floor incessantly. "What do you mean?" Suddenly, inviting the man whom she destroyed into her home didn't seem safe.

Only Sebastian's lips moved. "I missed an important meeting because of your little stunt, and I was fired." His stare pinned her, and she sat motionlessly.

She gasped and cupped her mouth and then dropped her hand to her lap. "Sebastian, I... I didn't know..." She lowered her chin to her chest. "I'm very sorry." She couldn't face his stare.

Relaxing, he slumped into the sofa and issued a coy smile. "There is something you can do."

Ashley's nipples pebbled though the man's words were hardly an innuendo or an invitation. *Horny, selfish bitch. The last thing Sebastian wants is you.*

She closed her eyes. "Okay. What can I do?"

He leaned forward again. Eyes deadlocked on her. "I need your best work on this marketing plan. For the next eighteen months, you're mine. I want access to you around the clock. You'll do as I say, when I say, with no questions asked."

Ashley nodded. "Yes, of course."

"If you fail me, I will see to it that your ass is fired. Are we clear?"

Intimidation rarely worked on her. Sebastian's unwavering stare fueled by his desire for revenge proved to be the exception. *I need to tread lightly.*

She nodded again. "Clear."

A grin stretched across his face. "Good. I expect the first draft of your plan by tomorrow morning."

Ashley opened her mouth to argue. Sebastian jerked his head back and arched a brow, silently reminding her that she had no room to negotiate.

She inhaled a deep breath instead, looking across the wide, open room at large green numbers on the stove in the kitchen. "I need to get started now. I don't have much time since it's already after ten o'clock."

"I think you should get some rest first. You can get me the plan late tomorrow afternoon." Sebastian leaned down and pulled off his brown leather loafers. "Mind if I leave these here?" he asked, sitting his shoes at the side of the sofa.

Ashley's eyes widened in surprise, watching him swing long legs up to the cushion as he lay down and stretched out. "Sebastian, are you staying?"

He lifted his head slightly and issued a coy smile. Mischief flashed behind those gray eyes. "Of course I'm staying. You'll need my input and information about the project. Since I'm here, I might as well give you what you need." At the hint of their passionate night together, need ached between her thighs. *He's taunting me!*

"Um, okay." Apprehension must have spread across her face like weeds spread across a field of Bermuda grass at the start of spring.

"Ashley, I'm not here to harm you."

She let out a breath and stood. "Okay. Do you mind if I ask you some questions?" She walked to the kitchen bar and gathered a notepad and pen.

His finger grazed her hand as he reached for the items she held. "Not now. Later. You should rest. I'll sleep here. Our minds will be sharper after some sleep."

Shrugging rounded shoulders, she snatched her hand away. Her palm ran down her hip. She couldn't wipe away the tingling sensation that spread from his touch straight up her spine. "All right. If you need anything, I'll be on the other side of the wall," she said, pointing to the ten-foot divider that separated the loft's bedroom area from the sofa where Sebastian relaxed.

Ashley spread a blanket across the air bed. Replacing the sullied mattress she had discarded hadn't been a priority. She crawled into her makeshift bed and pulled the comforter over her head, ducking in shame and guilt. With Sebastian on the other side of the wall, restlessness gnawed at her insides. She hadn't been able to stop thinking about him or their last night together. Learning that she had caused him to lose his job added to her anxiety and upped the guilt rolling through her stomach in waves. Ashley closed her eyes and tried to quiet her mind. The alarm clock would sound soon enough, and she would have to face Sebastian again.

Ashley's eyes fluttered open at the sound of a male clearing his throat. Sharp angles of Sebastian's face came into focus. He squatted beside her. His smile almost appeared genuine.

"You have something against the traditional bed?"

She rubbed her eyes and released a little yawn. "No. I haven't had time to replace the old mattress after..." she paused. Sebastian peered down at her. The early morning light spotlighting his chiseled jaw shot a memory of their passion straight to her sex.

"After what?" he said, his forehead wrinkling.

"Nothing. I need to get one, that's all."

"Did you have another mishap with a man trapped to your bed?" His eyes turned cold.

She winced and turned away. "Sebastian, I'm really sorry about what I did to you. I had no idea that my actions would cause you to lose your job."

He ignored her apology. "What happened to your bed?"

She pulled the blanket closer to her, shielding herself from his scorn. "I threw it out. That's all."

"Why?"

Ashley rolled her eyes. Sebastian wasn't going to let this go without an answer. "Because I caught my ex in bed with another woman." *There, she said it.* Maybe Sebastian would stop badgering her about the bed.

"Ah. I see," he said, light flickering behind dull eyes. "Come on. I made breakfast for us. You owe me a marketing plan." Glad that he didn't ask anything more about the mattress or her situation with Paul, she rolled out of bed.

Ashley strolled to the breakfast bar. She couldn't remember the last time a delicious smell came from that kitchen. He had prepared a feast, evident from the pots and pans stacked high in the sink.

Sebastian handed a plate of eggs, sausage, toast and jam to her. "Here. Eat up."

"Shouldn't I be the one to make breakfast, considering?"

He placed a fork on her plate. "The next time."

The next time? She wondered. How often did Sebastian plan on spending the night at her place? Her insides tingled.

She opened her laptop and began typing. "Tell me a little about your plans for the Carlisle. I know the building is being converted to accommodate retailers. What's the strategy behind your plan?"

Sebastian talked. Ashley's fingers flew across the keyboard. His plans included the conversion of the entire first floor to make room for twenty retail outlets ranging in size from two thousand to over ten thousand square feet. Every apartment would be renovated. Floors ten and higher would include high-end lofts and condos for sale. Expansion into the adjacent vacant building would add twenty additional rental units and amenities including a fitness center and indoor pool, resident café, event space, and a media lounge equipped with computer work areas and coffee bar.

"The Carlisle will be all about luxury, convenience and entertainment. I want to create a space that residents love to come home to." Sebastian paced the kitchen floor with exaggerated steps, his expression indicating his excitement. "I'm already in conversation with several retailers and hope to lease space to a small grocery-store chain, a dry cleaner, a postal center and a few restaurants."

"That's great, Sebastian. The plan sounds fantastic. I renewed my lease after speaking to Cassie in the front office."

Sebastian hand-massaged his chin. "So what ideas do you have about marketing?"

"I think you need a rebrand. Radio and TV spots. A website. Maybe promote some giveaways to incentivize condo sales and apartment rentals. I definitely think you'll need a housewarming and grand-opening celebration. Are you open to another name? What about parking and transit?" Ideas flowed out with ease, like honey from a tap. She tried to temper her excitement in her delivery, but there was no use. Talking about the project made her nearly giddy.

A smile touched the creases at the corners of Sebastian's eyes. "I like your enthusiasm. Yes to rebranding, advertising, incentives and the grand-opening celebration. I'll have to think about renaming the property. There will be a new parking deck to accommodate tenant and guest parking." Sebastian stopped pacing and leaned against the counter, facing Ashley. "You're really getting into this." Elbows pressed into the granite, a full-on grin settled on his lips.

Ashley peeked up from the laptop. "Yes, I like what I've seen and heard so far. I think your plan is great."

"Thank you. Now, what was your thought concerning transit?"

"Traffic in Atlanta is a major issue. What about offering a shuttle service to the Marta station and other businesses within a five-mile radius? Or what about creating a fee-based carpool service for residents or offering rental vehicles on an hourly basis?"

He paced the floor again. A hand stroked his chin, deep in thought. "Wait, slow down. I'm not sure I want to be in the transit business."

"Understandable. But, you could lease space at a discounted rate to someone who is an expert in the business to offer these services. You've got to offer something more attractive than the competition."

"I like the way you think." Sebastian strolled to the opposite side of the bar and swiveled Ashley around in her seat toward him. "What are you doing today?"

Ashley's eyes crawled up his tall, muscular frame. "Working on your plan. Why?"

"I want to take you somewhere. There's something I need you to see." Sebastian leaned close. "We have unfinished business between us that has nothing to do with the Carlisle or the marketing plan." Sensual heat radiated from him straight to her core. "But today is all about business."

Squirming in her seat, she swallowed hard. Confirmation that the desire she felt was returned by Sebastian raised her anxiety. "Sebastian." Her stare past his shoulder landed on the photo of Chris on the shelf. She closed her eyes. Sucked in a breath. "I'll do whatever you want me to do to market your development, but we need to keep our relationship strictly professional."

Amusement tinted his eyes. "Remember, I own you. Every inch of you for the next eighteen months." His smug expression infuriated her instantly. "Luckily for you, I'm not interested, at least not in the way you think I am." Sebastian headed to the front door, his hand parked on the knob.

Relief floated over Ashley, followed by a sense of regret. *Damn!* When would that night in the Keys stop haunting her?

She wiggled down from the stool, keeping a safe distance from Sebastian. "Where should I meet you?"

Sebastian leaned against the doorframe. "Bring your laptop." His broad shoulders filled the space. "Meet me in the lobby at two o'clock. I'll be out front, waiting. Don't wear a dress and be prepared to get messy."

In the hallway, Sebastian reached for his cell phone. The text message he sent to Daniel was short and direct.

I need another favor. Can you get a mattress for me? A king. The best one you've got.

Daniel fired back a response immediately.

You got it. Already banged your way through the new one you just purchased, huh?

Sebastian didn't respond to Daniel's rhetorical joshing—although the thought of banging his way through a mattress with Ashley did awaken a certain part of his anatomy.

Chapter Fifteen

Ashley gulped down the last of her green tea. She grabbed her keys and red clutch from the sofa table and headed out the front door. Her laptop bag relaxed at her hip. Sebastian would be there to pick her up in five minutes. The elevator doors opened, and she strolled across the freshly painted lobby to the newly renovated entrance.

Sebastian waited in the driver's seat of his silver and black Jeep Wrangler. As she approached, he hopped out and jogged to the passenger side and opened the door.

He extended a hand and took hold of her bag. Indulgent eyes roved her fitted shirt to her worn jeans. "Hello."

Ashley climbed into the vehicle. "Hi." She couldn't help ogling Sebastian's defined arms and strong hands resting on the door. Chiseled pecs peeked through his perfectly pressed dress shirt. "I thought you said I should wear something that I could get messy?"

He flashed a smile, closed the door, and headed back to the driver's side. He leaned back into the seat, his probing gaze stalled on hers. "You look great." A glimmer of mischief in his eyes.

Sebastian reached behind the passenger seat. She frowned at the rustling sound of plastic. He placed a T-shirt on his lap. "I'll change into this as soon as we get there." His eyes seemed to laugh at her.

"As soon as we get where?" Ashley asked.

"My office," he said. "We'll work on the presentation. Later you're going to help me paint."

"Paint?" She didn't understand. Wouldn't he hire professionals to do that sort of thing?

"Yes. Paint." Sebastian handed the tattered shirt to Ashley. "Hold on to this, would you?"

Ashley stuffed the plastic bag into her oversized Dooney. "Sure."

He glanced at her. "I enjoy painting. It's relaxing," he said, as though needing to explain. "Helps me manage stress."

Her head tilted and shoulder shrugged, "I understand."

They drove five miles north up Peachtree Street. "My office is there," he pointed to a high-rise across the street.

Ashley shouldered her handbag and exited the vehicle. She followed his heavy steps toward the elevator. They rode silently to the twenty-second floor. The doors opened into an open office space brightly colored in shades of yellow and teal.

"Come with me." Sebastian walked down a hall lined with offices overlooking magnificent views of the city. Inside she could see trendy office furnishings. Some offices showed signs of being occupied. Others were untouched, having nothing on the desk surfaces or walls. They approached a closed door at the end of the hall.

He rammed his shoulder into the smooth surface and opened the door. "This is your office whenever you need to work with me or my staff. I hope you'll be comfortable here."

Ashley scoped out the large room. The office was the largest of all the ones she had seen. "Sebastian, this is a great space." Her open palm pressed flat against her chest. A tiny gasp seeped from her lips.

"Great. I'm glad you're pleased." The flat tone of his deep voice didn't match the look in his eyes. Each sweeping glance devoured her body. "Each office has an accent wall. After we finish the plan, we'll paint your wall. The color options are teal or yellow. What's your preference?" Ashley stepped away, putting distance between them.

She spun around. Her office at A.C. Advertising was nice, but didn't have views as breathtaking as the views in Sebastian's office. "I like teal."

"Then we'll paint the wall teal." Sebastian hadn't moved from the entrance. "I'll be in my office at the end of the hall if you need anything."

"Sebastian," Ashley called to him as he turned to leave. "Thank you." Her words were sincere. Considering the many days and nights that would require her presence there, she appreciated his thoughtfulness.

In a flash, his mood changed. "Don't thank me," he snapped. "Get to work. I want the first draft completed by five o'clock. Can you do that?" His frigid tone slapped her back into reality. Sebastian had no other intention than to ensure she delivered what he wanted.

She unzipped the bag, pulling the laptop from its sheath. "Yes. I can do that."

"Good." He turned, and then he was gone.

Exactly ten minutes before five, Ashley hit the send button. Her stomach growled ferociously. She stood and stretched her arms wide, her back to the office door.

Sebastian cleared his throat as he leaned against the doorframe. "How's it coming along, Ashley?"

She whipped around. "I e-mailed the first draft to you seconds ago," she said, surprise marking her tone.

"Excellent. You must be starving. I ordered pizza and sodas. The food should be here at any time. Follow me." Sebastian disappeared faster than she could respond.

She hurried down the narrow hall after him. "Sebastian, I think you'll like my ideas." She couldn't help admire his swagger. The man knew how to pick a pair of jeans. And he wore them even better.

He strutted into the last office on the right. As she entered the room, he dipped into a chair behind a massive desk and swiveled around to face the computer screen.

The arrow glided across the screen at the command of his mouse stroke. After several clicks, the presentation popped up. Sebastian's mouth formed a hard line, eyes narrowed and brows bunched. Ashley clasped her hands, twisting them nervously as she stood peering over his shoulder.

Like the contrail from a jet soaring high, lining the sky, a sly grin streaked his cold expression. "This is a good start. I do want you to make a few tweaks, but overall..." He glanced over his shoulder. "Impressive," he said with flames flaring behind his eyes. "Hey, why isn't this working?" he asked, pointing to a stalled animation in the presentation.

Ashley leaned down. "Here. Let me drive," she said, attempting to take command of the mouse. Slender fingers clasped over his large hand. A hand that stayed fixed. She jerked away. "Oh! Sorry." Her voice pitched. "May I?"

Sebastian righted his posture. "Uh, hmm." He cleared his throat and then positioned his hand on the desk beside the mouse pad. "It's all yours."

She grabbed hold of the mouse, leaning closer to him. Inhaling Sebastian's masculine scent, she became woozy. Her breasts pebbled into hard beads. As though an apocalyptic ice storm had frozen him in place, Sebastian stilled. Even his breathing seemed to cease. Her supple bosoms pressed softly against his bare forearm, the obvious culprit.

A groan, deep and summoning, emitted from the pit of his gut, like despair. With a slight turn, his eyes centered on hers. Face-to-face, inches away. "Ashley." Her name rolled off his tongue like a dope fiend craving his next hit.

"Yes, Sebastian." Her words met his. She hadn't felt as strong as she did then since being humbled by his intimidation tactics the day before.

His forehead wrinkled and lips twisted into a smirk. "My pants are buzzing." Sebastian's bass reverberated through her core.

She paced her breathing, boldly keeping his gaze. "I've never heard that line before."

The glint in his eyes sparked laughter. "I meant the pizza is here." He chuckled. Fury boiled her blood.

Ashley shifted away. Her rear end planted on the wooden credenza at the side of the desk. She huffed. Sebastian stood. Her eyes followed his rise and then drifted to the floor. Humiliated. She scooted to the very edge of the cabinet as he neared, distancing herself, yet close enough to see the pulsing vein in his neck and to feel the searing heat of 98.6°F against her flesh.

Cheek to cheek, his breath brushed her earlobe like feathers. "We'll finish this later," he said. His mouth twitched, a wisp of a smile exposing delight in her torture.

Her throat went dry. Her mind went blank. Ashley shut her eyes. Sebastian toying with her libido spelled danger for them both.

"Come on." He said over his shoulder at a pouting Ashley, who remained glued to the furniture. "Let's eat. I know you're hungry for it."

Sebastian swooped up the last slice of pizza, nearly cramming the entire piece into his mouth with a single bite. He stared blatantly. He couldn't stop gawking. Ashley's dark brown eyes captivated him since that first night on Peachtree Street. What thoughts floated around behind that pretty face?

"Are you full?" he asked, pushing back from the round break room table.

Still chewing a mouthful, Ashley nodded. "Uh, huh," she mumbled before swallowing.

"Good. Then it's time to paint." He whipped out his cell phone, glancing at the time. "A quarter till six," he blurted out. "Do you have any other plans tonight?" He asked, not that he really cared about her answer. Based on their understanding, Ashley would do as he pleased, whenever he pleased. Sebastian wondered how far the limits of his power over her extended. His pants tightened around his crotch, his imagination running wild and rampant with naughty thoughts.

"No. I don't have any plans this evening," she said, releasing a small sigh.

He licked his lips, remembering her sweet tangy bitterness on his tongue. Sebastian had never relished the taste of a woman as much as that night. "Perfect. We can take our time and go slow." Circling his index finger on the table, his stare stayed fixed on her.

Ashley inhaled a deep breath. The rise and fall of her breasts mesmerized him. "That's the best way to do the job right," she said. Sebastian's cock twitched. He liked that she wasn't flustered by his unambiguously suggestive remarks.

Instead, she played on. Underneath the table, Sebastian's foot rubbed against her ankle. She didn't flinch or move away. He knew he could have her sprawled out on his desk, on his bed, or anywhere else he pleased, begging for him, whenever he wanted. For now, he would enjoy playing mind games.

He glared at Ashley, flashed a deliberate smile. "Nice and slow," the mellow tone flowed out from his lips like the seductive sway of a belly dancer's hips. "That's the only way I do the job."

Ashley's reach extended toward the ceiling, covering the last patch of neutral beige wall with teal paint.

He frowned. "I didn't know you'd be such a perfectionist." Sebastian leaned against the desk, arms folded across his chest.

She whirled around. Paint splatter from the roller in her left hand splashed across his face and doused his shirt. As though she aimed intentionally, paint missed the furniture, only splattering on him. Droplets of teal paint puddled on the hardwood floor.

Ashley's fingers curled over her mouth, shielding a snicker. "Oh! Sebastian, I'm sorry." The roller descended into the paint tray as she released the handle. "Here, let me help." Wiping her hands on her jeans, she approached him.

"Ugh!" Sebastian released an irritated groan as he raised his arms and lifted the paint-covered T-shirt over his head. "Don't you get tired of apologizing to me?"

Ashley froze, and then her eyes stalled on his naked, cut torso.

His mouth twisted into a smug half grin, eyes deadlocked on her. "What?" he asked coyly and used an unsoiled area of the shirt to wipe his brow clean.

The twilight skyline as her backdrop beyond the large paneled glass, the amber glow of the setting sun sparkled off her bronzed complexion. Sebastian basked in her beauty, radiating a mesmerizing aura.

Light bent around her curves, highlighting the angles and peaks of her fine figure. The woman had a body meant for a man to enjoy. He tossed the shirt on the desk and then took a step forward toward her. Their distance barely a foot apart.

Ashley's eyes fled his leer. "Stay right where you are, Sebastian." An expression he hadn't seen before graced her face, shimmering in the fading sunlight. Timid? No. Maybe hesitation. Whatever the look, Sebastian hadn't expected that reaction from his feisty temptress.

Throwing his head back, he laughed hard. "I told you we'd finish later. Did you think I was talking about the presentation?" He nodded his head. "No. You're an astute woman. You knew exactly what I meant, didn't you?"

Before she could counter in protest, Sebastian took another step and pulled her into his embrace. Head dipped low, his mouth descended over hers. Their tongues collided. The force of passion gripped him so hard that the feeling teetered them. He guided her fall, bringing her gently to the floor. Landing on the paint-splattered tarp, he quickly assumed control. And with haste, he mounted her.

Sebastian wedged himself between her thighs. Ashley's small hands took a firm hold of his biceps, nails digging into solid-muscled flesh. She moaned in surrender, her body giving way to his as a twig would snapped under the weight of a heavy snow.

Sebastian's hands cupped her face, deepening their kiss. Her scent. Her touch. Her taste. Stimulating nerve memory, his groin throbbed with pure carnal desire. A firm erection poked her stomach. Her nipples returned the favor, piercing his pecs. He wanted her. Then. Now.

Jostled by a hard shove to his chest, Sebastian stilled. Ashley turned away from his kiss.

He reared up, resting on an elbow. His hand clutched hers. "You make me so hot. I want you now, Ashley." Sebastian's lips grazed her jawline. Stern opposition met his seduction. Thwarting his attempt at another kiss to rekindle the mood, her lips remained sealed like a vault. "Look at me. I know you want me too," he begged, eager to resume the interrupted moment.

"Get off me, Sebastian!" The shrill that came from her lungs rattled him. He stared down at her. He hadn't been wrong about the desire and passion between them.

Sebastian rolled to the side and sat up. Confused. Frustrated. Horny. He frowned. "Ashley, I don't understand. I know you want me as much as I want you."

Ashley mimicked his position, joining him in an upright pose. Leaned back against the desk, she crisscrossed her legs and tugged at her shirt that had been mussed in their skirmish. There. She had that look in her eyes again.

"We share something special." Desperate, he would try anything, including intimidation. "Remember, you belong to me." He would make up for his brute behavior when he made love to her.

An inferno hotter than hell blazed in her eyes, met his longing gaze. "I'll do anything to make up for what I did to you. I'll work around the clock. I'll allow you to call me names and insult me." Anger flavored her words, the intonation of her voice matching her flared temper. "But, I'm not your ebony whore." Boiling rage in her eyes threatened to spill. "You tricked me once. I refuse to be fooled twice."

His eyes stretched wide. Sebastian didn't speak. He studied her, watched the way her mouth moved, the way she spoke with her hands. She was angry. And something else. An emotion he had never seen before on the face of such a beautiful woman. Ashley wasn't hysterical. He knew how a hysterical woman behaved. Ellie had been hysterical many times when she hadn't taken her meds or for no good reason at all. As quickly as the thought came, Sebastian forced the memory back and rejoined her in their moment.

He spoke gently. "How did I fool you? I recall being the one left handcuffed to the bed."

She leaped up, arms flailing in defense. "That was only after..."

Sebastian followed, standing a fingertip away. "After what?" He frowned, tracing her chin with his finger.

Ashley huffed. Stalked toward the window. "After I saw *that* message on your phone." Arms circling her trunk, as if they offered protection from him, she turned to face him. "You got what you wanted. A little taste of chocolate." Her accusation soured his gut.

His head jerked back. Sebastian stroked his chin, thinking. "Text message? Taste of chocolate? What are you talking about?" He frowned.

Her arms tightened. "I wasn't snooping. I needed to make a call. Your phone was on the bathroom counter. As I dialed the number, a text message from Daniel came in, asking if you had banged that ebony chick." He could see hurt and disappointment in her eyes.

Sebastian's lips drew tight. He cracked his knuckles. "And ruining my life was a better, more acceptable option than asking me about that text?" His voice raised. "What Daniel said was stupid and offensive, but he wasn't speaking for me. He was just being a guy. There was never supposed to be anything more. But that isn't what happened, is it?"

Ashley's chest heaved hard. Her eyes glazed with a light sheen of moisture. "I never expected anything from you," she yelled, making her way toward the door.

His wide gait overtook her steps. Sebastian lodged himself in the doorway, intercepting her escape. "And that's what bothers you. There is more. More than either of us expected," he fired back.

He knew her reaction before the lie formed on her tongue. "You and I had sex. Nothing more," she said.

Sebastian shook his head. Stepped forward. Ashley stumbled back. "Then what difference does any of this make?" He crushed her body with his, anchoring her to the wall. "You wanted me then, just as badly as you do now. And I want you. That doesn't make me a bad person. That makes me a man."

He could see her visible struggle, fighting the urge to scream. "I can't do this anymore," she said, the anger in her words fizzling out.

Sebastian covered her left breast, molding her mound with his firm hand. He spoke tenderly. "What can't you do anymore?"

She released a quiet moan. "I can't have meaningless sex." Her hand raised to her forehead.

"Do you want me?" He lowered his head, nestling his face in her bosoms.

Ashley responded to his touch with a whimper.

"You didn't answer my question. Do you want me?" His lips traced her cleavage.

Barely audible, she gave a breathy reply. "Yes."

"Who says sex between us has to be meaningless? I want you too." He unbuckled her jeans.

Panting softly, "Sebastian, I... I can't," she stammered.

"Yes, you can. We'll create rules."

"Rules?" Her eyes sparkled.

"Ashley, we both know this thing between us can't be stopped. I'm not offering you anything more than I can give, and I don't expect anything in return. As long as we both know where we stand, nobody will get hurt." His hand dipped into her panties.

She angled her head to the right. "Ahhh! Sebastian," she whimpered as he massaged her, readying her for his invasion.

Ashley tilted her head back. "I don't know. I don't want to be your black whore." Her sultry eyes didn't match the rejection that sprung from her lips.

His forehead wrinkled as his eyes searched her face. "I won't lie. The color of your skin captivates me. You're beautiful. I wish you didn't feel that way about yourself. That's not at all how I think of you."

"What do you want from me?"

"I want you as my lover, until the project is complete. Exclusively. That has nothing to do with race," he rasped hoarsely.

"And what happens after the project is done?"

"We walk away. Continue to live our lies." His voice cracked. "Lives," he corrected, heat warming his face. "Can you handle the arrangement?"

"I think so," she acquiesced. "Can you?"

His question posed back at him hadn't been expected. He hesitated. "Uh-huh," he muttered, taken by the sensation of her supple flesh under eager fingertips.

Sebastian's vigorous stroke forced the words from her lips. "Oh, you feel so good."

Tattered jeans fell to her ankles. Sebastian dropped to his knees, tugged her panties down. "Amazing," he whispered.

Hands dangling at her sides, her neck arched back. Sebastian's tongue glided across her moisture.

Two fingers pumped into her. "Ahhh," she released. "Sebastian."

He smiled. "Don't worry, darlin'. I'm going to give you what you need."

Chapter Sixteen

Ashley didn't remember how she had gotten home Saturday morning. The only thoughts floating in her head were of Sebastian and how good his body felt molded to hers, thrusting into her depths. She had never been with a man who made her ache with need the way he did.

The next few days, they worked side by side each day, taunting and teasing each other. At night, when the work was done, the lights were low, and there were no distractions or interferences, they couldn't keep their bodies apart. Like a drug, she wanted him day and night, couldn't get enough of Sebastian Stone. At least common sense and self-control, what little she had left, won in the end, sending her home instead of staying the night with him as he had requested on occasion.

"Hey, Kerri." Ashley chimed into the phone.

"Ash, where have you been? I haven't heard from you in weeks. You never ignore my calls."

A grin larger than she could control spread across her face like stars spanned the Milky Way. "Sebastian has been keeping me busy… working on the presentation," she paused. Merely saying his name made her pulse quicken. "Among other things." A hand flew to her cheeks covering her blush.

Like a chasm, quiet grew between them until Kerrigan shattered the silence. "Among other things?" she asked.

"Sebastian and I… well, we have an arrangement." Thinking about how she would explain their fling, she stood and moved toward the large window in the living area of her loft. Construction vehicles lined the street below. "We have unbelievable chemistry," Ashley said, defense clinging to her words.

"Yeah, I know. I was there in the Keys, remember?" Kerrigan teased. "And?" Her tone goaded Ashley for an explanation.

Ashley flattened her palm against the warm window pane. Workers patrolled the sidewalks, moving heavy equipment and tools. "And we agreed to continue seeing each other until the project is done."

Kerrigan couldn't contain her shock. "Really? Exclusively?"

Ashley smiled. "Yes, but don't go all sentimental and mushy on me. After the project is done, we'll go our separate ways."

"Will you be able to walk away? What if Sebastian wants to continue your relationship?"

"This isn't a relationship. This is an arrangement of convenience."

"Fine. What if he wants a real relationship with you?"

"Kerri, he won't. This is only about sex to Sebastian. My feelings aren't invested. I'm not hoping for more."

"Ash, I thought you wanted more than another fling? I thought you were trying to move on?"

"Kerri, I'm being realistic. I'm not like you. Love isn't meant for me. That doesn't mean I have to be lonely. Sebastian is the most amazing and attentive lover I've had. I can't describe the feeling. I'm just enjoying the time I have with him." Kerrigan didn't say much, only listened. Ashley imagined the self-righteous frown that Kerrigan always wore whenever she disagreed with her choices. "Kerri, are you judging me? Please don't."

She sighed. "No, of course. I'm not judging you. I'm worried about you. Eighteen months. That's a long time to be with someone and then just walk away. What happens if you fall for him or if he falls for you?"

Ashley waved dismissively. "Nah, that won't happen. We'll never be more than what we are right now." Just saying the words aloud, Ashley felt a pang roll through her stomach. "This is a long-term fling," she said, trying to convince herself as much as Kerrigan. "I have needs. He's a human dildo with a few extra parts," she teased.

"Yeah, a few extra parts like a human heart," Kerrigan scolded.

By this time, the workers had cleared the sidewalk. Construction debris littered the roadway. She nodded at Kerrigan's warning as she turned in the direction of the knock at the front door. "I'll keep that in mind." Changing the subject to avoid the lecture being given her, "Sebastian is nothing like Paul," she said, making her way toward the entrance. "He's not loafing off me for money or a place to live. I know what I'm doing."

"Ash, this is one game you shouldn't play. I don't want to see you hurt anymore."

Another knock sounded at the door. An intense wave of nerves radiated from her belly to every limb and faltered her steps. "Thanks, Kerri. I'll take that under advisement. Gotta go. I'll call you later."

Ashley hadn't expected what waited on the other side of the door.

"Miss Turner, I have a delivery for you," said the man who introduced himself as Joe.

The delivery and setup went smoothly. The new mattress and bed were up and ready in less than an hour. Surprised, Ashley still couldn't believe that Sebastian had done this for her.

"Just sign here, miss," Joe said, handing her a chewed ink pen.

She quickly grabbed a more sanitary option from the table beside the door and smiled. "Got it."

When Joe and his crew left, Ashley lay across the new bed, smiling. Sebastian would be coming by later. In fact, she had thought the knock at the door had belonged to him. Wheels turning in her head, the giddiness faded away. What was Sebastian thinking? More importantly, what was she thinking? His motive had been clear, the mattress the very evidence of his intention.

Sebastian stood beyond the threshold. A black canvas tote slung over his right shoulder rested casually against his back. Black gym pants hung seductively low from his waist. A sly smile parted his lips. "Hey, baby. Are you ready?"

Ashley couldn't help the feeling that grounded her feet to the floor, immobilizing her movement. "The name is Ashley, not baby," she quipped, her tone salty. Kerrigan had given good advice. She needed to keep her emotional distance from Sebastian.

He waltzed into the room and tossed the bag to the sofa. "You didn't have a problem with me calling you baby last night. What's gotten into you?" His aggressive advance sent a shiver up her spine. She flinched.

A hand flew to her hip. "You bought a mattress and bed for me. A very expensive mattress and bed." Steam rose from her pores.

"You needed a bed. I bought one for you." His frown dragged the corners of his eyes down into a puppy-dog expression.

Ashley rolled her eyes. "I'm not your girlfriend or your sidepiece. You don't need to buy expensive furniture for me."

Sebastian wrapped his arms around Ashley's waist, pulling her to him. "You're equating yourself with a chicken dinner. Are you all right? Did I do something wrong?"

"Ugh!" She released an exasperated sigh. Ashley struggled to break free of his grip, a useless attempt at independence over his dominance. Her hands shoved firmly against his chest. "Let go of me, Sebastian."

He dropped his hands to his sides. His expression seemed to convey hurt. "All right. Since you don't want to tell me what's bothering you," he paced toward the shelving unit opposite the kitchen, "why don't you tell me about him?" Anger burned in her stomach as Sebastian lifted the picture of Chris from the shelf.

Ashley bolted across the room and attempted to snatch the frame out of Sebastian's clutch. "Put the frame down, Sebastian," she demanded. "You have no right getting into my business."

Sebastian's eyes widened. He held the frame behind his back. "Who is he? Are you in love with him?"

Her heart pounded at his accusation.

Her throat dried. "He's none of your business. Now stop with the games, and put my goddamn frame back where you found it," she yelled, lunging toward him.

He must have recognized fury in her eyes. Sebastian quickened his gait, skirted past her. Ashley whirled around and reached out. She caught the end of his shirt sleeve, tugging his arm from behind him. Sebastian's grip loosened and the frame crashed to the floor, shattering glass in all directions. He froze.

The full force of breath in her lungs exerted, Ashley belted out, "Damn you! You broke my frame." Her arms fell limp at her sides.

Sebastian didn't hesitate. He turned, pulled her into his embrace. "I'm sorry, baby. I didn't mean to upset you. I didn't mean to break the frame." Like an anaconda, his arms wrapped around her, tightened. "I must admit, my woman having feelings for another man makes me a bit jealous."

Ashley squirmed, anger greeting his gaze as she lifted her face to him. "I'm not your woman. I'm your arrangement."

Her words, screaming for dignity. Her expression, lacking light in her eyes. The mood, sobering as quiet fell between them. Sebastian released her from his hold. "You're right." His jaw tightened, returned a cold glare. "I overstepped." He reached into the bag on the sofa and handed a folder to her. "I want these changes made and delivered to me later this evening. Meet me at my house at seven."

Sebastian didn't give her a chance to respond. He headed to the front door and paused before leaving. "I made a mistake. It won't happen again."

Ashley threw on her favorite pair of jeans and baby blue crop top. She grabbed the folder from the counter, slid on red sling back wedges, and headed to the elevator. She jabbed the L repeatedly with her knuckle, taking out her frustration on the helpless backlit button.

Maybe Kerrigan was right. The arrangement might be more than she could handle. On the drive to Sebastian's house, Ashley mulled over the situation and her options. Thirty-five minutes later, her car pulled in front of a grand craftsman-style home. Her fingers clung to the steering wheel as she stared at the earthy, moss-colored house. Drawing in a deep breath, she opened the door and planted a foot on the driveway. As she made her way over to the large wraparound porch, inspiration struck. Strength girding her, she knew what to do next.

The door swung opened before her foot landed on the step's first tread.

"Right on time." Sebastian's charlatan smile made her stomach roll. "Come on in. There's something I want you to see."

Sebastian standing in the door, dressed in khaki shorts and casual T-shirt, almost made her forget her reason for being there.

Ashley sputtered a quiet, "Oh, okay," and then followed him into the house that was more like a bachelor's pad than a home.

She had never been to Sebastian's house. The walls were bare. The tattered sofa must have survived his college days. Ashley wore her thoughts on her face.

"I moved in a few days before I left for the Keys. The place needs some work," he said, as though reading her mind.

Ashley handed the folder to Sebastian. "You can say that again. I suppose the renovation of the Carlisle building doesn't help." She shrugged tight shoulders. "At the very least, you should get rid of the frat-house sofa." She pointed to the plaid monstrosity that occupied two thirds of the living room.

His gaze followed hers as she panned the room. "I could do that," he said, a smile formed on incriminating lips.

"You need to," she said, a disapproving head nod returned.

"Darlin', I'd invite you to come sofa shopping with me, but I don't want you to get the wrong idea about us," he teased. "Wouldn't want you to act like my girlfriend."

Ashley rolled her eyes. "Knock it off, Sebastian."

No pictures or knickknacks were anywhere in sight in the room. He led them to the back of the house. As they whisked past the family room, she noted that even the mantel above the stone fireplace had been left bare. A small chair and table were the only items in the room.

"I hope this space is more suited to your standards." He raised a brow and held out a hand, making an introduction to his home office.

Ashley's sweeping glance scoped the room. "This is much better," she said, an approving grin his reward.

Sebastian swiped a hand across his brow, illustrating pretend relief. "I'm glad to have your approval. Please have a seat."

Ashley eased into the high-back, upholstered chair. Sebastian rifled through the folder and sat in the matching seat beside hers. He studied the contents of the folder quietly. Ashley's eyes danced throughout the space. Across the room on his desk, a small silver frame caught her eye. She squinted, trying to make out the image in the frame.

Sebastian lifted his head. "This is really good. I'd like you to present the plan at the meeting on Monday afternoon."

Ashley tore her eyes away from the frame with lightning speed. She shifted in her seat and adjusted her gaze to him. "Great. I'm glad you like the adjustments I made to the plan."

Sebastian needed to invest in better quality T-shirts. Either the thin material welded to his chest or Ashley's nerves for what she prepared to do next had caused a warm sensation to flow through her chest and spread to her stomach in waves.

Breaking her internal musing, "I have something to show you. Follow me," he said and then stood.

Ashley stayed fixed to the seat. "I want you to tell me about her." She spoke softly,

Sebastian stopped. He braced the door frame. "Tell you about who?" His voice tensed.

"Your wife. Tell me about your wife, and I'll tell you about the man in the photo."

"You mean my late wife," he said flatly. "No." His terse reply filled the room as he turned toward her.

Ashley rose. Stern eyes met his grimacing mug. "Why not? You asked me about the photo."

His forehead wrinkled. Sebastian brought a hand to his brow as though he could massage away the hurt held captive behind his icy glare. "Because," he said, his tone relaxed. "I don't want to talk about her. Whatever you read or heard about Ellie is all you need to know." Just saying her name seemed painful for him. "Besides, you were right…"

"He was my fiancé," Ashley interrupted. "We were supposed to be married on my birthday."

"Ashley," Sebastian said, a frown plastered to his lips. "You were right before, at your place." He bounded toward her. "I don't need to know about him. You don't need to know about Ellie. Let's keep things between us simple, uncomplicated." His hands rested on her hips.

Ashley's heart sank. Despite his subtle delivery, his meaning had been clear. "All right. Fine. We don't need to get too personal." She raised a dismissive hand, creating space between their compressed bodies.

"Come with me. There's something you need to see." His hand dropped to his sides. Sebastian turned and made his exit.

Ashley followed him. As they neared the end of the hall, a faint sound came from the last door on the right. The familiar sound grew louder as they approached.

Sebastian paused in front of the door. Slowly he turned the knob. Catching her eyes, he smiled. "I think you're really going to like what I have to show you."

Ashley raised a curious brow. "Okay, enough with the build. What's behind that door?"

He opened the door. She made a quick assessment, her eyes scanned the large room and landed on the source of the sound she had heard. Ashley cupped her mouth in disbelief. "Copper! Oh, Copper!" she yelled, and bolted across the floor, scooping the little fur ball into welcoming arms. Cooper barked and wiggled, tried to lick her face.

Ashley whirled around. Sebastian, stood at the door, a hand remained on the knob. "How did you…" She couldn't hide the excitement that burst from every pore. "Where did you find him?"

"Remember the red robin I told you about?"

Ashley rolled her eyes. "Yes. What does that stupid bird have anything to do with your finding my dog?"

"Well," he said, as he strolled toward her. "I had asked my buddy Daniel to help find Copper, but he didn't find any leads. I went to the building Thursday morning to handle some business. I was standing on the curb talking through some details with a few of the construction crew when the robin caught my eye. The little thing had been fluttering frantically around one of the shrubs at the front of the building, almost like it was trying to get my attention." He stared past her, as though remembering the moment. "I walked to the shrub, and that's when I saw Copper. He was curled up underneath the bush."

"Really?" A hand mounted her hip. Ashley gave Sebastian a skeptical grin. "Copper never goes to strangers willingly, without a fight."

"I'm not finished." He lifted his right hand. "I learned that the hard way." His hand wore the mark of his scuffle with Copper. "I saw his leash attached to an adjacent lamppost. A woman on a cell phone a few feet away came barreling toward me. She asked if I was Copper's owner. I said no, but I told her that I knew his owner."

"She just gave Copper to you?" Ashley asked as she placed an overly excited Copper on the floor.

"Not exactly. She seemed suspicious of me even after I told her my name and that I own the Carlisle. Thankfully, Cassie walked by us on her way into the office. She spoke to me first, confirming my identity. That's when Mrs. Wright handed over the leash."

On the floor, Copper ran laps around them, circling their legs as he panted and yelped for attention. Ashley peered down at him, an uncontrollable grin spread across her face. Rising on tippy-toes, "Thank you," she said, and threw her arms around his neck. "My hero."

Sebastian's hands found her waist. He peeled her off him, forcing her back so that he could look into her cheerful eyes. "You're welcome," he said, closing the distance between them with a tender kiss planted on her forehead. "I would have given him to you sooner, but I wanted to make sure he was Copper. I had his microchip checked. I also had a vet see him. He's perfectly healthy."

"Sebastian, I can't thank you enough. Copper is the only joy in my life. I've had him since he was a puppy and I've been depressed without him. He's the only good thing I've got in my life."

His head jerked back. "Well, thanks," he said. "I guess I'm useless."

Ashley lowered her head and then met his frowning face. "That's not what I meant, but you and I… well, you know." She halted her words, and turned her eyes down again. "I just meant that Copper is the one thing in my life that has been steady. A girl needs a little stability in the uncertainty of life," she said, her smile meeting his focused stare, eyes set deep beneath a wrinkled brow.

Sebastian looked as though he wanted to counter her remark. Instead, he remained quiet, only continued staring at her. "You're welcome, all the same. If you really want to make it up to me…" He stopped and reached for Ashley's hand, pulling her from the spare room.

Giggling, Ashley went willingly down the hall with him. Copper followed, yelping and playing behind them.

Sebastian scooped up Copper. "Oh, no you don't. You can have her back when I'm all done," he said, giving

Ashley a smoldering look that shot sensations straight to her girlie parts.

Chapter Seventeen

Under the conference table, Sebastian tightened his hold on Ashley's hand. He leaned to the side, whispered in her ear, "Hey, are you okay? There's no reason for you to be nervous. You've done a fantastic job. Do it just like we practiced. You'll be fine." She smelled like heaven. The sweet and spicy fragrance she wore matched her grit and determination.

She squeezed his hand in return and leaned into his right shoulder. He couldn't get enough of those big brown eyes now peering up at him, seeking approval. "Thank you. I have a lot riding on this project as you know. Axel won't ease up, and I really want this promotion."

At the mention of his name, Axel waltzed into the conference room. Ashley loosened her hand from Sebastian's grip and sat up straight. Sebastian knew Ashley would be nervous, especially being the only woman in the room. Not helping matters, Axel's permanent scowl and transfixed stare pierced a hole through Ashley. The only time the man seemed to soften had been around his wife Kerrigan.

Around the table, Sebastian, six other businessmen, and Ashley's boss Axel all turned eyes on her as Axel spoke. "Ashley is here to present our plan for the Carlisle. I know she and Sebastian have spent countless hours drafting and revising the plan that you are about to see."

Sebastian squeezed her knee. Ashley cleared her throat. "Gentlemen, I know your interest today is in how we plan to market the Carlisle. Each of you gentlemen is considering entering into lease agreements based on how much potential traffic and business this plan will generate. I do appreciate your coming into town to tour the facility and to see firsthand why we are excited about this property."

Axel arched a brow.

Ashley smiled, and addressed him. "Axel, earlier this morning I took Brian and Sam on a tour of the property. This afternoon, John, Michael, Bob, and Ryan will join me for a tour."

Axel gave an approving nod, indicating for her to continue.

"Well, for starters, we've decided to rebrand. The Carlisle brand has both good and bad name recognition. We want to preserve the good and eliminate the bad, pay homage to the past while forging ahead to the future. Therefore, the property will undergo a name change and rebrand." Ashley jabbed the button on the slide advancer. "Welcome to the future. Welcome to Carlisle Place, a destination and a place to call home."

"The property is absolutely magnificent," Brian Evans said. "We're set to begin negotiations this week. Our attorney will contact yours." An endorsement from the vice president of real estate development at one the nation's largest restaurant chains would be an added bonus.

Ashley smiled. "Thank you, Brian. Residents and future patrons have always flocked to cafés, and we are glad you see the potential in this property."

"Your website is quite informative, the data compelling, and the creative package you sent to my office captured my attention right off. We definitely want a presence at Carlisle Place."

"I have to agree with you, Brian," Sam Williams chimed in. "We are very close to executing our agreement as well. Atlanta, and this zip code in particular, has a healthy appetite for wellness and health. We feel confident that our organics grocery store will do well in this market. We hope to pilot a larger store here at Carlisle Place."

For the first time since meeting Axel, Sebastian saw him smile. Axel exposed teeth and gums. Ashley continued her presentation, showing compelling demographics and psychographic data and projections.

"I'll skip the renderings since you all saw those on the interactive website and will see them in person today. Are there any questions?"

"Yes, can you talk more about space for arts and entertainment?" Michael Blake, head of development for Metro Movie Cinemas, asked.

"Yes, of course. There is space for up to twenty-four amphitheater-styled auditoriums that will each boast sixty-foot screens. Your sales consultant from Carlisle Place will go over specific details with you later today. Currently, other entertainment venues include six bars, four galleries, an outdoor amphitheater for concerts, and we've signed thirty-two other retail partners."

Sebastian grinned at her and nudged her knee with his. Ashley advanced the slides again. "Here are details on our media campaign, beginning in two months." The slide showed high-level information about ad placements in local real estate and entertainment publications, and on the Internet, radio and television. "An additional way we'll promote Carlisle Place is through events. The Carlisle Place events management team is also working to book several events in the future."

"Are there any other questions?" she asked.

Heads nodded around the table. "The tailored package you delivered answered most of my questions," Michael said. "Our team is conducting an audit of the market, and we'll be reaching out for more details soon. Thank you."

Others around the table commended her and also extended their thanks.

"Great." Ashley rose, her graceful frame stretched tall and confident. "Gentleman, please excuse me. I need to make sure everything is set for your afternoon tour and meetings."

Ten minutes later, she returned and the meeting ended.

Sebastian turned to Axel. "May I have a word?" In the six months of working with Axel, Sebastian hadn't seen him as jovial.

"Sure. We can stay here. Is everything all right?" Axel asked, his forehead wrinkling.

"Yes. I wanted to tell you how thoroughly impressed I am with Ashley's work. She has been beyond accommodating, and I can't tell you how much I appreciate having her in my arsenal."

Axel smirked. "I'll bet she's been accommodating."

"Well, I wanted you to know. I know she's after a promotion. If you don't offer that promotion to her, I just might have to make an offer to her myself. She's become an invaluable member of my team."

Axel leaned back in his seat, his arms folded, crossed his chest. His grin hinted at the secret he held. "Would the nature of your offer be professional or personal?" Axel waited for a reply that Sebastian refused to give. "Don't give me that look, Sebastian. I see the way you two look at each other." Axel unfolded his arms, leaned his forearms along the table's edge. "I found myself in a similar position not too long ago." He smiled.

Ashley had told Sebastian about Axel and Kerrigan, and how the two had meant, fell in love and married. While their story had been heartwarming, the last thing he wanted was to fall in love or to remarry.

Sebastian pushed away from the table. "Axel, I won't lie to you, I do have a personal interest in Ashley, but my interest isn't what you think—or maybe it's exactly what you think. In either case, the thing between us isn't long-term, and it isn't anybody's business except ours. Any offer I make to her would be strictly professional." A knot formed in his stomach.

"Hmm. Interesting." Axel's hand massaged his chin, rubbing as he seemed to think. "You're right. Your relationship isn't my business. Care to join me for a drink to celebrate?"

Sebastian's taut facial muscles loosened. The knot in his stomach untied. "The meeting did go quite well. I'll drink to that."

Axel fiddled with his smartphone as he spoke. "Ashley did an outstanding job. She's always had great potential, but under pressure, she would always cave. With you, she has a new confidence."

Sebastian shifted his position. "Just to be clear, she isn't with me. We work well together."

Axel raised a brow. His fingers glided across the screen. "She'll be excited about the promotion. She's worked a long time for the senior account manager position. What you two have cooked up will require her exclusive, dedicated focus long into the unforeseeable future."

Inside, Sebastian couldn't help the sense of excitement and pride he felt. He knew how much the promotion meant to Ashley. "That's great news, Axel. She'll be ecstatic."

"You're welcome," Axel smirked, mischief in his eyes. Sebastian frowned at his remark, not sure what Axel meant. "I just texted the good news to Ashley, though I suspect she'll be sharing the news with you soon," Axel said.

As though Axel had orchestrated Ashley's actions, Sebastian's phone buzzed seconds later. A text from Ashley.

I got the promotion! The clients LOVE Carlisle Place. Best day ever!

Sebastian glanced up to meet Axel's knowing grin.

Axel stood. "Later you and Ashley can celebrate together, privately. Like I said, you're welcome. Now, why don't we go get that drink?"

Ashley stepped out of her stilettos and kicked them to the side of the door where her other after-work shoes lived. Sebastian didn't respond to the text she sent earlier that day. He stated clearly that their relationship didn't mirror convention. Trying to keep her expectations and emotions in check, she tried to squelch the waves rolling through her insides.

Eager fingers couldn't dial fast enough. Kerrigan answered on the second ring. A shrill poured into Ashley's ear through the cell phone. "Axel told me," Kerrigan squealed. "Congratulations, Ash! You've worked so hard. I know you wanted this for a long time. I'm so happy for you. Are you and Sebastian going to celebrate?"

Disappointment anchored in her belly. "Thank you, but my world doesn't revolve around Sebastian. I'm quite satisfied to celebrate my promotion without involving Mr. Stone," she lied and walked across the dark room. Ashley peered through the large window at the city lights twinkling in the distance.

At that moment, the sound of feet scuffing the floor came from the other side of the wall separating the living area from her sleeping area. She stilled. Panic struck her heart like a spear. "Kerri, keep quiet. I'm not alone. Someone's in my house," Ashley whispered. Clammy palms struggled to keep the phone from slipping out of her grasp.

Through the blackness, she tiptoed from the window to the kitchen counter. Reaching across the cool granite surface, her fingers curled around the slick handle of a long butcher's knife. "I'm going to my front door. If you hear me scream, call 911." She pocketed the phone in her slacks.

Taking feather-light steps, Ashley reached the front door. Her hand covered the knob. Before she could unlock the deadbolt, hot breath singed her ear. A masculine hand reached around her trunk and cupped her breast. Her heart pounded in her chest. A hard body trapped her movements, pinned her to the door. His thick erection pressed against her backside. His other hand squeezed her wrist and pinned her hand to the door at her side.

"Don't be afraid, baby." He spoke softly in her ear. "I'm going to make you scream, but you won't want any police interference." He released her, and stepped back. "Congratulations on your promotion."

Sebastian's voice melted away her fear, replaced by a deep ache, a longing for his touch. His mere presence gave her a premonition of his thrusting pelvis between her thighs, soothing her pain. "Sebastian, you, you... I almost stabbed you," Ashley whispered, stammering and spun around on shaky legs. Blood raced through her veins. Moisture readied between her thighs. She leaned back, her foot propped up on the door.

"Not a chance, baby." He held up the knife pried from her jittery fingers. The would-be weapon went down on the table with a clink. "I was waiting for you to come home, to celebrate. From what I've heard, sounds like you don't want me here," he rasped, his stance strong and masculine, and he stood steadfast. Moonlight streamed into the room, beams gently caressed the crevices of his well-formed chest and abdomen.

"No, that's not true. I... I..." she stammered. Her greedy eyes devoured his naked, heaving chest. "Hold on a minute." She reached into her pocket. "Everything is fine, Kerri. I'll talk to you tomorrow." She ended the call. The lube mishap at the grocery store taught her to properly disconnect cell phone calls.

Sebastian lifted a remote control and hit the button. Slow. Soft. Sensual. The melodic tempo of Operate by ASTR started smooth, almost sluggish, filling the space with sound that lifted high to the exposed metal beams twenty feet above them. The bass boomed slowly, the melancholy tune vibrating in and around her, bouncing off solid surfaces in the loft. The remote dropped to the seat cushion.

He advanced. The collision. The explosion. Being with Sebastian made her lose all senses, and time ceased to exist. She didn't remember how she ended up on her new bed writhing and moaning, completely nude. Across the room, their clothes lay shed on the floor.

Sebastian's tongue massaged her, tasting every inch of her tender flesh, inside and out.

Ashley arched her back, pressing her head into the down pillow under her neck. "Ahhh," she moaned, and he dipped into her center, tasting her sweet, savory honey.

He forced the tip of himself into her slowly until he entered her fully. "If you don't want me here, just say the words and I'll leave."

Taken by his pleasure, Ashley moaned again. "Ahhh."

"What do you want, Ashley?"

"I want you. Please don't leave."

"I'm sorry," he said. "We'll go shopping tomorrow."

She lifted her head and frowned. "Huh?"

"You'll never forget this night. I'm going to break your bed tonight. I'm going to break you."

Ashley swallowed hard. "Shit," she mumbled under her breath.

Like the words floating around them and the seductive melody, Sebastian went to work.

He entered her deep and hard. "Ah. Ah. Ah. Sebastian." Ashley screamed his name.

Sebastian's relentless hammering, his cock mercilessly hollowing out her moist sex with his slow, powerful thrusts, forced her cry. Her legs, shaking violently, were spread wide, wrists and ankles shackled to the headboard on either side of her head.

"Don't worry, baby. I won't leave you here like this."

She could do nothing but take every inch of his thick cock as he slammed into her so hard that she shuddered and cried out his name with each blow.

"Sebastian. Sebastian. Sebastian," she whimpered. "I love y…" her words trailed off. A thud beat her ear drums. Booming, louder and louder. If her pounding heart slammed against her chest wall any harder, the organ would explode. She turned her head away, embarrassed. "I'm sorry."

His hand stroked her cheek, brought her eyes to meet him. "Don't be." He slowed his pace, writhing in response to his thrusts, and her sex, clenching around his shaft. They exchanged a tender gaze, lovers coming to terms with new, unexplored emotions. Sebastian loosened the restraints, releasing her from sexual bondage. He held her tight, pressing deep into her center, over and over as he whispered, "Don't be sorry, baby."

"Ahhh! Sebastian," she moaned.

After the first orgasm, she was exhausted, but Sebastian wanted more. He slid in and out of her slickness with such force that her head banged into the headboard, threatening a migraine from the mind-blowing sex he gave. The bed wailed, banging against the wall in sync with his rhythmic pounding.

Although Ashley considered herself to be an expert at sex, she realized she had never been fucked until tonight. Sebastian changed her world. He delivered on his promise. Up. Down. Sideways. Any way he could have her. She would never be the same again, never crave average sex. She wanted what only Sebastian could give. And he fucked good.

Pummeling her hard, a loud crack stilled his movements. "I think we broke the bed," he said and then chuckled.

Sebastian stood at the side of the bed, held out a hand. "Let's try a new position."

He pushed her against the wall. Lifting her, he forced her legs to wrap around his waist, his cock pile-driving into her moisture. Her hips circled around and around. Bearing down, she took him in fully. Surrounding his rod, her walls clutched tight. He sent her over the edge three times in this position, his tip stroking at just the right angle against her jewel.

Ashley's legs numbed. Sebastian fastened his hands to the wall on either side of her shoulders, supporting her legs, draped over his biceps. Her head fell limply onto his shoulder, too exhausted for her neck to support.

She pleaded for mercy. "Sebastian, I'm tired," she panted breathlessly.

Mercy did not find her. "We're not done."

He pummeled her deep and hard. Until ecstasy leaked from her eyes. Until sound could no longer escape her lips. After the fifth orgasm had shattered her, body shaking, mind eclipsing sanity in the rapture of his complete possession, Ashley fell limp.

She lost all control of her motor functions. Her arms dropped to her sides slapping hard against the wall, her legs dangled lifelessly, and she boarded dangerously close to unconsciousness. He knew he'd delivered on his promise, brought her to the brink, finishing her. She felt so good wrapped around his hard cock, her sex clenching and gripping his long, thick member.

"Ashley. Ashley," he rasped.

Pumping furiously into her, he found his release, filling her hot, moist haven with his essence. "Ahhh!"

Sebastian had never experienced sex as powerful, as satisfying, as intense. He gave everything in him, and she offered herself back to him in equal measure. Ashley hooked him the minute she let him inside. He craved her, needed all of her.

He slid out of her sweet heat, and her lithe body collapsed down the wall. Sebastian caught Ashley, gathering her in his arms, and carried her to the bed. Her languid limbs seemed lifeless. He kissed her gently, tenderly as he laid down beside her. Heavy lids covered her eyes. After her confession, he ravaged her with wanton desire, and he didn't think to take it slowly with her. Seeing her like this, lifeless and wiped, worry struck his heart.

"Ashley?"

"Yes," she said softly.

"Are you okay?" he asked.

"I've never felt anything like this. You're amazing." She barely managed above a whisper. A faint, tired smile painted her lips.

"I've never experienced anything like this either." He kissed her forehead. "We're amazing together."

Her moon-kissed skin shimmered in the night as she lay next to him, her naked bronzed body wrapped in white sheets. Ashley's beauty reminded him of the robin sent by fate.

Sebastian stretched his arms wide and headed to the kitchen. Careful not to wake her, he quietly pulled pans from the cabinets. Ingredients that he'd purchased were placed on the counter at his disposal. Half an hour later, breakfast awaited.

The faint sound of bare feet slapping against the hard, cold floor brought Sebastian's eyes to her as he whipped around.

Like a bee drawn to nectar, he stepped to her. "Good morning, darlin'." Sebastian's arms wrapped around her waist, pulling her in. He closed his eyes and inhaled the scent of their sex that she wore. The musky aroma made him stiffen.

Ashley pushed out of his clutch. "Sebastian, what is this? What are you doing?" She gestured, pointing with frantic arm movements.

"I made breakfast. Hungry?"

She shook her head. "I see that." Burying her face in her hands, Ashley inhaled a breath. "I mean, why are you still here? Our arrangement... We have rules," she mumbled into her palms. Balled fists dropped to her sides, her forehead wrinkled. "This, you..." Stammering, a hand mounted her hip. She released an exaggerated "Ugh!" and paced the floor along the edge of the counter. "We agreed there would be no sleepovers. You're supposed to leave after we..."

"...make love."

She huffed. "Have sex," she said, sternly correcting him. "This is, this is..."

"...this is what you want," Sebastian finished. His confidence hadn't been rattled by her rant. "Baby, your eyes, your body, say it all. You want me, and not just in your bed at night." He walked toward her, pulling her back into his embrace. Her chest heaved, nervous brown eyes lifted to his. His head descended, lips captured her willing kiss, slow and tender. "Now go ahead, lie to me and yourself. Tell me I'm wrong. Tell me you don't want more than this arrangement."

She squirmed loose, distanced herself from Sebastian. "Thanks for breakfast," she said softly, surrendered. "I really do have a busy day ahead. Lots of things to do today. I'm leaving in thirty minutes."

If Ashley wanted to be rid of him to avoid talking about whatever was happening between them, she'd have to try harder. Sebastian's bellow bounced off rafters, yelling to her as the bathroom door shut. "I'm free today. I think I'll rest and relax here, unless you want the company." He heard the shower come on and he waited.

The bathroom door flew open. Ashley poked her head out. "No, and no! Sebastian, you need to go home."

He chuckled. "There's no way I'm leaving you. We have to talk, especially after last night."

Her eyes widened, as if the memory rushed to the forefront of her thoughts. "I'm sorry. What I said last night was…" At a loss of words, she fanned herself with an open hand. "Was…"

Sebastian strutted toward her, watched her brace the door as he neared. Towering over her, he leaned forward, "What you said last night was the truth."

The door slammed shut behind him, sealing them together in the tiny steam-filled room. Two hours later, Ashley emerged from the bathroom, exhausted, on shaky legs. She tugged the beige towel around her sopping wet body.

Sebastian exited the bathroom after her and tossed himself on the bed. A sheet draped the lower half of his naked frame. He propped himself up, resting on elbows, grinning with satisfaction. "So, I'll see you later this afternoon?" She caved to him without hesitation.

At the foot of the bed, Ashley squeezed into a pair of jeans. "I should be back by five."

"I'll be here, baby," he said. Her surrender gave Sebastian a major ego boost and the upper hand. He'd do the necessary to tame her beast.

Chapter Eighteen

When she faced the truth, which had been rare considering the deliberate efforts made to cram her schedule with little seconds to spare, emotions overwhelmed Ashley. The truth was more terrifying than the lie she had been telling herself for months.

Kerrigan sat on the bench, bouncing baby Alexa on her knee. "Hey, Ash!" she said as Ashley rounded the corner and made her way to the restaurant's waiting area.

Ashley's frown greeted Kerrigan. "Hey," Ashley muttered, eclipsing her friend's upbeat tone with rotten grapes. Ashley wilted into the seat next to Kerrigan and folded her arms across her chest.

"I never imagined things between Axel and I would turn out as they have." Kerrigan smiled, pearly whites beamed at Ashley. "Are you and Sebastian still pretending?"

Ashley's head jerked back. "Pretending?" she asked, her question a piercing screech. Inside, her stomach somersaulted and twisted into knots.

"Yes. Pretending." Kerrigan said and then pursed her lips. "Or have you two finally admitted the truth?"

Ashley's mouth dropped open. Before words came out, Dahlia approached

"Hey, ladies," Dahlia said, waving a long, slender hand. "Look at that baby! Head full of hair, hazel eyes. Kerrigan, she looks just like you. She's beautiful." Dahlia leaned down, her face distorting as she cooed at Alexa. The baby greeted her with a gummy grin.

"Hey, girl. I haven't seen you in months." Ashley stood and embraced her friend in welcoming arms. "I told Kerrigan that Axel was only the sperm donor," she said, glancing at Kerrigan's amused expression.

Dahlia nodded her head in silent agreement and then held out waiting arms. "Let me hold that baby." Uttering gibberish, Dahlia's silly expressions and funny sounds earned her another toothless smile, and Kerrigan placed Alexa into Dahlia's cradled arms.

A loud voice rang out, breaking their conversation. "Kerri, party of three. Your table is ready."

Gathering Alexa's bag, Kerrigan stood and headed to the host station. "Did Ash tell you about her new boyfriend?" Kerrigan asked over her shoulder.

Waving a dismissive hand, "I don't have a boyfriend. I have an understanding," Ashley defended.

Dahlia elbowed Ashley's arm. "I leave the country for a few months and you've already landed a new man? What happened to Paul?"

They reached the table. Dahlia handed Alexa back to Kerrigan. She draped her jacket over the back of the seat and slid into the chair across from Ashley.

Ashley cleared her throat. "That's a long story," she said, rolling her eyes and then sighed. "Paul was a joke. I don't know why you're surprised."

Dahlia shook her head. "I'll never understand why you insist on wasting your time with losers. What you need is a foreign affair," she said and then tossed her head back, laughing. "Javier would change your mind about a lot of things."

"Not everyone is like you, Dahlia." Ashley growled, her scowl aimed at Dahlia. "I don't speak four different languages, and I'm not interested in globe-hopping."

"But you are interested in real estate, particularly those assets belonging to Mr. Sebastian Stone," Kerrigan teased, grinning at Ashley. "Dahlia, Ash is in deep, but she refuses to admit her feelings."

"Really?" Dahlia glanced at Kerrigan and then at Ashley, her eyes stretched wide. "Have you moved on?"

Stubby fingers curled around a pitcher, lifting and filling a glass with water. "Welcome, ladies. I'm Tammy. I'll be your server this afternoon. I can take your drink orders now and come back, unless you're ready to order."

"We're ready," Dahlia spoke for the group. "We always get the same thing when we come here." Their bimonthly ritual included lunch at Sam's Tavern accompanied by girl talk.

Tammy scribbled on the pad in her hand as they took turns rattling off their orders, and then she left.

"So?" Dahlia asked again. Her eyes flashed with delight. "His name is Sebastian? I like."

Ashley couldn't stop the smile that trailed across her face. "Like I said before. We have an understanding."

Kerrigan laughed. "Yeah, I understand that you two spend almost every waking moment together and can't keep your hands off each other."

Ashley couldn't deny the truth. She swallowed hard. "Just stop, would you both?" Under the table, she rubbed clammy palms on her cream dress pants.

The waitress returned, setting bread and salads on the table.

Kerrigan turned to Dahlia, cocked a brow. "You should hear the ridiculous arrangement these two have concocted."

"Oh? So what's the arrangement?" Dahlia asked, returning a smirk.

"Well," Kerrigan began, giving Ashley a snide glance and then rolled her eyes. "They've been working together on a project for about eight months. Supposedly, they will stop seeing each other when the project is done, about a year from now. Cold turkey." She leaned in. "Since these two are crazy about each other, I don't know how that will ever happen."

"Uh, sounds delusional to me." Dahlia's puckered lips and wide-eye stare forced a wave of nerves through Ashley's stomach. "How did you two meet?"

Ashley replayed the sordid affair, giving her every grimy detail from their very first encounter on Peachtree Street to their topsy-turvy time in Key West and then to the present day. She omitted the parts about fate, the red robin, and the fact that sex with Sebastian was abso-freakin-lutely-and-hands-down amazing.

"Are you in love with him?" Dahlia asked.

"Of course, she is," Kerrigan chimed in, wiping drool from her daughter's mouth.

"Will the both of you back off?" Under normal circumstances, Ashley would be a barracuda, attacking with the sharp-edged bite of cunning words. A trait that made her proud. Instead, she slumped in her seat. Backed into a corner on the topic of Sebastian by best friends numbers one and two, she felt more like a guppy.

"Ash, do you love that man?" Dahlia pursed her lips, coldcocked Ashley with a piercing glare. She lifted questioning hands into the air, palms up.

Ashley tilted her head back, catching a glimpse of the corrugated tin ceiling. A long, winded sigh seeped out of her, deflating puffed cheeks. "Ugh! What the hell," she muttered under her breath, shaking her head from side to side. "I like him, a lot. I've never had feelings this strong for a man." Feeling ten pounds lighter after her admission, tension in Ashley's rounded shoulders dissipated and squared off her posture. "Okay. Maybe I love him, a little."

Kerrigan's mouth dropped open. "Ash!"

Dahlia smiled the kind of smile that know-it-alls and friends-with-perfect-lives smiled. "Love doesn't come in sizes. Either you love him or you don't. Acknowledging the truth is the first step. The second step is finding the courage to share your feelings. So…" She planted an elbow on the table. "When are you going to tell him that you're in love with him?"

Ashley's right palm covered the fingertips on her left hand. "Time out." She would never tell them that the words had nearly slipped out of her mouth like a sinner in a confessional. "Sebastian doesn't want a relationship, and he's made that very clear to me."

Air sucked between Dahlia's teeth made a hissing sound. "Sounds like an excuse to me. If you want love, you should go after him."

Ashley expected Dahlia's judgment. Being superhuman, her friend didn't have mortal flaws or human concerns.

"You shouldn't be too hard on Ash. Admitting her feelings is a huge step." Kerrigan's reassuring hand covered Ashley's shoulder. "You need to tell Sebastian how you feel. He might surprise you. What if he has feelings for you too?"

"What if he doesn't?" Ashley asked, secretly probing her friends for permission to be wrong.

Dahlia rolled her neck. "If you open your heart to Sebastian and he doesn't say the words back, then..." She leaned in close, wielding an index finger like a gavel, the final judgment made. "...then you know where you stand."

The words slammed into Ashley's stomach like a battering ram. She lifted a proud chin, pointed at the prosecution, and ignored the gaping hole in her center. Last night, the dreaded words bled from her soul, almost poured from quivering lips, almost filled lifeless arteries left barren from despair. Almost. The fact remained, Sebastian didn't say *I love you* back.

"Well, I don't know if that's true," Kerrigan said, shrugging off Dahlia's damning verdict.

Ashley's shoulders drooped. The drought inside withered her confidence. "I'll get over my puppy love. I'm a big girl," she said, eyes flitting between Kerrigan, Dahlia and the most captivating linen napkin to ever grace a place setting. If Ashley knew regret spread like a weed, she would have been more careful with her garden. Sebastian planted seeds that had taken root in her heart. And only the good Lord knew what would bloom.

Kerrigan rolled her eyes as she patted Alexa's little back. "Ash, I've watched you stumble from loser to loser. You and Sebastian have a natural chemistry that's hard to come by."

"Yeah, but he's nothing like the man I imagined for me."

Dahlia huffed. "Oh, thank goodness," she muttered under her breath and gave an exaggerated sigh. "I've seen your default man. Not impressive."

Kerrigan coughed. "White men may not be able to jump, but they can do everything else. And quite well," she emphasized.

As though their bodily movements had been synchronized, Dahlia's hand gave the table a firm smack, followed by Ashley's echoing assault. They snapped their heads in Kerrigan's direction, both giving her the bitch-must-have-lost-her-damn-mind look. "You've been slamming in the sheets for a hot second and now you're an expert, huh?" They never had to wonder about Dahlia's opinion.

A sly smile gathered the corners of Kerrigan's mouth. One of those smiles that spoke volumes without ensuing words. Words that weren't needed when she hoisted her left hand in the air, but she spoke anyway. "Well, I'm the only one at this table rocking a wedding ring."

Ashley shook her head and then laughed. "That's not a wedding ring." She squinted, focused on Kerrigan's ring finger, giving a serious expression. "See how those smaller diamonds orbit the center stone? That's a damn galactic event on your hand."

Kerrigan clutched her sides, laughing. "I may be newer than both of you at closed-door activities, but what Axel gives me in the bedroom is out of this world." She waved her hand, flaunting the enormous diamond. "Alexa is what makes me an expert," she said, gently rubbing her daughter's back.

Ashley rolled her eyes. "Bitch!" she said, laughing with her friends.

The raucous laughter calmed. Dahlia didn't miss a beat, picking up from an earlier point in their conversation. "So, you're in love. Now what?"

"She's going to move on." Kerrigan's look scolded Ashley. "She's going to let go of Chris and be happy. She's going to take a risk and let love happen."

Seconds later, Ashley's cell phone rang. "What now!" she blurted out. One hand reached into her handbag.

Sebastian's number on the phone's display forced her slack posture to attention. "Excuse me." Ashley shoved away from the table, eager to disband the double-teaming and frivolous conversation. A private moment away from her love-obsessed friends was the oxygen she needed. The excuse she needed to survive the attack.

Ashley brought the phone to her ear. The rumble of Sebastian's voice and the throaty rasp as he said, "Hi, baby. When are you coming home?" made her stomach flip.

Something deep within forced her courage, gave her strength, gave her emotions a voice. "I'll be home in thirty minutes. I'm…"

A rush of air seeped through the speaker, lungs gasping for breath. "Baby, we have some unfinished business. We really need to talk." His words conveyed warming, warning, wanting. Wanting what she had easily given, wanting what she could no longer give without a cost.

The aroma of freshly stewed tomatoes flooded Ashley's senses when she entered the loft that evening.

Sandals kicked to the side. Handbag tossed to the sofa. Hasty steps carried Ashley to the thermostat. "Something smells great," she said, disguising hesitation, trying to soothe nerves that boiled to the point of perspiration. She lowered the temperature to cool her hormones.

Large soiled hands ran down the front of an apron tied around Sebastian's waist. "My grandmother taught me to make stew like nobody's business." Sebastian's lighthearted tone tugged muscles in his face. A smile that said she might survive another evening without a broken heart.

She returned a faux grin, barely lifting tight facial muscles to accomplish a smile. "Sebastian, I'm not very hungry. I've already eaten. Sorry."

"Just a taste then?"

She couldn't resist his pleading, playful eyes. "Yes. Just a taste." The connotation of those infamous words was an indictment. A taste of Sebastian Stone in her so-called attempt to teach him a lesson landed her right where she stood eight months later. Now she had become the student.

"After dinner, I need your help. One of the contractors just called me. Major plumbing work has to be done before the expansion can start. The cost will eat into the budget of the amenities I had hoped to include. Can you help me brainstorm some other options?"

"Okay. Sure."

Sebastian pointed to the bar. "Have a seat. Your sample is coming right up." He flashed a sexy grin hot enough to melt the elastic waistband on Ashley's panties. She would stoop over to raise them from the floor, along with her jaw, when he wasn't watching her like a hawk.

Sebastian set the countertop with real dishware and utensils, unlike the Styrofoam containers and plastic sporks that usually accompanied her meals. He dished out steaming hot stew into bowls, placed soft rolls on a plate, and poured freshly squeezed lemonade into two glasses.

Sebastian lifted the apron over his head and hung the protective cover on a wall hook. He strolled to the counter where she waited and hoisted himself onto the stool next to Ashley's. "Try some." Sebastian planned for dessert. The look he gave said she was it.

She scooped a spoonful of the hearty stew and raised the spoon to her lips. Delicious flavors melted on her taste buds. Her eyes widened. "Hmm. This is good," she mumbled. "You really know your way around a kitchen."

Sebastian chuckled. "I'm glad you like my stew." His leer roved her body and then met her gaze. He wanted her to enjoy more than his stew.

"So," she began slowly. "What's up with the plumbing situation?" Diffusing Sebastian's lust, a necessary move played to precision.

He pushed away his plate and swiveled the seat toward her. Eyebrows squeezed in, nearly touching. Distress saddled the look of desire. "As soon as you're done with dinner, I'll show you."

The spoon clinked the edge of the ceramic bowl. "Done." She held up her hands. "Let's go."

Before she could spring from her seat, Sebastian reached over and grabbed Ashley's arm. She lifted her eyes to his. She didn't have time to protest. Sebastian crushed his lips to hers. His tongue entered her mouth. Hungry lips gently caressed hers with his kiss. The room whirled around her, spinning faster and faster. Seconds later, Sebastian released her.

"Thank you," Sebastian grinned in a way that said he was only getting started.

Ashley gulped. "For?" Every cell in her tingled. Every nerve in her pulsed. Every inch of her wanted him.

"You're amazing." Sebastian cradled her face. His thumb stroked her hairline as his eyes trailed the invisible mark he left. "Thank you for everything," he said softly.

Something about him seemed changed, different in some way. Vibrant sensations coursed through her belly. Her mind void of thought, she couldn't form an adequate response. "You're welcome," she whispered. "I'm simply following your demands." Ashley cringed as soon as her voice reached her ears.

He flinched. The blunt words hit him like iron being struck by a blacksmith with a grudge against his profession. "Right." Sebastian withdrew, his lips pulled taut, arms tucked into the pockets of his sides.

"Sebastian, wait. That came out the wrong way. I'm glad you appreciate my work." She placed a gentle hand on his forearm. "I'm sorry."

He nodded and stepped away. No tone, no inflection, "You're right," he said, between gritted teeth. An emotionless stare replaced the passion that had glinted behind sparkling eyes. "You wouldn't be here with me like this if I didn't have the upper hand." Spoken with the cadence of a robot, he'd win an Emmy for best male text-to-speech voice actor.

Nervous, fidgety hands tumbled in circles. "I'm enjoying this project. Remember, I asked for this assignment."

Uncertainty weighed down his jaw, tugging his lips and every other facial muscle in the same direction. "You asked for the project before you knew you'd be working with me."

"Eh, true. I still enjoy working with you."

"Is that the only thing you enjoy doing with me?" Sebastian locked crossed arms over his chest.

"No," she said, leveraging the power of the two-letter word. If Sebastian wanted her, she'd let him be the aggressor tonight.

Like a slack rubber band, the tension in his brow relaxed. His arms dropped to his side. "Do you enjoy our conversations?"

"Yes."

He stepped closer. "Do you enjoy spending time together?"

"Yes."

His finger danced along her arm, up to her shoulder. "Do you enjoy my touch?"

"Very much."

"Do you love me?" His question hit her in the belly like a battering ram.

She held the side of the seat to prevent her fall. Words caught in Ashley's throat. Silence.

Not letting up, his brow raised, and he stared without flinching, awaiting her reply.

Ashley swallowed hard. "The thought of loving someone frightens me. I love the moment." She turned away, hiding the lie on her face.

"Love frightens me too." He guided her eyes back to his. An unwavering stare. "I've been thinking. Maybe we can learn to conquer our fears, together."

The walls closed in around Ashley. The meaning of his words, like the dawning sun, rose inside her, bringing light and newborn hope. Hope that quickly withered. Sebastian's offer should have been accompanied by joy. Instead, fear camped in her heart.

A thin smile, unsure and forced, greeted him. "Maybe some fears can't be conquered."

"Darlin', love conquers all fear," he said.

"If love is the thing we're afraid of, how can love conquer itself?"

"If you and I are in love, we have to conquer our fear."

"Do you know what I fear more than love?" she asked.

"What, baby? What's more frightening than love?"

Her eyelids fluttered, rapid blinks. "The pursuit to conquer love."

"There's no failure in trying. That's all we can do."

"But there is fear of failure." She closed her eyes, breathed a heavy sigh. "Sebastian, I think you're going to take me down."

"Baby, sometimes, you have to reach your lowest point to rise again."

His words were meant to be soothing, but she couldn't escape the feeling gnawing at her insides. Sebastian Stone would take her down. In the end, she thought, *Will I rise again?*

Chapter Nineteen

When Sebastian opened the door, the city stood at Ashley's feet. Lights shimmered and glittered in the distance like diamond dust sprinkled over a sea of black. She had never seen a more spectacular view than this one from the penthouse.

Sebastian headed toward the living room. "Come on in," he turned to face her.

The apartment boasted a modest selection of furnishings.

She eyed Sebastian's proffered hand, glancing around the space again. "Why are we in the penthouse?" A hand flew to her hip.

He shuffled past the espresso-finished sofa table and sunk into a stylish tan sectional. A slight dip of the head, his eyes lifted up, pleading with Ashley to take his hand. "That view is inspiring, don't you agree?"

"Yes, the view is amazing." She couldn't hide the hesitation in her voice. "What's this have to do with the plumbing situation?"

"You know, this apartment is more than double the size of your new apartment."

"I can see that." Across the room, on the balcony, she spotted a table set for two. "Why are we here?" She held her breath.

"Have a seat, Ashley," he commanded from his roost.

She couldn't respond. All her brain power prevented the lashing of a sharp tongue and bodily movements. Movements that now rioted her thoughts. Thoughts that told her to run. Victorious over her inner protest, her legs buckled at the bend and Ashley went down unwillingly.

"That's better," he said, as she squirmed beside him. "The reason I brought you here is the same reason why I can't get enough of you."

Fingers curled around a pillow. The roller coaster inside her stomach reached the maximum speed. If the damn thing didn't slow down, it would fly off the tracks, compromising his safety.

"I brought you here because I'm ready to conquer my fear."

Fear. Excitement. Anxiety. The emotions crowded her head when they should have taken residence in her heart. "What does that mean, Sebastian?"

"You know exactly what I mean. I'm talking about taking a real next step. Going to the next level without the bullshit and games."

"The next level? When have we been on any level? All you ever wanted from me, I gave." The roller coaster slipped the tracks. The force of its load aimed at Sebastian. "You said you wanted sex without strings. I gave you sex without strings. Now you want to tie me down? Where is this coming from?" Her cadence rose with each word, matching the terror compounding inside. Inside, new construction was underway. A wall that could not easily be removed.

"Stop fighting. Stop running. Stop thinking. Just stop." Each word he uttered was a nail, drilled into reinforced-steel walls erected around her flimsy heart. "I'm sorry. If I could, I'd take back my actions, my words, the way we found each other," he said, lecturing himself as much as entering his plea. A burly hand caressed her cheek. "This isn't easy for me. Guilt has been my companion for years and I..." He looked away, eyes glazed over, captured by a memory filed in folder number five thousand six hundred and ninety-two in the cabinet of his mind.

The drilling inside stopped long enough for Ashley to feel her heart pulse and pound. Her heart ached. Ached to love, to be loved. "Guilt?" She understood the feeling too well.

Snatched back into the present, Sebastian sheltered her hand, keeping anxious fingers still beneath his own. Stormy gray eyes found her, stole her full attention. The depth of his emotion, raw and visible and strong. "Ellie was my world. Met her my sophomore year in high school." A smile, resurrected from the past, faded as quickly. "She was the new girl. Her family had just moved to Houston. I remember how scared she looked that first day." He tightened his fingers around Ashley's small hand as if clinging to her fortified him. "The thought never crossed my mind that I would be without her."

The name perched the edge of her tongue, on the verge of leaping into the air. She understood how Sebastian felt. She understood his anguish. She simply understood. And yet, Ashley couldn't find the courage, the resolve to say Chris's name aloud.

"Sebastian, Ellie chose to end her life."

He looked away. "I know. Ellie had emotional demons that I didn't understand. She was tormented. I took on the job to protect her. The pain became too much for her. She gave up."

"So you feel guilty?"

Sebastian shook his head. "No. I know her suicide wasn't my fault. I did everything I could do to help Ellie, to be there for her, and that was the basis of my love." He stole another glance at Ashley. "I feel guilty because I didn't think I deserved to feel the way I do now, but here you are. I love you in a way that I never knew would be possible, in a way that I never loved her."

The room went silent. In the quiet, Sebastian's guilt transferred to Ashley. How could he betray Ellie's memory? How could she betray her memory of Chris? Inside, her heart played tug-of-war with her mind, logic pulling in one direction and feelings and longing yanking her back.

"Sebastian, I don't know what to say."

"Just tell me how you feel."

Her chest tightened. "I don't know what I feel." Her cognitive abilities fled the instant she entered the apartment. Hell, the instant he entered her life. She couldn't articulate her feelings even if they were scribbled on notepaper.

Low light cast shadows, wrapping the definition of a fine jaw, and tension wrenched his brow. "You won't admit how you feel, but we both know," he whispered. "Every part of me wants every part of you. I'm in love with you."

Sebastian leaned forward, lifted her chin. A kiss. Tender, sumptuous, lusty. Sebastian groped her behind, ready to feast. Ashley's nails dug into his forearm.

Harsh, ragged breathing escaped his lungs and he withdrew his kiss. "Did you feel that?"

Scared to love him. Scared to lose him. Scared to be loved. Vulnerability became her defense. Ashley pushed away from him. "Why did you bring me here?" she asked again, the toxin in her venom less potent.

"Because this is where I want us to make a new life together. I thought we needed a place in this world that's just about us, just ours. No evidence of the past to haunt us, only new memories to make, neutral ground. I don't need an answer tonight, but I'll try my hardest to convince you."

Sebastian stood and then swooped Ashley into his arms.

If she wanted to protest, the feeling ripping her apart inside would not allow the action. He carried her into the bedroom. A large canopy bed dominated the center of the room. White sheers hung around all four sides of the bed and pooled to the floor. He lowered her onto the mattress.

"Sebastian, we can't do this."

"Shhh, baby. There's nothing you can do to stop us."

Ashley's head sunk into the soft down pillow. She stared up at the smooth white ceiling. Sebastian's touch, his smell, the force of his passion constricted her better judgment.

"Ahhh," she gasped, as he entered her.

He met her release. "Ashley," he groaned, pumping himself into her hard.

Sebastian lifted her legs, placed them into the crook of his elbows. His face nuzzled against her neck. Her back arched as he reached her end, pounding into her heat, his motion unrestrained.

She gripped his shoulders, bracing for the next thrust. The emotional weight of his lovemaking forced another release. "Ahhh. Sebastian," she whimpered. "Too much."

He lifted himself to see her. A tender gaze witnessed her panic. Sebastian slowed his tempo to a halt. "Let me love you, Ashley."

She turned away. "I can't." She heaved, gasping for air. Heavy emotions weighed down her breathing.

Sebastian lowered his hand to her cheek, brought her eyes center to his. "Why?" Glossy pain coated his eyes.

Pressure that had been building for the past six years burst from the dam in her soul. "I can't," she snarled.

She loosened Sebastian from the shackles of his past, and yet freedom didn't find her. His love laid at her feet waited to be taken, and she trampled him. "His name is Chris."

Emotion burned Sebastian's chest. A salty tear slid from the corner of his eye. And then another. "He's the one in the photos?" Red eyes stared at her, awaiting an answer.

She nodded. "Yes."

His heart turned liquid, his erection remained strong. "If you love him, why are you here with me?" Sebastian impaled her hard. "You love me. Tell me you don't."

He gathered her hands, pinned her wrists to the bed. His eyes pleaded for an answer. His heart pleaded for rescue. "Tell me you don't love me," he repeated, his agony compounded by her silence.

Ashley shrunk into the pillow. She struggled free of his hold. "We were engaged." She pushed against his chest. "I don't want to talk about Chris."

Familiar sadness in her eyes caught his attention, resounded in his heart. Sebastian eased out of her, and sat upright. "You have to open up to me. Let me inside. Let me know you."

"I… I… I can't."

"For so long, I felt empty, lost. You've freed me. Freed me to love you. Let me free you."

Ashley gathered the sheet in her hands and covered her naked bosoms. "Take my body and do what you want. I… I can't give you anything more."

Moonlight shimmered off her mocha flesh. *She's so beautiful.*

He turned away from her. "I want everything, and instead you'll giving me nothing."

"Sebastian, I'm sorry," she sobbed. "You made the rules. I've played by them. Now you're changing the game." Her eyelids fluttered, tears swelling. "I'm sorry. I don't know how... I can't..." She sobbed harder.

Sebastian never tasted pain so bitter. "All right. I'm done." He tossed his hand into the air, defeated. "The apartment is my gift to you for all you've done. Take it or not," he said as he scrambled out of bed.

"Sebastian..." Ashley shot up. "I'm sorry. I can't love you the way you want me to." She shook her head and buried her face in her hands. "I'm so sorry," she muttered in deep sobs.

"Me too." Her bare hands reached into his chest and squeezed the life out of his heart. As he approached the doorway, "I expect you to continue working with me. Get dressed," he called back, refusing to look at her.

On the other side of the door, Sebastian fastened himself to the wall. His eyes closed. Soft mutterings from the room where Ashley was held up garnered his attention. His ear pressed against the door. He heard the truth roll off her tongue.

"Oh, I do love you, Sebastian," she sobbed. "I do, but I can't."

If Ashley refused to give in to their love, he would force her heart. He would take control.

Sebastian burst through the door. Ashley curled into a ball, her knees folded into her chest, and she rested against the headboard. He sat down beside her and held out a hand. "Hi. My name is Sebastian Stone. You are the most intriguing woman I've ever met. You're stunning. You're smart. I'd like to get to know you better."

Ashley jerked back. He could see the light flicker on behind those bold brown eyes. She met his handshake. "Hi, I'm Ashley Turner." Her smile stole away his angst.

"Hi, Ashley. What sorts of things do you enjoy doing?"

"Well," she paused, appearing to fight against the tug of her lips. "I'm very athletic. I like jogging. I play racquetball. I hike. And my absolute favorite sport to play is basketball. What about you?"

"Hmm. Interesting," he said, giving her hand a squeeze. "I jog every morning. I play basketball on the weekends. I don't hike or play racquetball, though."

"We all have our flaws," she teased.

"Some more than others." Sebastian scooted closer. "Have you dated a white man before?"

Laughter broke through the anxiety. "I don't discriminate. Something tells me that you're not like any man I've met before, white, black or other."

"I've never dated a black woman. Black women have always intimidated me. Beautiful, strong, intelligent. You're all those things. How's a guy supposed to react to all that?"

"Just like he would react to any other woman."

"So, did you always want to go into marketing?"

A pained expression replaced her joy. She sucked in a breath. "No! I wanted to be an engineer."

"An engineer? Why didn't you chase your dream?"

Exhaling, "I was strongly encouraged to find a more realistic career by my demanding mother," she said. "She also told me that I needed to give her little brown babies while she was young enough to enjoy them and that no man wanted a woman whose job was more demanding or paid better than his."

"Little brown babies, huh?"

"That's what you react to?" She shook her head. "Well, would you date a woman whose job paid better than your own?"

He stroked his chin. "Let's see. Technically, I'm unemployed. I won't draw a salary until my construction project is done. So, yeah. I'd date a woman whose job paid better than mine. That is if she'd be interested. Now, about those brown babies..."

She shook her head again, and rolled her eyes. "Do you want kids?"

"Of course, but I can't give you little brown babies."

"I don't want to talk about kids. I'm not ready for them."

Breaking script, he whispered, "You do realize we haven't used a condom the last few times." He swallowed hard. "You could be pregnant."

She shook her head. "I've got us covered. I get birth control shots."

"Oh, thank goodness." Sebastian wiped his brow. "I want kids someday, but I'm not ready for them now. Besides, I need time to convince your mother that little tan babies are every bit as lovable as the brown ones."

She laughed again. "You'd be willing to meet my mother?"

"Yes. I love all of you, including your overbearing mother. Don't worry. I have a way with mothers."

"You've never met Ericka Turner."

Puffing out his chest, "Ericka Turner's never met me," he said.

They continued talking, watched television, and enjoyed each other. Sebastian hadn't seen Ashley as unguarded as that night.

"Can I ask you a question?"

"Yes. Of course," she said back.

"Did Chris hit you? Did he hurt you?" He thought back to their encounter in the elevator. He thought back to times when he had been sure he had seen fear in her eyes.

He watched her shrink and then turn away. "Sebastian, you wouldn't understand."

Fever ran in his veins. His blood passed the point of boiling. "Where is he now?" Tempering his rage, he closed his eyes and opened them slowly.

"I don't want to talk about him. He'll never be able to hurt me again." Ashley winced as the admission slipped out.

Sebastian inhaled a breath, struggling to control his anger. "If he ever comes near you or tries to hurt you again, I don't know what I'll do."

She touched his chest, calming the beast within him with her gentle caress. "He can't hurt me anymore." She nestled against him. "Can we please stop talking about him?" Ashley didn't say anything else.

They made love into the early morning hours. She gave herself completely as he gave himself in return.

"I love you, baby," he said breathlessly, after their last round.

Silence met his tender gaze. Sebastian knew the road ahead wouldn't be smooth or easy. Rough and hard would be the road they traveled. His determination was strong enough to carry them along the journey.

Sun peeked through the windows the next morning. Ashley rose first, tip-toeing from the bedroom into the living room. Only when his stomach growled did Sebastian remember that they hadn't eaten the night before. He watched as Ashley headed to the kitchen.

A sound that he recognized stopped her where she stood. Giving a sidelong glance, she spotted the red-feathered friend fluttering and pecking at the sliding glass door. Ashley strolled gingerly toward the door and placed an open palm on the glass. The little bird didn't frighten.

Sebastian leaned against the doorframe, stroking his chin as he silently watched her. He enjoyed the way her dark hair cascaded over the curve of her shoulder. The outline of her shapely frame shone through the thin sheet wrapped around her.

And then, as if slashing his heart the night before hadn't been enough to ensure his death, she minced it with her next words.

"Little red robin, I can't love Sebastian. Chris still holds my heart."

Hurt swelled inside him, forcing his retreat and he ducked into the bedroom. He had confessed his love, and Ashley rejected him. Pain unlike any feeling he had experienced struck his chest. His heart exploded. A flood of emotion brought the giant to his lowest point and he wilted to the bed.

Wiping away the evidence of his brokenness, a new man emerged. Sebastian wouldn't be yo-yoed. Wouldn't suffer at her whimsy. Wouldn't be wound up to be let go. She chained him and then unshackled the desire within him. An idea began to form in the darkest part of him. As wrong as Ashley pegged him, she had been right about one thing. He would take her down.

Coming Soon

The story of Ashley and Sebastian
continues in **Down With You,**
the fourth book in the *Suits in Pursuit* series.

About Lauren H. Kelley

Lauren H. Kelley is the bestselling author of sizzling hot contemporary romance across the color lines. She aspires to bridge the racial divide with provocative storylines that arouse the senses and transcend race, focusing on issues that unite us all through our shared experiences in love. She currently resides in the Southeast where she is an active member of Romance Writers of America.

Visit **laurenhkelley.com**
for other titles in the Suits in Pursuit series.

Pull Me Closer
Closer To You
Take Me Down
Down With You (coming soon)

Find Lauren H. Kelley:
laurenhkelley.com
Facebook.com/authorlaurenhkelley
Twitter: **@laurenhkelley**
Watch book trailers at **youtube.com/authorlaurenhkelley**